Praise for *Wired for Murder*

"**Wired for Murder** is a fast-paced read and definitely not for the squeamish. Yet once you begin, do not expect to be able to put this novel down. It's one that will keep you talking about it long after you've read the final page.

—Judy Candis, Freelance Writer for the *Florida Sentinel Bulletin* and Author of *Colorblind* and *Still Rage*

"*A nail biting, easy to read, straightforward novel. The sex scenes were hot, intense, and steamy. Betty keeps you guessing as to who is the killer. You think you know, but...surprise! Betty's first novel is really something. Look for her soon on any "best seller's" list. Can't wait to read what she's cooking up next!!!!!! Looking forward to future work.*

—Dr. Idelia P. Phillips, Author of *Star Light, Star Bright*

"*With short chapters plus a narrative style that is colorful and at times conversational and crisp, the plot of* **Wired for Murder** *moves forward nicely…. Betty Bradford Byers is a fresh, new risk-taking voice in African American Literature. And her readers will no doubt stick around, waiting for her next novel and for other mystery stories that will flow from her pen.*"

—Vee Williams Garcia is a Tampa-based writer and the Author of *Forbidden Circles* and *Whatever It Takes*

The Big Payback

Micah McCall

She's a vice president/designer for the *MJP* design team that is an off-shoot of her mother's successful McCall Fashion and Design Center. She's self-assured, commanding and the self-appointed leader of the pack. Her personal decisions shape the course of events she finds she cannot avoid, and her choices lead to unforgettable adventures and a gut-wrenching conclusion.

Juanita Sanchez, aka *Nini* Sanchez

She's hip, bold and full of bravado, and she has a fondness for men with a tough, street-savvy edge. As a vice president/designer of the popular Atlanta design team, *MJP*, her biracial Peruvian ethnicity sets her apart and on a whole new course.

Pepper Hankerson

An emotional affliction proves to be her downfall. She's a vice president/designer of the *MJP* design team, and her stunning beauty and innate sexuality attract unusual men who she finds she *will not* and *cannot* resist. Her secret penchant hurls her head-on into a titillating series of twists that she finds difficult to escape.

Edmond Waverly Windbrook, III

The extremely wealthy international conglomerate heir who weaves a deceptive web that entraps and destroys the weak and less fortunate. He works his whole life to prevent the one thing he holds most dear, and his ultimate fear becomes his destiny.

Johnny Diamond

Handsome and dynamic, he's a charismatic womanizer who meets his match and finds himself entrenched in a love affair that he vows never to escape. His reputation as a notoriously tough and decisive nightclub owner attracts the attention of one he adores and one he prefers to forget.

Universe Publishing
by
Betty Bradford Byers

Ask your bookseller for
the book you have missed.

Wired for Murder

THE BIG PAYBACK

THE BIG PAYBACK

Betty Bradford Byers

Writers Club Press
New York Lincoln Shanghai

The Big Payback

Writers Club Press
an imprint of iUniverse, Inc.

For information address:
iUniverse, Inc.
2021 Pine Lake Road, Suite 100
Lincoln, NE 68512
www.iuniverse.com

Any semblance to actual people and events is purely coincidental. This is a work of fiction.

Author's Contact Information:
Betty Bradford Byers
2108 Whitlock Place
Dover, FL 33527
(813) 681-9562

ISBN: 0-595-25615-5 (pbk)
ISBN: 0-595-65215-8 (cloth)

Printed in the United States of America

For my husband, James A. Byers, Sr.

To you, James, for without you to carry on, I would not have written *The Big Payback.*

Acknowledgements

First and foremost, praise be to **God**, for without him, *nothing* could have been possible.

I am especially grateful to my son, Roshie Jones, for his design of all my promotional materials as well as for his collaboration on **The Big Payback** and to my son, Derek F. Jones, for his reading of all my work and his encouragement of whatever I pursue.

I am indebted to Dr. English Bradshaw, my publicist, for his patience, dedication and guidance and for sharing his in-depth knowledge of the intricacies of the writing profession.

To Felecia A. Wintons, president and owner of Books for Thought, for her continued willingness to support my efforts.

To the Reverend J. Ricc Rollins, II for his promotional assistance and for just being there to keep me sane.

To Lucy Keith for the editorial assistance she so graciously provided.

To the members of the Nathari Writer's Group for their review and support of my literary endeavors.

To the members of the Ladies of Literature for their feedback and support.

To the ladies of The Tampa Bay Cotillion Group for their camaraderie and support of *everything* I have done.

To the Vintage Ladies for their encouragement and, most of all, for keeping me connected.

To my friend, Betty Gaston, for her willingness to go that extra mile.

To Ella N. (E.N.) Cusseaux and the Beta Sigma Zeta Chapter of Zeta Phi Beta Sorority for their acknowledgement and support.

To my extended family, friends and acquaintances for their prayers and many contributions.

Peace to all, and most importantly, **God** speed.

Prologue

St. Louis, Missouri
May 1989

Johnny Diamond was in seventh heaven. It was May 27, 1989, and he had just signed on the dotted line. He had a pocket full of money and big bucks in the bank. He had finally made it. He had just sold "The Bird's Nest," his popular nightclub. Now he wanted to celebrate with his ladylove. He would be leaving his hometown of St. Louis, and he and Tangela would be Atlanta bound, his dreams at last a reality. He opened the door of his brand-new, shining, navy Lincoln Continental and headed home.

Life is great. Couldn't be better.

He pulled into his driveway, entered the front door of his large ranch-style home and threw his keys on the kitchen counter. He walked the long hallway to his bedroom to awaken Tangela and found the door cracked. He walked in and was rocked! Tangela's curvaceous brown body was spread astride his longtime friend, Manny Blanks.

He surveyed the scene. Neither saw him until he spoke. "You double-crossing motherfucker," he said. His voice was level, but filled with rage. He stepped through the doorway, and Manny grabbed his gun from the bedside table and fired. Johnny, with his gun already in hand, crotched, and the bullet lodged in his bedroom wall. Johnny fired once, hitting Manny between the eyes. Tangela screamed and jumped from the bed, knelt beside it and pled for her life.

With his gun still in his hand, Johnny considered his options. He looked at her disbelievingly and walked from the room. He dialed the police and said, "My name is Johnny Diamond. I've just killed an intruder in my home. Send someone immediately."

Manny's death was determined to be justifiable homicide. Four months later, Johnny entered the city limits of Atlanta, Georgia. He has never returned to St. Louis, and he has kept his heart on lock down, allowing no one entrance.

✤   ✤   ✤

The inner-city public school of Atlanta, in which Juanita Sanchez's parents sent her, was rife with hip, wayward "gangstas." She captured the attention of Raymond Perry, a.k.a. Boogie, leader of the Southwest Blazers gang. They clicked instantly. She and Boogie were an item for two years, and their friendship remains intact today. Juanita fit seamlessly into their world, while keeping her privileged background under cover. In essence, she led two lives.

Juanita left Atlanta and Boogie reluctantly. Her parents sent her to the elite, all-girls' school, the Deauville Academy, just north of Atlanta to round out her education. They never knew of her alliance with Boogie.

Juanita's mother, Desiree, was a homemaker, and her father, Miguel, a renowned archaeologist. Desiree's heritage was biracial, a black mother and a Cuban father. Her disciplined, conventional upbringing appealed to Miguel, a Peruvian. He traveled often on research expeditions, and when he was home, he regaled his children with mysterious tales of his discoveries.

Juanita grew up with a deep love and respect for the unique and the unknown—a love that has remained a basic part of her life and has fueled her insatiable desire for adventure.

✿   ✿   ✿

Micah McCall lived with her parents and two siblings in a well-tended, Northwest Atlanta neighborhood, and she enjoyed a warm, loving relationship with them. She was popular and smart, and when her parents approached her with the idea of attending the noted Deauville Academy during her tenth-grade year, she was thrilled. She met Juanita and Pepper her second day at the school, and they have been friends ever since.

Lila, her mother, met Franklin McCall in Atlanta in 1972, the night the Ebony Fashion Fair arrived. Lila was one of three central models in the show, and she and two of her assistants were relaxing over a drink in Milo's, a small, secluded bar near Franklin's law office. When Franklin asked her to join him, she was drawn to him instantly.

Franklin's reputation as a lawyer in Atlanta was catapulted when he won a major legal case involving three black males who were charged with embezzling over a million dollars from the Andover Corporation, an investment company, in which they were fledgling investment advisors.

Lila spent eighteen months in Paris pursuing her dreams. She worked as a free-lance model and traveled extensively. She kept in contact with Franklin throughout her European sojourn.

She fell in love with a debonair, young French actor, and though it was a very strong, passionate alliance, she realized their different goals would make a permanent relationship impossible. She returned home to Chicago, and Franklin was delighted. She and Franklin pursued a long distance romance that lasted for over a year. They were married in 1975, and she returned with him to Atlanta.

Franklin was the love of her life, but her young Frenchman retained a corner of her heart.

❧   ❧   ❧

Pepper Hankerson was pure perfection. She was gorgeous, chic and smart. With Pepper, you either loved her or envied her. The odd thing was, no one hated her. She had a strange, appealing quality about her that both men *and* women recognized.

Pepper gravitated toward Micah and Juanita because they were vibrant and carefree, yet she felt she was inhibited and withdrawn. Her father, Frederick, was a doctor, and LaVerne, her mother, the senior seamstress at Lila McCall's fashion and design center. Fred and LaVerne lived quietly and well, the only African American family in their gated, upscale community. They were loving and kind and provided Pepper and her sister a solid, comfortable home life, but she craved for so much more.

❧   ❧   ❧

When Edmond Waverly Windbrook, III entered the Westmoreland Military Academy north of Atlanta in 1989, he made not one friend, and he never did. He met Pepper, Juanita and Micah his second year at the academy, and he became Pepper's nemesis the first night he met her. Their destructive relationship endured for the next twelve years.

CHAPTER 1

Atlanta, Georgia
March 2002

"Please, Edmond. Don't! It won't happen again, I promise," Pepper pled. Her mutilated face, now almost twice its normal size, would need extensive surgical repair. Her blood-soaked hair plastered her head, appearing dark auburn rather than its natural black-ink hue.

Backhanding her, Edmond sneered, "You don't understand anything but this," and then he smashed his fist into her left eye. His heavy, gold ring tore her flesh, and blood spurted from the slash just above her brow. She fell to the floor, her back against the ivory sofa. He wrenched her arm behind her, and she screamed in agony.

"So sorry. I love you," he heard her say through swollen lips. Controlled by his fury, he continued to unleash his pent-up anger, mauling her viciously. Her pleading and pathetic entreaties stimulated him.

"You black bitch," he said, "Who the fuck you think you are?"

He kicked her repeatedly and stomped her right leg. The bone snapped. His senses now heightened, he looked at her, filing away her helpless image. He captured the contorted face, registered her pain. He catalogued her eyes, now tiny slits, to relish when he wanted stimulation. She lay curled into a fetal position between the sofa and the coffee table, crumpled and silent before him.

Outside, the night storm raged, thrashing and moaning, whipping the waterlogged trees against the house. Scraping branches brushed the windows as lightening flashed, illuminating the dark room, spotlighting Pepper's ravaged body and the sumptuousness of his home. He looked down on her in disgust, rankling his nose as a strong urine scent assaulted him.

His arousal consumed him, and he needed immediate release. Touching himself, he erupted. His low-pitched moan penetrating the soggy night.

"Bitch! You never stop. You always push until I hurt you."

His release left him breathless, but the rage still racked him. His right eye twitched in rapid succession.

"Get her out of here." He spotted the blood-soaked carpet and bellowed to his two henchmen, "Jesus Christ. The carpet. Get the blood out…now! And do something with her. She's caused enough trouble already."

They had stood watching as he'd plummeted her fallen body. They had become accustomed to his outbursts, but his extreme reactions never ceased to amaze them.

Edmond Waverly Windbrook, III, euphoric and sated, welcomed the power that coursed through him. His mental state soared, everything back intact. These escapades were getting more frequent and violent, but they always bolstered his flagging self-esteem.

I showed her something tonight. Criticizing me. This will teach her to keep her fucking mouth shut.

He rubbed his swollen fist. He had cracked the crest of his onyx ring, a cherished family heirloom. He peered at it in the dim light, still visualizing her battered face. A lop-sided grimace creased his thin, dry lips.

As he inched up the mahogany staircase, he glanced about, surveying his expensive surroundings, his keen sense of order appeased. Everything aligned, everything in its rightful place.

As muted thunder rumbled in the distance, he lingered at the stair top and studied his reflection in an antique mirror. He stripped away his tailor-made shirt, exposing his pale, gaunt body. His emaciated appearance belied his extraordinary wealth and lavish lifestyle. But neither his financial state nor his possessions meant anything to him. He was back on top and in command, and those were the elements that propelled him. Now all he wanted was a long, hot shower and a glass of champagne.

CHAPTER 2

"Love you, too. See you at eight. Bye," Micah whispered.

Just as she hung up the phone, Juanita burst through the door. "Micah, that cashmere material we ordered is—"

"Noooo!" someone screamed.

"My God. What was that?" Juanita said, turning towards the door.

Micah was out of her chair in seconds. They rushed from the office, encountering Dana, Micah's startled assistant. "Who was that?"

"Don't know. It came from the seamstress galley," Dana said.

Running to the galley, Juanita reached the door first and flung it open. LaVerne rushed past them, tears streaking her face.

"What happened?" Juanita said.

"It's Pepper. Nicky just called and said Pepper's been hurt. She's at St. Michael's Hospital. They think Edmond did it."

LaVerne ran toward the elevator and stabbed the down button.

"LaVerne, wait. I'm going with you," Micah called.

"Me, too. Hold the elevator," Juanita said, cutting through the maze of dress forms to grab her purse from her desk. "I'll drive."

In the car, LaVerne couldn't stop crying. Edmond had gone over the edge. Pepper's long-standing boyfriend, Edmond Waverly Windbrook III, had beaten her into oblivion.

"My baby," LaVerne repeated. "I've never cared for him, and he knew it, but why did he hurt her?"

LaVerne told Micah and Juanita that a nurse called her 21-year-old daughter, Nicky, and said someone dumped Pepper at the emergency room door sometime during the night. Her husband, Fred, a doctor at the hospital, also called and told her Pepper had been beaten and was in intensive care. When an orderly discovered her, she was drifting in and out of consciousness. Pepper gave them her family's phone number and also said Edmond beat her.

As soon as they entered the hospital, they inquired about Pepper and were directed to her room. Fred was with her. He hovered at the foot of her bed, peering at her chart in silence. Two other doctors flanked him, talking in hushed tones. When he saw LaVerne at the window, he rushed to her side.

"What happened, Fred? Is she all right? Can I see her?"

"She's unconscious right now. She wouldn't know you were there, LaVerne. It was Edmond, he did it. I tried to warn her about him, you know I did. She just wouldn't listen," he said, anger washing over him.

Fred grappled with his emotions and tried his best to maintain control. He was a scrapper from the mean streets of Detroit, and when he saw Pepper's battered body in the emergency room, his first inclination, despite his medical oath, was to deal with Edmond Windbrook with his own hands.

"Is she going to be all right?" Micah asked, tears beginning to form.

"We don't know yet. She's in pretty bad shape, but we'll know something definite within the next few hours. All we can do now is pray."

"I can't believe it. I thought all this brutality was behind them," Juanita said. "It's been going on far too long. I thought she'd ditched that motherfu—"

"Juanita, please. We'll get to the bottom of this soon enough," Micah interrupted. "Where's Edmond now?"

"No one knows. He's disappeared, skipped town," Fred said. "The police are looking for him."

"My baby. I can't believe it. When she was at the house last night, she said she was going home and to bed," LaVerne said. "She must have gone to see him. Why would he do this? My God, just look at her, Fred." She buried her face in her hands and wept. Fred kissed the top of her head and held her, encircling her safely within his arms.

Micah forced herself to look at her friend. Wrapped like a mummy, with one eye visible, Pepper's whole body was in traction. She stared at her padded left eye and then at her raised right leg. From the angle of the cast on her right arm, Micah surmised correctly that it was broken in multiple places.

She must have suffered horribly.

Dr. Hankerson told them later that night, "If she survives, she'll be blind in her left eye. She has a fifty-fifty chance."

Upon hearing the doctor's report, Juanita said, "We've got to find him, Micah. He can't get away with this again."

"You got any ideas on what we should do?"

"I sure as hell do," Juanita snapped, whipping out her cell phone. "I'll get to the bottom of this right now."

CHAPTER 3

Acapulco, Mexico
April 2002

"Bring me another one," Edmond said to Angelo, his hefty, Italian bodyguard, indicating the smooth Johnny Walker Black Label scotch he preferred.

"Coming right up, boss." Angelo scurried, knowing full well the habits of his strange employer. He'd worked for Edmond for nine years, and he knew how to appease him, how to keep his temper in check.

"Acapulco seems to be the one place in the whole world where I can relax," Edmond confided. "Just wish I could find this kind of peace at home, but that is impossible. Too many distractions."

He stretched his long, thin legs and lay back on the padded chaise lounge, enjoying the warmth of the sun on his body for the first time in years.

"Yeah. Ya got that right. This is just what you need," Angelo said, placing the mellow, dark brown drink containing three ice cubes on the small table next to Edmond. "You beginning to get some color on you, boss. You gonna be darker than me in no time." Angelo sensed just the right thing to say.

Edmond smiled. "Yes, I will be. It won't take me long. You should have seen me as a kid. Mother would make me stay inside because she said I got too black for her taste."

Angelo laughed, but didn't comment. Edmond seldom mentioned anything about his past, especially about his parents.

"The trainer's due in an hour, boss. You want me to get anything for you while he's here?"

Edmond hesitated and then said in his usual, formal manner, "No, the hotel knows my preferences. They have everything here I need. Just relax. Go for a swim or take that cart and explore the premises. I am looking forward to beefing up again. If Javier is as good as his clients claim, he will have me in shape in no time. Hopefully, well before the three months we are to be down here are over. I am ready to get started."

"He's good, boss. You don't have to worry 'bout that. I can vouch for him," Angelo said, walking toward the *casita* to find his Speedo.

Edmond closed his eyes, and shifted his mind in gear.

Ah, Pepper, Pepper. I need you here. Everything would be perfect if you were just here with me.

He flashed his fondest memory of her in his mind's eye and felt an instant erection. He saw her lying at his feet, professing her love for him, battered beyond recognition. He remembered the sound of the bone snapping, and he couldn't control himself. His eruption exploded, and he sighed and relaxed. When he recovered a short time later, his right eye twitching, he reached for the thick towel and covered himself.

Wait until she sees me. She will not be able to resist. She needs me just as I need her.

He was already feeling the triumph he envisioned. His plans were in motion, and he was elated. Thoughts of Juanita and his well-laid plans overtook him, and he drifted into a welcoming, much-needed sleep. In his mind, he was once again the victor, and above all else, in total control.

CHAPTER 4

Atlanta, Georgia
June 1982

Jeanine and Edmond W. Windbrook, II entered their exclusive sub-urban neighborhood just north of downtown Atlanta, and she reached out and touched his leg. She peered through the darkened limousine glass and said, "It's good to be back. I'm always raring to go, but it's so good to get back home, don't you think?"

"I do. I think this home is the one I cherish the most," Ed answered in his clipped English accent.

Eight-year-old Edmond waited in his room for the arrival of his parents, aligning his toy soldiers. His hatred for disarray was already legendary. Everything he owned had to be immaculate and arranged just the way he wanted. He enjoyed the process of arranging, re-arranging and cleaning his possessions. He seldom used the myriad of toys and technical equipment that his parents heaped on him for the purpose they were intended. His enjoyment came from his con-trol over them. The soft knock on his door brought him back to real-ity. He had drifted into his own reverie.

"Your parents are home, sir. They're waiting for you downstairs," Anna, his *au pair*, announced.

"Thank you, Anna. I'm ready." He placed the last of the little sol-diers on his tabletop battlefield, adjusting them several times. He descended the stairs and heard his mother's voice. He followed Anna to his father's large, wood-paneled library.

"Here he is, sir," Anna said.

"Edmond, darling," his mother said, moving toward him. "We've missed you so." She ruffled his neat curls.

He wanted to comb his hair immediately, but thought better of it. "Hello, Mother. Dad. How was London?"

"Always the same. David sent his greetings." His father studied him, scrutinizing his appearance, but could find nothing amiss.

"Thank you, sir. I have not talked to any of my cousins in England in quite sometime. Perhaps we will while you are home," he said formally, aware of his father's careful inspection of him. It delighted him to no end that his father could find nothing of which to complain.

"You must tell us what you've been doing since we left. What have you done to occupy your time?" his mother asked, amazed at how much he resembled his father.

"I spoke with Jackson, Martin and Sophie. They asked if I could spend some time in Savannah with them this summer. I told them you and Dad would be home soon, and I would let them know. I would love to see them, Mother. Do you and Dad think I could go for a short visit?" he asked, looking to his father for the answer.

"We'll see. We've just gotten back. You'll have plenty of time for that later," his father said.

Edmond endured his parents while they were in Atlanta. He could not wait for his mother to find some new reason for them to be off again to one of their homes or to some social affair she wanted to attend. He looked forward to their frequent trips because he could live in his fantasy world without interference. When he was younger, he would have been devastated if she left him.

*   *   *

Edmond visited his cousins in Savannah and had a marvelous time. Jackson was two years older than he, but they had the most in common. They shared the same hunger for power and control.

"Let's go down to the creek. We might find something to do down there," Edmond said.

"Okay, we'll go through the woods. It's the quickest way," Jackson said.

The wooded area near their home presented Jackson a slew of opportunities. The thickness of the surrounding brush and the hanging tree branches provided perfect cover for their secret activities.

Last summer, the two boys scoured the area for rabbits and squirrels that they shot with their BB guns. They tortured them, burned them until they squealed. The stench from the burnings permeated their clothing and their nostrils. They dismembered them while they lived. Edmond's passion was his knife. He'd slice their throat and let them bleed to death. They enjoyed the fact they'd been responsible for the torture and the death. After the suffering and the animals' subsequent death, they would masturbate in the brush while the other looked on in awe.

"Look. Whose cat is that?" Edmond asked.

"Tina's. Why?"

"Go get it. This is going to be fun."

Jackson strolled into his neighbor's yard and picked up the cat. He stroked its head and smiled. "Okay, now what?"

They took it to the back of the house, and Edmond lifted the lid from the old barrel. He removed the cat from Jackson's arms, cuddling it as he moved.

"Watch," Edmond said. He eased the cat into the barrel of rainwater and submerged it. The cat scratched and squirmed, but he squeezed, struggling to keep it under. When he realized the cat was dead, his adrenalin spiked.

"Wow. That was amazing," Jackson said. "How'd you ever think of that?"

"I don't know, but it was terrific." Edmond was thrilled. He had won Jackson's respect. He would make sure he kept it.

Jeanine and Ed stayed in Atlanta for two weeks that summer. She grew up in the city, and her many friends and acquaintances still lived there. Her family home near the downtown area had long been torn down, and she no longer had family there. She use to visit her alma mater often, but her years at Spelman College now seemed so long ago. Her current world transcended that part of her life. She was still a faithful contributor, and she made sure her yearly donations were generous.

"I've got to go to Barcelona, Jennie," Ed said. "Ramon said I'm needed to close an international deal this week. I know we haven't been here long, but do you want to come?"

"Of course, I want to come. What about Paris? I thought you had something brewing there. Is it still on the agenda?"

"It sure is. I know you like that," he said, smiling at her.

"Now you know I do." She got up from her chair, eased onto his lap and kissed him. "I love you, Ed. I always will."

"I love you, too. Now what are you planning to buy for the upcoming season? I know you wouldn't think of entering Paris without prowling your favorite showrooms."

"I have a couple of things in mind, but I'm open to whatever strikes me."

Jeanine and Ed owned homes in Barcelona, London, Paris, Los Angeles and Atlanta and a huge apartment in the exclusive 515 Park Avenue tower in New York City. Their own private jet afforded them the freedom to move between them often. Jeanine had someone scouting for a place in Acapulco. She wanted to relax in some exotic, sun-drenched wonderland, and Acapulco piqued her interest.

Edmond traveled with them, on occasion, whenever they spent time in one of their homes. He was happy in Atlanta, and he was content to remain there. When the Acapulco home was bought and decorated, he adored it. He found some semblance of peace whenever he visited the city. It remained that way throughout his life.

Edmond sold the Acapulco home years later, but he continued to visit the city often. He now preferred the privacy of the Las Brisas Acapulco, and the mountaintop cabana was his choice when he was there.

Edmond thought often of his childhood. He had been extremely close to his mother for the first six years of his life. Jeanine devoted all her time to him. She told her husband, Ed, a mother's duty was to nurture her young, and she intended to give their son her undivided attention during the formative years of his life. In fact, she nursed Edmond until he was six. He had no friends, just a strong attachment to his mother.

When he turned six, his mother started spending most of her time with her husband, leaving Edmond resentful and depressed and in the care of his *au pair*. From age six on, Edmond lived in his own fantasy world, clinging to the memory of his previous relationship with his mother. He resented his father for taking her from him. Neither Jeanine nor Ed realized the trauma he suffered. They were unaware of how much he'd become affected by what he considered the loss of his mother's love.

The opulence of the Windbrook jet made travel a treat. Jeanine put down her magazine and took a sip of her wine. "Ed, I have such a hard time now showing my affection for Edmond. I love him dearly, but, I don't know, I just can't seem to show it as I do for you or as I did for him when he was younger."

"He's a hard one to fathom. You're a great mother, Jennie. Don't worry about it. You devoted six years of your life to him. He knows you love him."

"You think so? You can be distant with him, Ed. He's the spitting image of you, and I know you love him. I just worry about him sometime. He can be sulky and withdrawn. He's much too formal for such a little guy."

"He's smart and interested in a lot of things. He's fine, I tell you. Don't worry about it."

"He's interracial, and he doesn't fit well in either world."

"We'll send him to England next summer. He needs more contact with his relatives there. He'll like that," Ed said, ending the conversation by picking up his book and placing his glasses on his nose.

Unknown to his parents, Edmond's greatest wish was to be loved by his mother and respected by his father. He was reclusive. He compensated by creating an imaginary, magical world. He read voraciously, and he lived though all the adventures.

Jeanine's African American heritage was important to her, and it showed in her bearing. Her sophisticated and stately aura proved to be the envy of her friends. She stood almost six feet tall, and her pecan brown skin glowed from the expensive care she gave it. She was a statuesque, serene woman, and the perfect complement to offset Ed's highbrow manner.

When Jeanine met the wealthy and generous Edmond Waverly Windbrook, II, she fell head over heels in love. They met in a small restaurant in the Omni International Hotel in Atlanta. She was attending a real estate convention, and he was in the city negotiating a block of buildings. All rooms were booked that week, but Ed was fortunate to have found a room in the Omni. Jeanine did not know of his extreme wealth when she met him, and this intrigued him. She was attracted to the *man*.

When she and Ed married two years later, she vowed she'd remain true to her strong heritage, but the luxury of having everything she wanted, changed her outlook over time. She had instilled none of that proud heritage in her son; therefore, he floundered between both worlds—hers and Ed's. She was so right. Edmond fit in neither.

When Jeanine looked at her son, she saw a perfect composite of Ed and her. His hair was a mass of thick, bronze curls that he fought to contain, and he had his father's steel gray eyes and his perfectly straight nose. His glistening bronzed skin melded beautifully with his hair color. He was a miniature bronze god to those who knew him. At eight years old, he was already shaping his world to his specifications. He controlled his own world exclusively and ruled the household with an iron hand. He would have it no other way.

CHAPTER 5

Atlanta, Georgia
June–July 1989

Edmond spent his fourteenth birthday alone in his room. Anna did
her best to coach him from his retreat, but he refused to budge. Jeanine and Ed were in London, but called him that afternoon to make
sure he'd received the gifts they'd sent. "Happy birthday to you," Jeanine sang when he came on the line.

"Hello, Mother. Thank you. When are you coming home?"

"In a couple of weeks. Your father's trying to close his deal. As
soon as he does, we'll be on our way. Have you done anything special
today?"

"No, but Anna's planning a small celebration later."

"She told me. We wish we could be there with you. Your father's
thinking of slowing down his end of the business. When he does,
we'll be home a lot more. I'm looking forward to that. You and I can
catch up on everything we've missed. How would you like that?"

"I can't wait," he lied, his right eye twitching.

"Hold on. Your father wants to talk to you."

"Hello, Edmond. Happy birthday."

"Thank you, father," he said, still thinking of them spending more
time in Atlanta.

"We're leaving on the twenty-seventh. We don't have any more trips planned this year. I'm looking forward to settling in for a while."

"Yes, it's going to be wonderful to have you both here. I'm looking forward to it, too."

"Take care, son. We'll call you later in the week. Bye."

"Goodbye, Dad." He went into his bathroom, stripped off his clothes and spent an hour in the shower. Whenever he became agitated, he couldn't get himself clean.

❧   ❧   ❧

True to their word, Jeanine and Ed returned to Atlanta two weeks after Edmond's birthday. They arrived in a huff, generating all kinds of excitement. Edmond felt his world crumbling. He couldn't bear the thought of having them permanently in residence.

"Edmond, darling. We're home," his mother crooned, entering his room and finding him reading at his desk.

"Hello, Mother," he said, placing his book neatly beside him. "I didn't hear you arrive," he said, resenting her intrusion into his personal space.

"I'm so happy to be home. I haven't been in here in years it seems. You've changed things about," she said, roaming the room, inspecting as she moved.

"Just a bit," he said, walking to the door. "Where is Dad?" He wanted her out of his room that very minute. No one was allowed to enter. He'd made that clear to Anna. Now he had to contend with his mother. "Let us find him."

"He's in the library, I believe. Do you really want to go see him?" she asked, startled. She knew they were formal and distant with each other and was delighted Edmond wanted to see him.

"Yes, of course, Mother. I always want to see him when he comes. Did you not know that?" he asked as he started down the stairs.

"To be honest, I *didn't* know that. I just know we're going to get much closer when we've spent more time together. I'm really excited. We'll be like a real family from now on," she said, following closely behind him.

His heart sank, and he said, "Yes, I cannot wait."

His parents had been home three weeks, and Edmond was beside himself. He'd become morose and edgy, and he began to formulate a plan. He hadn't put it together completely, but he was close. Whenever he thought about it, he could feel his depression lift.

It will not take much longer. Everything will be back to normal.

He thought about his mother, touched himself lightly and ejaculated into his towel.

❦   ❦   ❦

After a month of his parents' excessive hovering, Edmond thought he was losing his mind. They were literally driving him insane. He was not use to their constant directions and intrusions. Since their return from London, he'd spent endless hours trying to sort through his options.

He struck pay dirt while reading one night. He picked up one of the many books on his shelf he had never read. He was interested in a variety of topics. The book he chose to skim was on automotive repair. Since he'd never had cause to tinker with a car, he'd promised himself by summer's end, he'd have at least a talking knowledge of them. While flipping through the book, he had an instant awakening. It was as plain as day. His plan lay before him.

He waited until near midnight and slipped quietly down to their massive garage. His parents planned to lunch with some of their friends in the city the next day. He'd memorized everything he needed to know to accomplish his mission. It took him just under an hour to finish his work. While in the garage, he was completely focused and in total control. That feeling of elation he craved flowed through him. He could barely contain himself.

When he finished his work, he entered the house and went straight to his bathroom. He removed his pajamas, conjured up his mother's image and fondled his aching shaft. An explosive hot rush overtook him, sending tremors throughout his body. He moaned softly and leaned against the sink, enjoying the subsiding ecstasy. He experienced the most exquisite feeling that night. Relief flooded him. He'd established this ritual years ago, but tonight was special. He'd triumphed again. Tomorrow would put things back in order.

He stepped into the shower and scrubbed himself thoroughly. He could hardly wait for the new life that awaited him. Finally, he was back in control, and that's the way it would remain. Of that he had no doubt.

The doorbell rang at 12:15 p.m. the next day, and Charles, Ed Windbrook's English butler, opened the door.

"Is Ed Windbrook, Jr. at home?" one of the policemen asked.

"Yes, he is. Whom may I say is calling?"

"Officers Valdez and Simpson."

"Please come in? This way," he said, as he turned toward the hall-way. He led them to the library. "Won't you have a seat? I'll let him know you're here."

"Thanks," they said in unison.

"Gentlemen," Charles said. "Just a word of caution. Please refer to Mr. Windbrook as *Edmond*. He detests *Ed*." He bowed his head and left to get his employer.

The policemen looked at each other, amazed by the warning.

Edmond entered the room, dressed in coat and tie. Both officers registered his appearance and stood to greet him.

"Hello, I am Edmond Windbrook. How may I help you?"

"Hello, Edmond. I'm Officer Valdez. This is Officer Simpson. We have tragic news. Your parents' black Mercedes careened out of control while descending the hill a quarter of a mile from here. We are sorry to tell you they were both killed."

"What?" Edmond said, tears stinging his eyes. "Killed?"

"I'm sorry," Officer Simpson continued, "From all indications, the car scraped the mountainous rock that lined the highway and was thrown out of control and over the edge. The car flipped several times. The tremendous impact and speed crushed the top completely. We have already launched an investigation to determine exactly what happened. At this time, we know nothing more."

Edmond was devastated. He appeared strange and formal, but deeply affected by his parents' death. Since he was still a minor, Jeanine's sister, Carolyn from Savannah, was his nearest relative. Jeanine and Ed's wills stipulated her as his guardian should anything befall them while he was a minor.

During the month before his death, Ed made final preparations for Edmond to enter Westmoreland Military Academy in Meads, Georgia, that fall. They'd planned for years that he would attend the academy starting his freshman year in high school. Ed's instructions were explicit, and his lawyers carried out his wishes to the letter.

Edmond insisted the house remain open when he was in school, and that the servants stay in residence. Carolyn and his lawyers followed his wishes. She and his cousins spent the rest of the summer in Atlanta, helping him as best they could. They left for Savannah the same day Edmond left for Westmoreland.

The Windbrook lawyers at Langley, Stanford and Wright paid the household expenses and dispensed his monthly income. While he was still in school, all of his holidays were spent in Atlanta in the family home with Carolyn and her children. Charles and Anna were always there.

The family lawyers stayed closely aligned with the police while the investigation of the Windbrook accident progressed. The case was closed within the year. Nothing afoul of the law could be determined.

CHAPTER 6

❀

Atlanta, Georgia
June 2002

Standing at the large plate glass window, the city lights glittering in the distance, Micah stood encircled in the arms of the only man she had ever loved, excluding her father, Franklin McCall. It was 8:10 p.m., and Armstead LaRue's long, muscular arms embraced her from behind. She leaned back against him, content to let the day's tension ease from her body.

"What are we going to do, Armstead? I can't believe all that's happened in the last three months."

"You've done everything you could. The police are involved now. You can't do anymore," he said, inhaling deeply, enjoying the vanilla scent she knew he loved.

"I just don't trust them with this case. The Windbrook name is like a mighty shield in this town. You know that."

"I know what you're saying, but you've got to let it go, Micah. It's been eating away at you since it happened. Listen to me. You can't do *anything* else," he said, turning her around and pulling her against him.

"I know you're right, but I feel so helpless. If you'd seen Pepper that first day, Armstead, you'd feel the same way I do. It was awful. She didn't deserve that. She just didn't. The strange thing is she said she would never press formal charges against him. I'll just never be able to understand that. If they ever find him, that is."

"That's all the more reason to let it go. She has some responsibility, too."

They were in Armstead's large, plush office, smack in the middle of downtown Atlanta. He was Vice President of Sales for Amstock Communications. He released her, and held her at arms' length. He saw the worry and frustration etched on her face. He turned and walked from her, moving towards his bar. He swung the heavy mahogany doors wide open and retrieved a brandy sniffer.

"I'm going to have brandy. You want one?"

"You got any wine? White, preferably."

"Uh-huh. Mattie put some in here yesterday," he said, opening his pint-sized refrigerator and getting the wine. Already chilled for you, too."

She turned around to observe him, admiring the back of the lean, strong frame that first attracted her. She realized just recently how much she really loved him.

You're my pillar of strength. The eleven-year age difference doesn't matter one iota. You're just what I need. I'm twenty-seven, you're thirty-eight. Big deal.

"A penny for your thoughts," he said, handing her the wine.

"I was just thinking how much I love you, that's all. You know I do, don't you?"

"I hope so. I've loved you from the start, Micah. From the very first day I met you."

He kissed her then, savoring her lips. She pulled him closer. Her kisses were urgent and deep, and he moaned her name, igniting that familiar flame, wanting to consume her.

During the two years since they started dating, Armstead brought up marriage to her twice. Both times, she skirted the issue. She just wasn't ready. She knew he understood. She also knew, when she made up her mind, she'd just need to tell him. At this moment, she had more pressing matters to attend to.

Got to call Mick tomorrow. He'll know what to do.

CHAPTER 7

Micah walked the long, carpeted hallway until she reached the door with the impressive stenciling, *Sutherland-Bailey Investigative Services*. It was still quite early, 8:05 a.m., and she hoped she could catch Mick before he became immersed in overseeing his heavy caseload. When she opened the door, there he stood.

"Micah," he said, clearing Sela's desk. He rushed to hug her.

"Mick, you ole devil. How have you been?"

"Great. Haven't seen you since the reunion at the academy. How long has that been?" he asked, using both hands to brush back his thick head of graying hair.

He still does that—still slicks his hair back when he's nervous or excited. "Almost a year. You look like new money. Still chasing all the women?"

"You'd be surprised. Think I found the one."

"Uh-uh. Not you. Who is she? Anybody I know?"

"Nope. Known her all my life," he said, nudging her toward his office.

"Come on in here. What are you doing in this neck of the woods? Thought you'd be locked up in that luxury apartment. Or maybe in that executive office you got downtown at the design center."

"Come on, Mick. I'm the same girl you met at Deauville. Nothing more, nothing less. Just a little older, that's all."

She couldn't imagine him being any better looking than he was nine years ago, but he sure as hell was. When she saw him last year, she thought the same thing. He still had that same killer smile and those mesmerizing green eyes. His shock of dark hair was now shot through with gray, but it made him so much more appealing.

Man, if Armstead weren't in the picture…oh, hell. Forget that. Wonder who could have pulled Mick in? If she can tame Mick, she must be some kind of woman.

"Where's Sela? Thought she'd be the first person I saw when I opened the door?"

"Still too early for her. She'll drag in here around nine. So will Hubert. You look great, Micah. Always have, though. How's everybody? Pepper and Juanita still with you at the center?" He motioned to a chair, indicating that she sit. He retrieved his cigarettes from his desk drawer. "Mind?" he said, flipping the pack.

"Go right ahead." *Wonder why we never got together in school? I know something was there.* She put her purse on his desk, and sat down to talk. "Yeah…well, Juanita's still with us. That's why I'm here, Mick. Pepper was damn near killed by Edmond Windbrook a few months ago." She still bristled when she thought of him. "Her family was able to keep it relatively quiet—just a few articles appeared in the papers."

"Must have missed them, I guess. I'm surprised she was still dealing with him after all this time. I always thought they were mismatched. Whatever he did, I won't be shocked. He was strange…always blinking that eye. Never liked him even back at Westmoreland. He acted too damn superior for my taste. What did he do to Pepper?"

"Beat her to a pulp. Literally. She's home now, though. She was at St. Michael's for a couple of months. He's always smacked her around, even when we were in school. It just got worse over the years. This time, he went wacko, it seems. She's blind in her left eye. He broke her right arm and leg. She'll always have a limp. She's got to have extensive plastic surgery to regain her looks. It's terrible, Mick. And he's on the lam. Skipped town, I hear. I need you to find him. I mean it, Mick. I wanna find him. We thought she might get better, but her progress is slow. That's why it's taken me this long to come here. I kept hoping she'd come around. Mick, I can't tell you how much I want him. He *won't* get away with it this time."

"Don't worry about it. We'll find him. *You* just take it easy. I know you, and I know how you feel. We'll handle him, make no mistake about it," he assured her. "The question is, will this beating convince her to stay away from him? It sounds to me like co-dependency."

"I don't know, Mick. We've tried umpteen times to get her to see the light, but he's like a drug to her. I don't understand it. I'm hoping this time she's learned her lesson. She says she has, so we can only hope."

When Micah left Mick's office, she felt a whole lot better than she had in months. She had confidence that if anyone could find Edmond, it was Mick.

> Micah met Mick when she attended Deauville Academy in Stanton, Georgia, and he was attending Westmoreland. Mick was 30 miles north of Stanton in Meads—the home of the great Westmoreland Military Academy. They met on the dance floor at the monthly Deauville social. It was the same night Pepper met Edmond. Edmond was rich, handsome and conceited. He and Pepper had maintained their rocky relationship for all this time—then the vicious beating.
>
> *It's still hard to fathom.* One of her best friends had been mutilated and in a coma for two months. Just to think Pepper would ever speak to him again was mind-boggling. *Totally, fucking unbelievable.*
>
> Micah's one regret was that she and Juanita could never convince Pepper how unhealthy her relationship with Edmond really was. Whenever he slapped her around, she would blame herself. Psychologically, they knew Pepper's attachment to him stemmed from something deep within her, knew there was an underlying cause for her insatiable need for love and approval, but they

couldn't uproot it. She and Juanita suggested therapy on many occasions, but Pepper would have no part of it.

"You think I'm wacked out, huh? Well, I'm not, so just drop it, will you?" she said the last time they'd mentioned it.

Pepper told them she felt a great void inside her. Her parents were upstanding and loving; therefore, Micah and Juanita couldn't understand her actions as far as Edmond was concerned. They suspected something unspeakable happened to her when she was younger, something she couldn't reveal.

Edmond was such a bastard. Few people found him the least bit likable. Pepper's continued fascination with him kept them baffled. Micah smiled as she remembered one night in particular, just before Pepper was hospitalized. They were well into one of their nights on the town at the Blue Palace when a dark, creamy chocolate brother tried to catch Pepper's eye.

"Pepper, front and center. Girl, you're too much. You're the beauty in this here bunch, and that 'hunka-hunka' man is tryin' to get your attention. Why don't you at least cast those smolderin' eyes his way?" Juanita said, her voice beginning to slur.

"Or better yet," Micah said, "walk over to the bar and show off that curvy bod and those long, shapely legs. You'll bowl him over without a word."

"Will you two quit it? He is *not* my type," Pepper said, "and I will not lower my standards."

"Lower your standards?" Juanita said. "Well, *excuse* me." Pepper was exasperating. Her eyes were for Edmond only.

Pepper was a beautiful, dark coppery brown, and she was extremely imposing, just a little less than six feet tall and very refined. She could turn any man's head. And she did. Often. When they made her aware of some man's obvious attraction, she'd shrug and move on, just as she did that night in the Blue Palace. She intimidated many because of her regal appearance and stoic manner. Had either one of them had Pepper's looks, they would have had many brothers groveling in front of them licking their bootstraps.

Micah's life was just so out of wack since Pepper's attack. Pepper's beating needed to be vindicated, and she seemed to be the only one to handle it. She needed to get her mind together. She would have to come to grips with the whole thing. She knew what needed to be done, but she couldn't seem to pull it together.

Juanita, on the other hand, was well aware of what needed to be done, and she'd put her plans into action. She needed Micah's help to implement the whole thing, with some side action from her street-savvy friends. Juanita was the rich kid who enjoyed a little bit of thug life. She was always enamored by the whole gangbanger lifestyle, and she was still in touch with Boogie. Her tales of her walk on the wild side while in public school often captivated Micah and Pepper long into many nights at Deauville. Her parents never had a clue.

It was time for her to approach Micah with her plan, but she had to be careful. Micah could be unpredictable at times, and Juanita wouldn't be surprised if Micah had plans of her own. She was often secretive until she'd made up her mind.

Hell, I'll just play it by ear.

The timing was right, and the longer she stalled, the further the goal loomed. Of that she was certain.

CHAPTER 8

"Hey, Mom. What's going on?"

"Micah, how are you? Nothing much going on here. Your father's cooped up in that office over there. He's in court on Monday morning, and you know McCall, Peterson and Knight can't go into court half-stepping. He said he's wrapping things up right now."

"That's good. Where are Skipper and Tania?"

"It's Saturday, so Tania and her girl, Keisha, are at the Regency. I can't think of the movie they're seeing, and Skipper is at the mall. So, everything's right on track for a Saturday afternoon here. What are you up to today?"

"Nothing much. Just feeling a little down, I guess. I think I've been depressed for the last few months. Armstead and I are going out tonight, so I'm looking forward to that."

"Why don't you come on over here? We haven't had a moment to talk about anything in a while. That office is so busy. You know Ruby would be delighted and will fix you anything you want. You haven't been showing her the love lately, so she's been complaining," Lila said, smiling at the thought of her cantankerous live-in maid. Ruby had been with them since Micah was a baby. Almost twenty-seven years in the next few months. She was a part of the family.

"Yeah, I just might do that. Tell Ruby I would love one of her big ole hamburgers with all the trimmings. I haven't had one in a long time."

"I'll tell her. She'll be delighted. See you in what…? An hour?"

"Yep. I just have to take a quick shower and throw on my jeans. See you later," Micah said, hanging up and heading into her bathroom. She still missed the activity of her parents' home after all this time.

Lila was happy Micah was coming over. She'd seen her at work, and she seemed just fine. She had no idea she'd been depressed about Pepper and her "condition." Oh, yeah, everyone was mad as hell, but Micah seemed perfectly fine.

I need to warn Franklin.

Micah and her father had a special bond. He'd always been able to help her through her various difficulties. Now Lila knew, he'd be able to help her through this current malaise.

Exactly fifty-five minutes later, the doorbell chimed, and Ruby rushed to answer it.

"Ruby, I've missed you. How are you doing?"

"I'm all right now," Ruby said, squeezing Micah. "Come on in here. Here comes your momma now."

"Hey, Mom. You got it all hooked up in that yellow. And, Ruby, you got it smelling good in here." Micah was a student of brevity. She'd just issued two compliments, all in one breath.

Her mother smiled, and Ruby beamed.

"Everything's ready when you want it," Ruby said. She heard Franklin's office door open. "Oh, oh. Your daddy's coming. You better get it while you can. You know he'll eat up everything and then some."

Micah stayed with them all afternoon and told them how distressed she'd been about Pepper and how she felt obligated to take matters into her own hands. Her father talked with her for a long time and told her the police were making headway in the case. What he didn't know was she had made up her mind to go ahead with her plan while she'd been talking with him.

When she got ready to leave, she said, "Thanks for listening, Dad. I feel a lot better already. Don't worry about anything. I'll be fine. I won't do anything crazy, I promise."

She knew the exact moment she'd made up her mind. She just needed to unburden herself before she could move on. Had her father known he'd helped her make the decision she'd been pondering, he'd be devastated. She would make sure he never discovered the truth. When she left, she felt free and unencumbered for the first time in months.

Micah needed to talk with Mick again before she made her move. He might have some answers that could alter her decision. After that, she would approach Juanita. Whichever way she played it, she was ready to roll.

CHAPTER 9

Acapulco, Mexico
June 2002

Edmond took a long swill from his Long Island Ice Tea and wiped the sweat from his brow. His silver-mirrored sunglasses slipped down his nose. The heat was oppressing. He lay on a white padded chaise lounge beside his private pool. His appearance had changed over the last two months. He'd gained a startling twenty-two pounds, and the sun had burnished his skin to a dark golden brown.

He looked down at his six-pack belly, now covered with a dull, oily sheen, and made sure it was displayed. Javier, his personal trainer, had lived up to his fierce reputation. He had worked Edmond day and night, and the results were in evidence. Edmond's sun-bleached hair was now streaked honey-blonde, and he was in the best shape of his life. He still had a month to go in his sun-dappled hideaway, the most expensive single *casita* in the whole mountaintop retreat.

"Angelo. Please arrange for a girl for me tonight. You know the type I like. Seven-thirty will be fine."

"Sure, boss. I'll get right on it," Angelo said as he headed for the *casita*, scurrying barefoot across the hot pavement.

When he entered the luxurious suite, he picked up the phone, staring at the old Windbrook family picture Edmond always carried wherever he traveled. He zeroed in on Edmond's mother, Jeanine, the woman he would describe to the agency.

"Aztec Escort Service. May I help you?"

"Yes. I'd like an escort tonight at seven-thirty *sharp*. I'm at the Las Brisas, *casita* 107. It stands alone at the highest peak. I'd like somebody dark with shoulder length hair, about six feet tall, and with plenty of curves, no hooker types. She must be...ladylike...and speak good. She gotta be dressed like...you know, like she got class. You got all that?"

"Yes, sir. She'll be there at exactly seven-thirty. Is there anything else you require?"

"Nah. Just make sure she's a looker," he said and hung up.

At seven-eighteen, Edmond emerged from his private suite. Angelo snapped to attention. Edmond was impeccable. He wore cream linen slacks and a heavy silk, cream shirt that hung loosely around his body.

"You want a drink, boss?"

"Yes, I think so. I am feeling great tonight. I will have some of that special scotch."

"You got it. You look great. Javier is doing his job *real* good."

"Yes, I am pleased with him. I would love to have him on staff. I have been thinking about offering him a job, but I have not made up my mind," Edmond said in his typical formal manner. He rearranged the marble figure on the coffee table and straightened the magazines.

"He'd like that, boss. I *know* he'd like the states," Angelo said, watching Edmond's reaction as he handed him his scotch.

Edmond surveyed the drink, making sure Angelo had three well-formed ice cubes in it. "Thank you. I will give it some more thou I hope that girl is on time. You know I get upset if I have to wait."

"Yeah. I told them seven-thirty sharp, boss. She'll be here then," Angelo said as he shifted his weight nervously, willing her to be on time.

"Good," Edmond said, pleased about his evening. He crossed his legs, sipped his aged scotch and sat back to await his guest.

At seven-thirty, they heard a soft knock. Edmond glanced at Angelo. "I'll get it, boss." He crossed the massive room and opened the door. "Hello, please come in," he said, stepping back to allow the tall, slender woman entrance.

Edmond stood, pleased with the elegant, refined beauty that approached him. "Hello, I am Edmond. Won't you have a seat? I am just having my first drink of the evening. Would you like something?" he asked, taking in her extreme loveliness.

"I'll have red wine," she said, her accent almost undetectable.

"Angelo, red wine for the lady. And your name is…?"

She hesitated, then flung her long, black hair from her face and said, "Consuelo."

Angelo nodded, knowing this would be his final duty for this part of the evening. He had served in this capacity so many times and in so many locations, and he knew the drill. He poured the wine, crossed the floor and handed her the drink.

"Thanks."

Angelo looked at Edmond and said, "Good night, boss. If you need anything, I'll be in my room."

"Thank you, Angelo. And good night."

He turned to his visitor. "Consuelo, I have a suite where we can talk more comfortably. It's just through that hallway. Why don't we relax in there?" He stood and reached out for her hand.

"That sounds cozy," she said, allowing him to help her to her feet. She followed him into the sumptuous bedroom suite.

"This is lovely, absolutely stunning, actually."

She moved to the balcony and inhaled deeply. The night breeze, perfumed and refreshing, caressed her cheeks. She could see the muted lights of the other *casitas* nestled among the greenery, scattered beneath them. *Casita* 107 was the most exclusive on the retreat. She could hear nothing from that height. Absolute silence and total isolation caused her to shiver, raised her antennae. An internal foreboding infused her. She turned, and he was at her side.

"It *is* breathtaking, thank you," he said, scanning his surroundings. "It's captivating here, especially at dawn and dusk. I visit often. This is the only *casita* I use. It is quite serene, and most of all, private."

They walked back inside, and she stood, trying to assess him. Her intuition had never failed her. Something was amiss, but she dismissed it because she was absorbed in the splendor. She had never seen such grandeur.

"Please make yourself comfortable."

She sat down on the green and beige floral sofa and crossed her legs, exposing a smidgen of thigh. She wore a silk crimson kimono with long side slits and stiletto crimson sandals. Her legs were bare. Edmond sat beside her, scrutinizing her face, noting the strong resemblance to his mother. She was exquisite—dark brown skin, flashing onyx eyes and full cherry-stained lips.

"You are very enticing, Consuelo." He lifted her hair from her face and brushed her lips. She smelled of soap rather than the heavy, exotic perfumes he'd become accustomed to expect.

"Thank you," she said, lowering her eyes.

"How long have you been with the escort service?" he asked, realizing she was new to her well-paid profession.

"Not long, I'm afraid."

Edmond found himself becoming aroused. He moved closer to her, held her face and kissed her, teasing her tongue.

He inhaled deeply, withdrew from the embrace and said, "Please get undressed. I would like to see you nude."

She stood in front of him and took her time. She unbuttoned the asymmetric kimono, revealing a soft, filmy red bra and matching thong bikini panties. She was arresting.

She reached to unhook her bra, but he stood and said, "No, allow me, please."

When he touched her, his passion flared, and he tore the bra from her body, destroying it in the process. He ripped the panties from her hips and flung her on his bed. He peered at her terrified face, absorbed power from her fear. He turned her over, spread her cheeks and entered her anal passage, delirium infusing him. She cried out in pain, but he continued, prodded by her pleading. He tortured her, ripped her internally, but he never released his semen. *That* would come later.

She hovered at the brink of unconsciousness, but she fought to hold on. When her struggles and pleas subsided, he pulled himself from her. She lay motionless beside him, a ploy she contrived for escape. She jumped from the bed to run, but he sprang into action, restraining her easily. She struggled and screamed, but his attack had left her weak.

He grabbed the heavy, marble bookend from the table and struck her once. Blood and matter gushed from her head, splattering his upper body, the headboard and the sheets.

"Ohhh," he moaned in rapture when he realized he'd killed her. He yanked open his bedside drawer, retrieved a condom and put it on. He lowered himself onto her, experienced a powerful release of semen and raped the corpse repeatedly. He lifted himself from her and arranged her body, using his mental camera to record the details.

He positioned her legs to reveal her most intimate secret. At first glance, she appeared the beautiful woman she had been. Upon closer inspection, she was a shameless, seductive vixen. She represented a strange duality that proved to be a significant clue to his psyche. She personified everything he believed his mother to have been.

"You look beautiful, Mommy," he said in a childlike voice. "Beautiful just for me." His mind snapped, hurtling him back in time. Back to the night he saw her enter his father's library dressed in a thin, revealing negligee. He saw her straddle his father's legs, enveloping him in her arms.

As he grew older, he found his mother to be incredibly beautiful and seductively alluring. He worshipped her from afar because she spent her time with her husband. He resented her love for his father, viewed it purely as a means to indulge her sexual fantasies. He envied his father because of it and detested their closeness and devotion to each other. Consequently, he felt abandoned and alone, desperately longing to fulfill her needs. These thoughts, above all else, shaped his personality and have been his lifelong torment.

The rapid, repeating sound of Angelo's buzzer jarred him from his sleep. He'd been expecting the call. He glanced at the digital clock in the darkness—9:10, the red numbers glowed. He pressed the intercom button and said, "I'm here, boss. You need me?"

"Yes, come now. To my bedroom."

"Right."

He placed the receiver down and then picked it back up. He dialed a memorized number and said, "Just got the call. Stay alert…I'll call ya back."

He leapt from his bed. He had responded in this manner on many occasions. He pulled on the clothes he wore in these instances, everything black—jeans, tee shirt, and tennis shoes—and scampered to Edmond's suite.

The door was ajar. "Boss," he said, opening it wider. Edmond was leaning over the woman, obscuring his view.

"Come in. I need help."

When he straightened up and turned, Angelo glimpsed the carnage. Blood covered everything, the beige sheets, now deep red in the faint light.

Angelo hesitated, but he rushed to Edmond's side, taking in the gruesome scene in its entirety. Splatters of matter speckled the headboard; matter he later discovered was part of the woman's brain. Her body lay face up, the right side of her head caved in.

"Take care of this. Call the agency…give them what they want…you know what to do," he said, his right eye twitching.

He wiped his red-stained hands on his cream shirt and hurried from the room, blood covering him all over. The harsh smell of fresh blood permeated the room.

Angelo surveyed the scene. No one would recognize the tall, slim body that lay sprawled across the bed. He was sure Edmond had arranged her in this position. Her long legs were splayed, and her dark hair fanned across the sheets. Her blood-covered face, obscuring her beauty, was turned to one side. Her left arm trailed haphazardly to the floor.

The whole scene was familiar, but it far surpassed anything he had ever seen or been required to clean up. His stomach lurched, but he recovered. The gruesome murder before him attested to just how far his employer's mental state had declined. No one would ever suspect Edmond's fiendish obsession. To anyone who met him, he appeared lucid and calm and in total control. That was his greatest feat.

Angelo would have to get rid of everything, including the blood-soaked mattress, but he was careful *not* to disturb anything just yet. He needed immediate help. He picked up the bedside phone and dialed the number he called earlier.

"Come now. This is much worse than I thought…I need a big van with tinted windows and a king-size mattress. Bring plenty of film. Now!"

He hung up and tiptoed to Edmond's bathroom door. He heard the water pouring from the shower. He knew Edmond would be occupied with his scrubbing for well over the next hour, giving him time to get what he needed, clean up the mess and dispose of the body. Things were looking up.

CHAPTER 10

❀

Atlanta, Georgia
June 2002

Juanita had rehearsed the conversation in her mind for days. The time was now—she was ready to approach Micah. She knocked and entered at the same time.

"Hi, there. How are you doing this morning? What's on your agenda today?" Micah had bolts of fabric strewn across her desk and over her chairs.

"Hey, I'm doing great. Got a couple of meetings before noon, but the afternoon looks quiet. I'm trying some new patterns together. What do you think?"

"I love these two," Pepper said, indicating the black and white conflicting prints.

"Yeah, me, too. What about you? Got everything wrapped up for the show next Friday?"

"Yep. We're making a few changes on a couple of the designs. LaVerne has that covered. Other than that, we're set," Juanita said, delighted to see Micah coming around. She'd been a mess since Pepper's beating.

"Thank the Lord," Micah said. "It's about time something started going right around here."

"Yeah, I'm with that. Let's do lunch. We haven't done that for a while. Can you swing it?"

"Why not? How about Slim's. We haven't had any of that artery-clogging food in a long time. I could use something filling. What do you think?"

"Sounds good to me. What time? Twelve-thirty?" Juanita said.

"Yeah, that's good. Meet you at the elevator."

"You got a deal. See you then."

When Juanita left, Micah's thoughts drifted to their sophomore year at Deauville Academy. Micah, Juanita and Pepper were fifteen years old. They gravitated toward each other because they had something in common—their love of clothes. It was evident in the way they dressed when not in class. Their styles were different, but their attention to detail was evident and similar. It set them apart from the others. Their friendship blossomed quickly.

Micah invited them to spend the Thanksgiving holiday of their sophomore year at Deauville with her family in Atlanta. They both accepted. When Micah took Pepper and Juanita on a tour of her mother's fashion and design center that weekend, they were smitten. Her mother, Lila, had been a Fashion Fair and runway model in Chicago and Paris before she married Franklin. She opened the design center in the heart of Atlanta when Tania, her youngest child, started elementary school. It was an immediate success.

That Thanksgiving weekend, the three girls made the plan that would help them fulfill their dreams. They worked their ideas for two and a half years before they revealed them to Lila, when they were seniors at Deauville. The professional, up-to-the-minute design sketches they showed Lila took her aback. They told her they were all going to attend the McMillan School of Design in Chicago when they graduated from Deauville Academy. Lila was delighted. She had worked with Janice McMillan during her years as a model in Chicago.

Lila and Franklin began plans to expand her business as soon as the girls graduated from high school. After Lila saw their designs, she was convinced they could capture the audience that had been reluctant to support her—the up-and-coming young professionals.

When the girls graduated from the McMillan School of Design in Chicago, they walked through the door of Lila's fashion and design center with their first clothing line already intact. They had spent the last three years of high school designing clothes they adored. Thirteen months after they started work with Lila, the *MJP* line was introduced to the public. The advanced hype and extensive advertising that Lila provided paid off big time. Their clothes were an instant success, capturing the attention of a younger, more affluent clientele.

Lila promoted them to vice president over their own lines. They were their own best advertisement. They had always dressed to the hilt, but now they were in their glory. They wore their own designs exclusively and made sure the clothes were always shown to their best advantage. They each had their own distinctive image, and their designs appealed to a broad spectrum of society.

Micah's *M* line reflected her personal relaxed, comfortable style. Her designs were semi-casual, but with a professional bent; Juanita's *J* line represented her hip, over-the-top dramatic approach to dressing. She designed the latest cutting-edge styles that appealed to those who were ethnic, exotic and fashionable. Pepper's *P* line veered toward the classics. They were chic, elegant and sophisticated, but most of all, they were always appropriate and current. When the *MJP* line was introduced, the three young designers became the darlings of the "wanna-bes."

Micah's telephone buzzer interrupted her reverie. "Yes," she said, aggravated by the intrusion.

"Mr. LaRue's on line one."

"Thanks, I'll take it."

"Hello, how are you doing?" he said.

"Good, this morning. What about you?"

"I've got a light day. How about lunch?"

"Oh, Armstead. I just made plans with Juanita. We haven't been to lunch in ages. How about a rain check?"

"Ahhh, I'm disappointed, but I'll survive. We still on for tonight?"

"I wouldn't miss it. Looking forward to seeing the *real* Armstead," she said, conjuring up all kinds of illicit thoughts.

"You got it. Just be prepared."

"I can't wait. See you at seven."

"Right," he said, ending with a smile.

As Micah and Juanita made their way inside Slim's, they had to stop a number of times to acknowledge their clients and fans. They caused a ruckus wherever they went in Atlanta since they'd become well-known local designers. Everyone wanted to see what they were wearing, reporters wanted to interview them and their clients demanded attention. That was the price of fame and fortune, but they had no real complaints. Their ultimate goal was to gain international acclaim.

"Good lord! Can you believe it took us fifteen minutes just to to our table," Juanita said to Micah while smiling and waving someone she'd never laid eyes on.

"I know. It can be a pain when you're just trying to do something simple. Armstead hates all the commotion. But you know we can't knock it. We could be out there starving and still trying to come up with the rent."

"Now that's a scary thought, but who wouldn't hate all the fanfare? I can understand Armstead's feelings."

"Me, too, but girl, don't we wear some bad-ass stuff? That's the good thing about our job. 'We da bomb,' Micah said, giving Juanita five.

"You got dat right."

Settling down, they reached for their menus. They hadn't relaxed and had any fun in over three months. Not since Pepper's calamity.

"I'm having the ribs special," Micah said after she glimpsed the menu.

"Me, too. We need some grease on these pampered fingers."

Just as they leaned back to chat while waiting on the waitress to take their order, Micah's cell phone rang.

"Damn. I meant to turn this phone off."

She retrieved the phone from her purse and saw Mick's name and number. "It's Mick. I've been trying to catch him. It'll be just a minute."

She flipped the cover and said, "Mick, where have you been hiding?"

She listened. "Right now? Juanita and I are just about to eat…No, just wait for me. I'll be right there. Bye."

Looking at Juanita, she said, "Mick is about to leave for the airport, but he has some news about Edmond that he didn't want to discuss over the phone. Order my food for take out, and I'll see you back at the office."

She grabbed her purse and left, leaving Juanita frustrated and curious.

CHAPTER 11

❀

Micah couldn't imagine what kind of news Mick had uncovered. She knew Juanita was pissed about being stranded at lunch and having to catch a taxi back to work, but Mick said it was important. He was headed to Acapulco, and said he needed to discuss his discovery with her in person. When Micah arrived, Sela was on the phone. Micah waved, picked up a magazine and took a seat.

When Sela placed the phone down, she said, "Lord! Didn't think I'd ever get her off the line." She came around her desk and squeezed Micah to her. She knew Mick had a special attachment to Micah, and for some reason, she felt the same way. "How are you doing? Mick told me you came by the other day. Sorry I missed you."

"Me, too, but it was early. I'm doing fine. You look terrific. I can tell you've been in the gym."

"I sure have. Fighting the weight is a full time battle."

"Don't I know it. Mick told me he had a plane to catch. He's expecting me."

"Yes, he mentioned it. Just go on in. I just wanted to see you before you disappeared into his inner sanctum."

"Thanks. We still haven't had that lunch we keep talking about. Call me, and let's get it on the calendar."

"I will. I'd like that."

She knocked and then peeked into Mick's office. "Hey, I'm here," she said, happy to see him.

"Come on in. I've been waiting for you."

"What's happening in Acapulco?"

"We found Edmond. He's down there. I'm leaving in a couple of hours. He's been there for two months. Staying at the Las Brisas Acapulco. I'm going to look around and see what he's been up to. Got an old buddy from Harvard down there looking into it for me. He'll have some info by the time I arrive. I'll keep you posted," he said, peering into her eyes.

"Mick, you don't know how much this means to me. Don't worry about the expense. Do what you have to…stay as long as it takes. Are you staying at the Las Brisas?"

"Uh-uh, too expensive. I'm at the Radison Acapulco. It's just right across the bay."

"Mick, stay at the Las Brisas. I insist. I want you right there with him. Buzz Sela now and have her make the changes."

"All right. You've twisted my arm." He talked to Sela and had her switch hotels.

"I'll call you from down there. Here's my cell phone number. Call me if you need anything," he said, writing down the number and handing it to her.

"You have all my numbers. Call me anytime on any of the phones. I want to know what he's up to—hiding out in Mexico. I know you're on a tight time frame, Mick. Don't let me keep you."

She stood to leave, and so did he. She felt a need to hug him, and she moved around his desk and pulled him to her. "Thanks so much, Mick. You've done so much already." She felt a stirring in her loins as she held him. He pulled her closer, moved into her.

"You don't have to thank me. I would have done it anyway," he said, reluctant to let her go.

She made the break, composing herself as best she could. "Take care of yourself down there. He *is* dangerous, you know."

"Yes, he is. And I will be careful."

She walked to the door and before she opened it, she turned and said, "Give me a call when you get there. I want to hear from you."

"Okay, but it'll be late."

"Call me anyway. Bye."

Micah thought about her conversation with Mick as she drove back to the design center. He didn't tell her anything he couldn't have said over the phone. Why did he insist she come to his office? She had been drawn to him when they were in high school, but her feelings for him today surprised her. She also detected Mick's reluctance to release her and the undercurrent of tension between them.

What's going on? After all this time, why now?

When Micah returned to her office, she found Juanita in the galley, revising a design to be used in the upcoming fashion show.

"I'm starving. Where's my food?"

"In your office," Juanita said.

"Good. Come on. I need to tell you what Mick said."

"Did he find Edmond?"

"Uh-huh, he sure did. In Acapulco, no less."

"Acapulco?" Juanita said. "I guess we shouldn't be surprised. He's always been a weasel. Always squirming out of something. Micah, we are *not* letting him get away this time. I was going to talk with you about all this at lunch, but you had to leave. I've got some plans."

"Some plans? About Edmond? Pray tell. Can't wait to hear all about them."

They entered Micah's office, and she headed straight for the food. "Okay. Tell me about your plans. How long have you been thinking about all this?"

"A while. Now don't go all ballistic, but I think I can get my boys to get to him. I mentioned it to Boogie, and he said they're in. Just waiting for me to give them the word," Juanita said, anxious to hear what Micah thought of the idea.

"Just what would you have them do?" Micah asked, licking her fingers. "Excuse my manners, girl. I haven't had a thing all day."

"Micah. Eat anyway you want. I'm serious about Boogie and the Blazers. What do you think?"

"Well," Micah said, wiping her hands, "I think you should forget about Boogie and the Blazers and concentrate on Johnny."

"Johnny? Now that's some *serious* shit. You know Johnny is for real."

"I know. And we're not? We ain't half-stepping, Nita. I think we should definitely get Johnny involved. You just said we can't let Edmond get away with this crap again, didn't you? I was going to ask you about Johnny, but I didn't know how you'd feel about it since you two have been…What have you and Johnny been, Juanita? Fuck buddies or is it more serious? You've been tight-lipped about him, so I thought you might have taken it to another level and didn't want me to know."

"Fuck buddies *only*, I assure you. Micah, I don't know about Johnny. I need to think about this a while."

"Well, you think about it. I'm positive he's the way to go. How long do you have to think?"

"I don't know. I'll get back to you on that," she said. "See you later."

"Bye. Hey, Nita…study long, you study wrong," she cautioned.

"Yeah. That's what they tell me. Bye."

"Hi, Johnny. It's me. I need to come over. You busy?" Juanita asked.

"Not if you're coming over. Is this a pleasure trip or is it something else?

"Something else, but it could develop into something you just might like."

"Well, come on now, then. You want me to order in anything ᵕ eat?"

"Lord, no. I ate at Slim's today. I won't need any food for weeks. See you shortly," Juanita said and hung up.

Juanita's parents would be shocked if they knew she had been involved with Johnny Diamond for the last two years. They gave her brother, Juan, a lot more slack than they ever gave her when she was his age.

Miguel, Juanita's father, emigrated from Peru during the 1950s. He met Desiree shortly after his arrival. They enjoyed a brief courtship and were married three months later. They were a tight-knit family with traditional values. Miguel talked of his life in Peru to his children often. Juanita set her goal to visit his homeland when she was eight years old. Machu Picchu, Peru, the famous mountaintop city that's considered "The Lost City of the Incas" has fascinated her all her life. She planned to take some time off from work over the next year to visit it.

Had her parents known she had been involved with the Southwest Blazers gang when she was in public school, they would have held her prisoner in their own home. She and Boogie, the gang leader, had a thing back then, but she kept the relationship secret from everyone but her schoolmates.

Juanita met the well-known, urbane Johnny Diamond at one of the *soirees* the design center hosted. He was rich and powerful, and he contributed generously to the design center whenever Lila, Micah's mother, needed to build up the coffers. He was strongly attracted to the gorgeous mocha-colored Lila McCall, but she didn't give him the time of day. Franklin was the light of her life. Johnny was a patient man. He was convinced she would come around. Not many women could resist him and his generosity whenever he became enamored.

When Juanita found out Johnny was Atlanta's most notorious womanizer and owner of the most exclusive nightspot around, Club Eden, she was intrigued. In addition to his reputation, he was exceptionally handsome and well dressed. He was what she would consider an older man, but who the hell cared? She wasn't looking for a husband, just a man who could hold her interest.

When she spotted Johnny talking to Lila at the *soiree*, she honed her way in for an introduction. She flirted outrageously, and he invited her out for breakfast. She was young and determined, but most of all, spunky and vivacious. He recognized her for what she was, but he found her a delight. He knew she was drawn to excitement and adventure, but so was he. That was two years ago, and they have been seeing each other ever since—not exclusively, but whenever they felt the need. They were both pleased with the arrangement.

Juanita rang Johnny's doorbell, and he opened the door immediately. "Come in, pretty lady," he said.

"Hi, Johnny," she said. She walked right up to him, put her arms around his neck, moved against him and gave him a kiss that rocked.

"Wow! And this is no pleasure trip? You coulda fooled me," he said, grinding into her. Johnny was a man who liked hips, and he found Juanita's curvaceous and appealing.

"Just thought I'd let you know who was boss," she said She knew he liked bad-ass girls.

"You don't have to convince me. I *know* who's boss, he said, smiling down at her.

She backed away from him, sat down on his expensive, tan leather sofa and crossed her legs high. "See anything you like?"

"Damn right, I do. You know I do, too." He stood looking down at her.

"Since we got all that straight, let's talk."

"Yes, ma'am. What can I do for you?"

"I need your help?"

"That's a first. How so?"

"You know my girlfriend, Pepper? The one that was beaten by that fucked-up boyfriend of hers a few months back?"

"Yeah, you told me about her."

"I think I need your people to deal with him."

He sat down beside her. "You sure about that?"

"Hell, I don't know, Johnny! I'm trying to make up my mind. What would they do, if I agreed to go for it?"

"Anything you wanted them to."

"I see. Would you have it done for me?"

"Damn right, I would. Just say the word," he said, realizing she'd never have the courage to go too far.

"All right. This is where I am. I'm thinking about it, but I don't know what I want right now. I've never done anything like this, you know that," she said, her voice quavering.

"Yes, I do. I also know, you like walking the edge. You like the excitement. That's why you're attracted to me. Don't you think I know that? I also know you like a little roughness on the sheets," he said, knowing she'd be embarrassed by his comment.

"Oh, shoot! What are you talkin' 'bout? Don't even go there," she warned.

"Okay, just joking, but you know it's true. Can't say I mind accommodating you, either. How 'bout it? He moved closer to her. "Come on, baby. We haven't been together in a couple of weeks. What'll you say?" he asked, nibbling her ear.

"Come on, Johnny. Let's get this straight, and I can think about that pleasure trip you're so willing to take later."

"All right. What do you want me to do? Make up your mind, Nita. We got more important things to do."

"I'll let you know soon. Just need to think about it a little more. How about that?"

"All right. Whatever you want. Now, come on over here and show me how much you appreciate me."

She stood up, unzipped her skirt and flung it into his face. He took it away and stretched out his long legs, making himself comfortable for the show. She did a slow strip tease for him, knowing he liked a sexy build-up. When she was naked, she reached out to him.

"Come on, big boy. Show me what you got." She led him to his bedroom and stayed all night.

CHAPTER 12

Acapulco, Mexico
June 2002

Micah's phone rang at 2:20 a.m. She was sound asleep, but she knew it was Mick.

"Hello."

"Hey. Sorry to wake you, but I just got in. I'm bone tired, but I'm tucked into the Las Brisas. We were stuck at the airport for hours. Haven't talked with Keith yet, so I don't have anything to relate. Just wanted you to know I'm here," he said, his heart racing because he was talking to her.

"Okay, Mick. Get some sleep and call me when you talk with Keith. I've got an eleven o'clock meeting in the morning, but other than that, I'm free, I think."

"Okay, I'll call you tomorrow...or rather sometime today."

"All right. Mick?"

"Huh?"

"Take care, and...I miss you," she couldn't believe she said.

"Hmm. I miss you, too," he said in the deepest, sexiest voice she'd ever heard. "I'll call you soon. Bye."

"Damn," she said to herself. "I'll never get back to sleep now," and she didn't get another wink all night. She got up and made a cup of tea and picked up the novel she had been reading. She couldn't concentrate on that, so she put it down and concentrated on what was going on between Mick and her. Things were heating up pretty fast with them. She felt excitement creeping into her life, and she hadn't felt that in a long time.

Mick was tired, but he couldn't sleep either. He tossed and turned until he saw the first rays of light streak across the bay. He walked out on the balcony, mesmerized by the red and gold dawn suspended above the treetops, far off into the horizon. He inhaled deeply, taking in the fresh, heavily scented morning air. He detected the mingling perfume of tropical flowers, a heady mixture that he enjoyed. He could see the pink and white *casitas* nestled among the hillside foliage. The muted sunrise held him captive.

The Las Brisas Acapulco was magnificent. He was happy Micah insisted he stay here. It was worth every penny, and he decided to pick up the tab for the hotel expenses. It was the least he could do. He had work to accomplish, but he preferred to just sit and think. His life was about to change, he could feel it. He knew he had some decisions to make, and he had stalled long enough.

CHAPTER 13

❀

Atlanta, Georgia
July 2002

The doorbell rang, and Micah put down her spoon, wiped her hands on her kitchen towel and removed her apron. She stopped at the foyer mirror and brushed a wisp of hair from her temple. After a closer glance at her face, she opened the door.

"Welcome," she said with a seductive smile. "Come in." She pulled the door wider, allowing him entrance.

"Something smells good in here," Armstead said, stepping inside.

"I've been slaving all day. Only for you would I even attempt to do this," she said.

He turned and pulled her to him, "I've been watching the clock all day. I had to stop myself from leaving at noon. I've missed you." He kissed her, nibbling her lower lip.

"I've missed you, too." She loved his masculine smell—faint cologne mixed with pure man. She kissed him again, lingering in his arms.

"You should have called and told me. I would have been over here in a flash," he said.

"I didn't want to interrupt your day. I played hooky to prepare for you. It's been a long time since I took a day to myself. We'll do it together the next time."

"Sounds like a plan to me."

She pressed her body to him, giving him a prelude of her evening plans, then disengaging herself, pulled him into the kitchen. "If you'll pour us some wine, I'll check the oven. Are you hungry?"

"Just for you," he said, fondling her from behind as she bent to tend the roast.

"Let's just relax awhile in the family room. Everything's ready when you want to eat."

He poured the wine and carried the glasses to the family room. She left everything on warm and joined him on the sofa. "I had a great day," she said. "Got up late, took my shower and had breakfast on the balcony. I could get used to that real fast."

"It sounds great, but knowing you, you'd be bored within a week."

"You think so? I don't know...I could do it for a while if I could keep Juanita from calling me so often."

"Did she call you today?"

"Uh-huh. She wants us to visit Pepper tomorrow. I'm looking forward to it even though we talk everyday."

"How's she doing?"

"She says fine, but we'll see tomorrow. When we saw her last week, she had the patch over her eye, and she's still using the cane. The worst thing is her flagging spirits. She hasn't snapped back the way I'd hoped. I think she needs some therapy, but...I don't know. I'm not feeling too good about her whole situation."

"Is that the way Juanita feels, too? Is that why she suggested the visit tomorrow?"

"I don't know. She's been tied up all week working on the fashion show. We'll get a chance to talk tomorrow."

Armstead removed his shoes and put his feet up on her big leather ottoman.

"Comfortable?" she asked.

"Uh-huh, but I want you."

"Ditto," she whispered, leaning to kiss him.

He sighed and relaxed, letting her take over. She removed his tie, unbuttoned his shirt and lifted his tee shirt. She tweaked his nipples and caressed his chest.

"That feels good," he said as he closed his eyes and enjoyed the softness of her lips. When he could stand no more, he stood up, took her hand, and led her into her bedroom. She followed, ready to accommodate him.

"The food…don't you want to eat?"

"Just you," he replied, without a second thought.

The phone startled Micah and woke her. It took her a moment to adjust. Armstead turned, wrapping her in his arms. Memories of their lovemaking flooded her. She smiled and reached for the phone. "Hello."

"Micah, it's Mick. Did I wake you?"

"Uh-huh, but that's okay. It's Saturday, and I can always go back to sleep. How are you?" she asked hoarsely.

"I'm fine. Just wanted you to know we've come up with quite a bit on Edmond. He's been a busy boy since he's been down here."

Now alert, she asked, "Oh? How so?"

"He's changed his appearance, for one thing. He's gained 20 to 25 pounds since he's been here, and he's lived in the sun. He's very dark. I would have never suspected he could tan like this without any trace of redness. If you could see his before and after pictures, you'd never recognize him. It's incredible. Keith and his team are looking into the disappearance of a young woman, a lady of the evening, if you will, who might have been involved with him. They're trying to make a connection. If they do, that might throw a whole new light on things. Oh, and I think he's planning to leave here sometime soon, so we've got to move fast."

"Has he purchased tickets?"

"No, but his bodyguard inquired about departing flights to Atlanta yesterday."

"I see. Good work, Mick. Just keep me in the loop every step of the way. She hesitated, but said, "You okay?" She wanted to say more, but couldn't because Armstead had her encircled in his arms.

"Yes, I am." His voice softened, and he continued, "How about you? You doing all right?"

"Yes," she said. She could tell he wanted to talk more intimately, but she couldn't respond because of Armstead's presence. "Things have been complicated, but we'll talk about that when you come home."

"Okay, we will. I'll keep you informed…let you know what we find out."

"Call me anytime, Mick. Bye," she said, hating to let him go.

"What's happening in Acapulco?" Armstead asked.

"Mick thinks Edmond is preparing to leave to come back here."

"Have they been able to pinpoint anything?"

"Not yet," she said, readjusting her pillow and shifting in his arms.

I don't know how this is all going to work out, she thought. Her mind went back to Mick. She thought about what it would be like to make love to him. The thought was nothing new. She'd fantasized about them when they were teenagers. She felt a stab of guilt, as Armstead pulled her closer, allowing her to feel his desire. He fondled her breast, indicating his rising passion. She did nothing to discourage him, simply responded in kind.

CHAPTER 14

❀

Juanita rang Micah's doorbell at noon. Armstead was reading the paper on the balcony, and Micah was pulling her hair back into a ponytail when they heard the chimes.

"I'll get it," Armstead yelled. He opened the door and smiled at Juanita. "Hey, come on in. Micah's just about ready, I think. How are you doing?"

"I'm doing great." Micah told her earlier that Armstead was there, but they were still on to visit Pepper, so she wasn't surprised to see him. "What about you?"

"Working like the devil, but other than that, I'm doing great. You look good. Micah told me you were into your fitness routine. It's paying off. Keep up the good work."

"Thanks. I've got the weight-thing down, but containing these hips is another matter. Can you convince Micah to get with the program, even though she looks great not doing one thing? She gets on everybody's nerves with that. I have to work like hell to keep these hips half way in control."

"Now who can convince Micah to do anything she doesn't want to do? You know how she is," he said.

"Yes, I do. Forget I even said that." She turned towards Micah's bedroom and called, "What up? You ready to roll?"

"I'm ready. Just looking for my black cap. It's here in the closet somewhere," Micah said in a muffled voice.

"Armstead, she might be ready when you pick her up, but I've yet to have that honor," Juanita said in feigned exasperation.

Micah walked into the room. "I heard that. Let's hit it."

"Look at you. Girl, you make me too sick. Looking all fly and all. We're just going to see Pepper. I can't stand you," she said.

Micah was lean with an athlete's body. Where Juanita was curvaceous, Micah was straight. They each envied the other's figure. Micah pulled her baseball cap down and adjusted her ponytail through the hole in the back. She looked at Armstead, who stood watching them go through their usual ritual, and she said, "See you when I get back. You going to do any work today?"

"I'm doing nothing but relax. Take your time. I'll watch TV and just do whatever. Say hello to Pepper for me."

"All right, we will. Bye, sweetie," she said, pecking his lips.

As soon as they were out the door, Juanita said, "Things must be heating up between you two, huh?"

"Why do you say that? Because he spent the night?"

"Well, yeah…and you both seem so content."

"Things are going pretty well between us, but…oh, hell, Juanita. I know this is going to blow you away, but I think a little some'um, some'um's going on between me and Mick." Micah had always had her unique expressions, but "some'um, some'um" had been one of her favorites for years.

"Huh? You and Mick? He's still in Acapulco, isn't he?"

"Yeah, he is, but we've been talking. He called this morning when Armstead and I were still in bed. We've both kind of indicated an interest in each other during some of our other conversations, and I could tell this morning he wanted to say something or have me say something, but Armstead was right there. He didn't know that, however. I know he must be confused about me. I've always been attracted to him, remember? At Deauville, remember how we flirted, but never did anything about it?"

"Yeah, I remember. What are you going to do? What about Armstead? Girl, you just better tread lightly," she admonished.

"I know. You know I damn well *better* know. I'm just having some fantasies about Mick, that's all. Just don't want to get caught up in the moment."

"Well, we've both been known to do that. Just take it day-by-day."

"Yeah, I will."

"It'll be good to see Pepper," Juanita said, leaving Micah still thinking about Armstead and Mick.

"Huh? Yeah...it will be," Micah said, stepping into Juanita's black sports Mercedes.

"I talked to Johnny, and he's ready to roll just as soon as I give him the word. I don't know, Micah. I don't know if I'm with all that."

"Well, you just better get with it. That's the way it's going to be. You and I both agreed we wouldn't let Edmond get away with that beating he put on Pepper. Not again. We're doing it, Juanita. Get used to it. Call Johnny back and tell him to move it."

"How far are we talking, Micah? That's what I'm talkin' 'bout."

"Johnny's boys will have to wipe him out, Juanita. Otherwise, Edmond will have her under his spell in no time. She's weak for him. She just can't help herself where he's concerned."

"Are you willing to have that on your conscience?" Juanita asked.

"Yes, I am. I've thought about it, Nita. I don't know if I could do it, but just thinking about what he's done to Pepper, I would be tempted. We're talking about our best friend. A permanent limp, blind in one eye, scars all over her face. She'd do the same for us if we were in her shoes. I'm convinced of it. So, let Johnny know to get on the stick. Mick said Edmond would be back in town soon. So, let Johnny know. Okay?"

"Yeah, I know you're right, but...*killing* him? That's some rough shit, Micah."

"Hello? You're the one who craves all this fucked-up crazy shit…the thug life, the shoot 'em ups. Not me. What the fuck are you talking about now? Come on, Nita, don't get me going. It's too damn early in the day for all this shit."

"I know I'm attracted to a lot of that gut-bucket bullshit, Micah, but I've never even *thought* about killing anybody."

"And you think I have? Well, get used to it. That's the way it's going to be," Micah said, allowing no further comment. The decision had been made.

They didn't say another word until they rolled up into the Hankerson driveway.

"Okay. You all right?" Juanita said.

"Yeah, I'm fine. I'm sorry about losing it back there, but we've already talked about this, Nita. So, let's go on in here and just act normal. We got to get Pepper back on track."

"Right. I'm cool. Let's go," Juanita said.

Dr. Hankerson saw them drive up and opened the door before they rang the bell. "Hello, ladies. I saw you pull in. Pepper's in the family room. Come on inside."

When Micah and Juanita saw Pepper sitting on the window seat, staring into space, their hearts broke.

"Hey, girl. How you doing? Did LaVerne tell you we were coming over?" Juanita asked.

"Oh, hi. Yes, she told me. Don't you both look great? Where're you off to?"

"Just here. We thought we'd see if we could get you out with us today. What do you say to that?" Micah asked.

"Out? Where? I don't think so. I don't want to be seen like this. I don't think I could face anyone looking like this."

"Come on, Pepper. We'll just ride around, go to the park…or anywhere you want to go," Micah said.

"Uh-uh. Not until I've at least had some work done on my face. What would people say? I don't want anyone seeing me like this."

Juanita and Micah exchanged glances. The plastic surgery would prove beneficial, but her eye was gone. She'd either have to get a false eye, wear the patch or both. Micah thought the patch would add a lot of intrigue, a whole shitload of mystery. What man in his right mind could resist a woman who lived the kind of life in which her eye was destroyed, and she looked and acted like Pepper—all ladylike and proper, yet with an eye missing? Please. Not a goddamn one. They'd get off big-time on that kind of mixed message, have all kinds of bedroom fantasies. She was certain of that. The patch would be her suggestion.

The therapy would help the limp, but her doctors said she'd never get rid of it. That might even be another plus.

Damn. Pepper's got it all, and she can't even enjoy it. She'll be as good as new as soon as she has her face fixed.

"All right, Pepper. We're going to spend the day with you. What shall we do?" Juanita asked.

"I'd love to catch up on some movies. I want to see *Monster's Ball*. I know you've seen it, but could we watch that today?" Pepper said, looking at them both.

"*Monster's Ball*, it is. You're going to be surprised, but I won't spoil it for you. Just let us know what you think of it after you've seen it, okay?" Juanita said.

"Deal," Pepper said, smiling.

Juanita left to get the movie from Block Busters and stopped by Kroger's to get some beer. When they finished watching the movie, Juanita said, "What did you think of that love scene between Halle and Billy Bob? Was it realistic?"

"Yes, I think it was. I know it was a bit graphic, but a woman like that, who has nothing in her life anymore, might approach any man under the right circumstances. I've learned to 'never say never.' She just wanted a little affection, and he'd been nice to her. Remember that line Sammy Davis use to say, 'Nobody knows where the nose goes when the doors close'? That scene was a perfect example."

Juanita countered, "Chile, what kind of shit is that? I'm with Angela Bassett. They just created that scene. That's just some fantasy in some white man's fucked-up imagination. Come on. Get real."

"Juanita," Micah said, "We can't pigeon-hole all black women nor all white men. Nor all of any specific group of people for that matter. You know for a fact, we have not always used common sense, even when we knew it was called for. Thua! Didn't we just have this conversation? Don't get lost in the moment? What's up with you? Don't let me act all crazy up in here," she said, getting more pissed off by the minute with Juanita and her off-the-wall bullshit.

"Come on, you two. This is *not* a major catastrophe. It's just a movie," Pepper said, trying to restore order in the house.

Nita is getting on my last good nerve. We're all uptight. I just need to let it go.

They ordered in pizza, and Juanita and Micah drank the beer Juanita bought. They knew Pepper would never go near the beer. In fact, they never understood why she loathed beer so much either. She could be *real* strange in some ways when you got down to it. Pepper seemed fine, but Micah sensed things were not as great as they appeared.

Johnny would be able to help put some of the pieces back together. It was time they moved on. Micah knew she'd have to take Juanita kicking and screaming along for the ride where their plans with Johnny were concerned. That was her minor role. Her big plan could not be verbalized. Not to a single soul. She was willing to bear that burden alone. She prayed she could avoid what loomed ahead for her, but that was yet to be determined.

CHAPTER 15

Acapulco, Mexico
July 2002

"It has to be tonight. We're leaving tomorrow afternoon, so spread the word. Keep everything tight, just like we planned. Ya got all that? Okay, wait for my call," Angelo said, and hung up.

Angelo sat alone in his room, rehashing his plans. They had to be careful. Edmond must have no inkling of anything. The element of surprise was crucial to their success. He paced the room, analyzing the risks. His buzzer sounded, immobilizing him. He answered, "Yes, boss. I'm here. You need me?"

"Yes. Please come to my suite."

"I'll be right there."

When he arrived at Edmond's bedroom door, he knocked and said, "It's me, boss."

"Come in. Are we ready for the return trip tomorrow?"

"Everything's done. We just have a few things left to pack. That's it."

"Good. I've asked for a light meal tonight—just a salad with shrimp. I'm planning to go to bed early. It's your last night. You're free. I'll need nothing else tonight. Perhaps you and Javier might do something. Whatever…just wanted you to know that."

"Thanks, boss. That's nice. Might try to reach Javier. It might be fun to paint the town. I'll let you know if I leave."

"Good. I'm going to take a shower and just relax and read. Have fun, if you decide to do anything."

"Thanks, I will." Angelo lingered, just long enough to hear Edmond's shower raining water. He went to the kitchen for a hand towel to muffle the sound, returned to the front door and tapped the small glass sidelight pane from the outside with his knife. He left the room, satisfied his plans were in full bloom.

Two hours later, Angelo dialed his contact. "He's in his room reading. Everything's done. Make it one hour tops," he said, hanging up. One hour later, Angelo heard a light tapping on his window. He cracked it open and heard the whisper, "We're here. They're already inside."

"Thanks. Stay put. I'm going to lie down now."

His contact nodded. Five minutes later, the buzzer sounded, and Edmond was frantic. "Something's wrong. Someone's inside, I think. Hurry. Now," he whispered, panic overtaking him.

"Be right there," Angelo said, slamming the phone down, retrieving his gun and walking to Edmond's bedroom with his gun pointed, scanning as he moved. He saw the masked intruder. He trained his gun on him, but someone from behind knocked him out. Three masked assailants overtook Edmond, forced him face down on the bed and tied his hands behind him.

They sat him up and spread the telltale photos before him. He looked at them in shocked horror.

How did they get these pictures? They must be destroyed.

They were horrendous, blood everywhere. The woman was still in the pose he arranged, her long black hair fanned across the bed, her head bashed in and turned to one side. Her long legs, seductively open, allowed him the glimpse that he desired. Edmond couldn't take his eyes away. He was remembering the scene, savoring its horror. His intruders watched him, deciphering his thoughts.

"You sick motherfucker," the tallest man said. He threw a hard punch, knocking him backwards and across the bed. Edmond recognized the New York accent.

A New Yorker? Down here? What's going on?

"We want one million dollars or these pictures go straight to the police. We want the money by 1:00 p.m. tomorrow. Do you understand?"

"Yes, I understand. It might take me a little longer. The money has to come from the states," Edmond said, his right eye already twitching.

"By 1:00 p.m. tomorrow or else! We'll contact you." One of the men snatched up the pictures, and they vanished.

"Angelo. Angelo," Edmond called. Angelo was still unconscious. When he awoke a short time later, his head throbbing with pain, he called, "Boss? Are you all right?" He rose from the floor and staggered into the bedroom. He saw Edmond's panic-stricken face. "Are you okay? Are you hurt?" Angelo asked.

"I'm all right. We need to call someone...not the police. My hands are tied...saw you on the floor...just waiting for you to come around...make the call," Edmond said, rambling, still petrified from the attack. "Javier. Call Javier. Have him come now."

"I'll try. My head..." He lifted the receiver and dialed the memorized number. The phone rang, but no one answered. "No answer, boss. I'll try later," he said, still holding his head.

"Angelo, have the hotel get a doctor. You need to have your head looked after. Call the front desk."

"I don't need—"

"Angelo, call them now."

"All right, but it's nothing," Angelo said, dialing the front desk. "Please send a doctor. We need some help." He turned back to Edmond. "They're sending someone. Did you see anything? Did you hear any names?" Angelo asked, still not thinking clearly.

"Nothing that would help. One was a New Yorker. That's a fact. Didn't hear the other two talk. Who could it be? A New Yorker down here. The night of the murd…with the girl. Did you ever leave the bedroom when I took my shower?"

"Just went to the van several times when I was cleaning up. Why? Did anything about that night come up?

"Yes. They had pictures of the girl sprawled on the bed…pictures of the bed and the room when the girl was moved…they had the whole thing. The pictures were taken in segments. They must have taken pictures each time you left the room. We've got to get them. We need the pictures and the negatives."

"Don't know no New Yorkers down here. Coulda been anybody, I guess," Angelo said, discounting Edmond's observation. Angelo took out his pocketknife and cut Edmond loose.

Angelo called Javier off and on for over an hour, but could not reach him. The doctor arrived and said Angelo had a mild concussion. He prescribed a painkiller and bed rest. Angelo took the medication, but didn't give the bed rest another thought.

As soon as the doctor left, Angelo turned to Edmond and said, "We gotta do somethin' now, boss."

"I know. I've been thinking. I'll call Langley. He'll be able to handle this. He picked up the phone and asked for Thomas Langley in Roswell, Georgia. Mrs. Langley answered.

"Theresa. This is Edmond Windbrook. It's urgent. I've got to speak with Thomas. Is he there?"

"Yes. Just a moment."

He heard a muffled conversation, and Thomas came on the line.

"Edmond? Where are you?"

"Still in Acapulco. I need your help. I've been attacked, and the attackers are asking for a million dollars. I need the money now. Tomorrow morning at the latest. I'll explain later."

"What is it? Do you want—"

"No. No one is to know. Get the money here tomorrow morning. You've got all the information you need. Let me know when you send it. We're leaving here tomorrow afternoon. Four o'clock, I believe. Do you understand? Do not notify anyone."

"Yes. First thing in the morning. I'll call you when it's done."

"Thanks, Thomas. See you when I get home."

Thomas Langley was a partner in Langley, Stanford and Wright, the oldest and most respected law firm in the state. Keeping Edmond Windbrook as a client was Thomas' main concern. He would do whatever he had to do to accommodate his request. When Edmond hung up, Thomas went to work. He set everything in motion that night. Getting the money to him in the morning would be his first priority.

Mick and Keith heard the whole thing. Keith planted his surveillance equipment in Edmond's *casita* the week Mick arrived in Acapulco, but in spite of that, they had been unable to connect him to the missing call girl. Tonight was their lucky night. They saw the intruders enter, heard their conversations and followed them when they left. They confiscated the photos and negatives from the blackmailers and turned them over to the police *after* they'd copied everything and obtained the information they needed.

At 7:30 a.m. the next morning, a loud knock awakened Edmond. He looked at his clock and decided not to answer. The knocking continued, and he got up, threw on his silk robe and answered the door.

He was agitated. When he flung open his door, he said, "Who are…" He stopped short. He saw two uniformed policemen. "What is it? What's wrong?"

"Are you Edmond W. Windbrook, III?"

"Why…yes, I am," he answered, worry taking hold. "What is it? Is anything wrong?"

"Yes. We've got a warrant for your arrest. For the murder of Consuelo Menendez. Please get dressed, sir. We need to take you downtown…to the station."

"What? Who is Consuelo Menendez? I don't know a Consuelo Menendez. Come in. Let me get dressed. I need to call my lawyer. I'm an American citizen…Angelo!" he bellowed. "Get out here. Have a seat. I need to get dressed."

Angelo entered the room; hair disheveled, and froze in place when he saw the policemen.

"What's wrong, boss? What's going on?"

"Call Langley now. Tell him I'm being arrested for the murder of a Consuelo Menendez. Tell him to come now. Today."

He placed his hand over his right eye to stop its rapid twitching, but couldn't control it.

"Right, boss. Don't worry. He'll be here today," Angelo said, heading straight for the phone.

Edmond showered for an hour. The policemen stood the whole time. They were anxious and ready to leave and told Angelo to get him. He entered the steam-filled bathroom and said, "Boss, the police are ready to go."

"Okay. I'll be right there."

They took Edmond to the station and held him all day. Thomas Langley and Daniel Wright arrived in Acapulco at 6:15 p.m. They went straight to the police station. They'd spent the last 24 hours working to resolve Edmond's issues. The Windbrook millions kept them in business, and they had no complaints.

CHAPTER 16

Atlanta, Georgia
July 2002

"Mick Sutherland's on line two," Dana said.

"Thanks, I'll take it," Micah said, brushing her hair aside and picking up.

"Mick, how are you?"

"Hanging in. Just thought I'd bring you up-to-date on events down here. Everything's broken loose. Three men broke into Edmond's cabana last night armed with incriminating pictures taken of the missing call girl I told you about. The pictures were of the murder scene that occurred in his bedroom. They want a million dollars for the pictures. Edmond has instructed one of his lawyers to get the money here today. He murdered the woman in cold blood. He's much worse than we thought—you couldn't begin to imagine the murder scene nor the acts he committed after the murder. He's a sicko—a real threat to society." Mick paused; he had so much to tell.

"Where is he now? I hope you'll be able to prove all that."

"Well...I haven't finished yet. Keith wired his cabana when I got down here, so we heard everything. We nabbed the guys right on the grounds of the Las Brisas. We turned them over to the police along with the pictures. Edmond's lawyer is on his way here because Edmond is in custody."

"Wonderful. That should do it then, right?"

"It should, but this is Mexico…a whole different kettle of fish. Of course, Edmond's denying everything, and our tapes can't be used as evidence. He's concocted some story about the three guys killing the woman and taking the pictures in order to blackmail him. The real deal is his bodyguard planned the whole thing to get the dough. It's complicated, and you can bet your bottom dollar his lawyers will get right into the mix. I've got to be in Atlanta on Tuesday, but Keith's here…. I'll get back down here as soon as I can. Hubert needs some help wrapping up a big case next week."

"When are you leaving?"

"Monday. I'm arriving at two-fifteen."

"I'll pick you up. I can't believe all this. I don't see how he's going to be able to get out of it. The police have everything they need. It should be an open and shut case."

"That's what you would think under normal circumstances, but we're talking Edmond Windbrook and his high-powered lawyers. Money talks you know, but Edmond's in real trouble regardless. We will just have to wait to see how it'll all shake down. We've done what we could."

"And you've done a great job. You ready to come home?"

"Yeah, I'm ready. It's been a long haul. You'll be at the gate?"

"Yes, I will."

"Can't wait to see you. I'm looking forward to that."

"Me, too. Call me again before you leave."

"Micah…we need to talk. I know that. I should have done it a long time ago."

"We'll have plenty of time to do that. But I know what you're saying."

"It's not going to be easy…a lot to work through."

"Yes, we'll talk about it all. Not now. Face-to-face," she said.

"Yeah, face-to-face. I'd better go, but I'll call before I leave."

"Tonight? Call me back tonight…just want to hear from you."

He smiled, liking what he had just heard. "So, you want to hear from me?"

"Oh, Mick, you know I do. I'll be home. Got to run. I'm already late for a meeting. Mom and Juanita will be down here in a minute, if I don't hurry. Bye."

"Bye…I'll call early." He placed the phone back on the hook, ran his hands through his hair and said to himself, "This is your last chance, Mick. You'd better not fuck it up."

❋   ❋   ❋

Juanita showed up at Johnny's house unannounced, and she sat beside his bed, stressed, but determined. She found him in bed, scrutinizing his accounts. He was also pondering his next move with Gia Cantoni. Gia had been persistent, and Johnny decided to confront him head-on.

"I've made up my mind. I want to go all the way," Juanita said.

"Go all the way? You mean you want the guy whacked?"

"Yes, that's what I mean. The sooner, the better. I'll let you know when, though. Mick called and told Micah that Edmond murdered a call girl in Acapulco, and he's in police custody right now. His lawyer is down there. It's a great possibility he'll walk."

He stared at her for a long time. He knew she didn't want Edmond killed.

"You sure? I know you, Juanita. You're not a killer."

"No, I'm not, but it has to be done. It won't work any other way. She'll never give him up."

"You're right about that." He thought about it for a long moment and said, "Then, I'll have him taken care of."

"Thanks, Johnny. I appreciate it."

He took off his reading glasses, placed them on top of his books and pulled his heavy bed covers back, revealing his gray charmeuse pajamas.

"Now get outta those clothes and come on in. I've missed you," he said, never taking his eyes from her.

"Yeah, I've missed you, too."

Johnny could thrill her like no one else, and he knew it. She dropped her black knit dress to the floor and crawled in next to him, still in her black bra and panties.

"So, you want me to do the honors, huh?"

"I sure do," she said, smiling up at him. No one knew it, but Juanita was shy underneath all her bravado. No one *else* knew, but Johnny had her number.

He turned her face down, lifted the hips he loved and removed her panties and bra. She lay with her hands underneath her chin, waiting for his strong hands to caress her, releasing the pent-up tension she'd harbored all week. He retrieved the oil from the bedside table, straddled her hips and rubbed it between his hands, warming it. He kneaded her shoulders, and she sighed.

"You have wonderful hands, Johnny. I can feel the tension waning. It feels so good."

"Just relax and let me take care of you. You feel good, too."

He handled her with care, oiling and caressing as he worked her whole body. When he finished his lengthy massage, he lay down beside her, and she nestled into his arms.

"You're something else, you know that? I'm beginning to want you here all the time," he said, totally out of character. "You're all the woman I need." He kissed her, drawing her to him. He removed his pajamas, and she moved above him.

"You're all I need, too, Johnny. I just want you to love me."

They made love long into the night. Johnny's cavalier manner disappeared. Juanita sensed a change, sensed a deeper, more satisfying exchange between them. Johnny longed for more between them, but he was afraid of the consequences. He'd been down that road before, and he wouldn't do it again. The hurt was too deep, still wrenching his heart whenever he thought of it.

Johnny and Juanita had enjoyed each other over the past two years, and neither wanted any restrictions. He understood the occasional booty calls kept them in touch physically, but he found the intensity of his feelings now surpassed his need for casual sex.

He was aware that Juanita enjoyed her independence, but he had felt her need for love. She wanted to belong, to reach out to him, but she was afraid to trust. He understood her perfectly, knew he could give her what she needed, but the risks were far too great. She met all his needs and desires—he was aware of that instantly, but she was young and defiant, still coming into her own.

> No one knew the thirty-eight-year-old Johnny Diamond. Juanita loved his ability to handle any situation he encountered. His physical appearance loomed large. He towered six foot five, and his commanding manner intimidated most people. He was heavily muscled and darkly handsome, and women were drawn to his strong, masculine aura. His clothes, tailored and conservative, quietly proclaimed his wealth. He was a tough, no-nonsense wheeler-dealer, and, consequently, he was both feared and respected.
>
> When he was younger, after he'd left St. Louis, he'd been a major player. He dallied with a variety of women. As he matured, he became more secure, willing to align himself with one woman, but his heart was kept off limits. He allowed no one in, but Juanita was another matter. She'd wormed her way in, unknowingly infused his thoughts, consumed him softly.

Just before Juanita left the next day, Johnny held her in his arms, kissed her as only he could and whispered, "You mean a lot to me, Nini. Don't stay away too long this time."

Something had changed between them. She felt warm and secure, but, most of all, connected. Johnny had drawn her in, quelled the storm she often felt raging.

She withdrew from his arms and opened the door. She kissed her index finger, placed it on his lips and said, "You don't have to worry 'bout that, Johnny Diamond, I *will* be back."

She sashayed away, sassily strutting her stuff. She envisioned his smile and felt him drawing her back.

He called me "Nini." Never heard that before, but I sure as hell like it.

The last two months had been troublesome for Johnny. Gia Cantoni, a Miami-based Italian mobster who recently set up his diverse operations in Atlanta, introduced himself and his various interests to Johnny and propositioned him about partial ownership in Club Eden.

Gia was a smooth operator, engaging and lethal. He entered Club Eden one night with two of his goons, and asked to see Johnny. He spoke with Rubin, Johnny's personal bodyguard, considered him a minion, and refused to divulge any information about his business. "I came *personally* to speak to Mr. Diamond," he said to Rubin, his coal-black eyes riveting, challenging.

Rubin stared him down, not relenting an inch.

"Do we have a problem here?" Gia asked, chuckling with his protectors.

"Not unless it's with you," Rubin said, not one bit amused. "I'll see if Mr. Diamond is free." He turned away, leaving them standing where they were. Rubin knew his kind, knew they were trouble.

In all the years of Johnny's dealings, he had never been confronted with the likes of Gia. Johnny was cordial, but firm. He refused Gia's offers, shaking his hand as they left.

"Give it some thought, Mr. Diamond. We're anxious to proceed," Gia said, not accustomed to being denied or treated so condescendingly. His immediate dislike for Rubin was mutual.

CHAPTER 17

A light misty rain drifted, blurring Micah's magnificent view of the Atlanta skyline. She had spent the last few days trying to determine which turn she wanted her life to take. Today would prove crucial to her elusive plan. Monday mornings had always been a dreaded challenge, but today was worse.

Mick was arriving from Acapulco in a few hours. Her heart skipped several beats whenever she thought of him. She had been happy that Armstead worked most of the weekend because she didn't know how she felt about him any longer.

Mick had brought about a lot of changes in her life already, and she was confused about the tight trio in which she found herself. The trio was a quartet because of Mick's current girlfriend, but she tried her best to exclude her.

Guilt-ridden and confused, she reached for the phone to call Armstead, but her buzzer sounded instead.

"Yes?"

"Mr. LaRue. Line one," Dana said, wondering why Micah was so morose.

"Thanks, I'll take it." Pausing a moment to compose herself, she said, "Hey, how are you doing this morning?"

"I'm dragging. I feel as if I've had one long, continuous work week. I apologize for allowing this project to monopolize my whole weekend."

"I understand. How's it coming?"

"Not too well. We're making no headway with the Jemison representatives. We might lose the account to Avalon. We'll know something this week. Can we do lunch today?"

"Uh-uh, I told Mick I'd pick him up at the airport this afternoon. I couldn't wait for him to phone me. I'll call you after I hear his latest news."

"All right, but Micah, don't get so caught up in all the hoopla. Don't forget the police are doing what they're paid to do and will handle the whole thing. Edmond Windbrook *will* get his comeuppance, I assure you."

"I know, Armstead. It's hard to let it go…but I'm trying."

"I know you are. Got to go, but I'll call you later."

"Okay. Bye." She glanced at her digital clock—9:52 a.m. Four more hours. *This is pure torture.*

Mick stepped from the airplane walkway and glanced about, frowning, looking for Micah. Her heart pounded when she saw him, and her knees buckled.

She waved her hand and shouted, "Mick, over her," several people obscuring her view.

He smiled and made his way towards her.

My God, just look at him. He looks wonderful.

Mick's thick head of mixed gray hair had grown several inches, and he had an easy, laidback presence about him. His sun-kissed skin glowed, and he looked as though he had just returned from a long, relaxing holiday.

"Micah," he said, dropping his unconstructed bag. He pulled her into his arms and felt an urgency overtake him. She hugged him, willing him to want her.

When he drew back, he looked at her with longing. "I've been dreaming of this moment."

She looked into his pale jade eyes, knew how much she wanted him. "So have I," she confessed. She touched his face and kissed him. He tasted of spearmint, cool and refreshing. She pulled him to her, and he responded as she'd imagined. He moaned, then sighed.

"Micah, I need—" he began.

"Not now. Just hold me. Should I take you home or to my—"?

"Home," he said. "Let's go home."

Armstead was desperate. He'd called Micah repeatedly, but could not reach her. He'd left a message on every one of her phones, but she had not responded. It was 11:15 p.m., and he'd been pacing the floor all night.

She's never done this. She's got to be all right.

Earlier that evening, at six-twenty, he dialed Mick's office. Sela answered. "Sutherland and Bailey, may I help you?"

"Yes. This is Armstead LaRue. May I speak with Mr. Sutherland, please?"

"I'm sorry. He's been out of the country for a while and hasn't returned to the office. May I have him call you tomorrow or would you like to speak with Mr. Bailey?"

"I'll call him tomorrow. Thank you."

Armstead knew Micah and Mick had been acquaintances in high school. He'd had an intuitive flash, but he rejected it. *No way! Micah's dead set against any philandering, especially with some white dude she's rarely mentioned.*

He knew it was late, but he looked up Juanita's number and dialed her. She answered on the first ring. "Hello," she said, hoping it was Micah or Johnny.

"Juanita, this is Armstead. I'm sorry to call you so late, but have you talked to Micah tonight?"

"No, not tonight. Why?" she said, trying to sound unconcerned.

"I've been calling her for hours, but I can't reach her anywhere. Do you know where she is? This is not like her, I'm getting worried."

"No, she didn't mention she had anything special planned when I talked with her this morning. She's probably in bed with her phones turned off. She's been tired lately. I wouldn't worry, though," she said, out of her mind with curiosity.

"No, I've been by her place. She's not at home. I'm sorry I disturbed you. Talk to you later. Bye."

Damn you, Micah. I'd like to whup your ass. I know you're with Mick. How could you just disappear knowing I'd have to lie for you? I ain't getting in the middle of this shit.

Armstead hung up, trying to be reasonable. He decided to shower, have a drink and get some sleep. He would talk with Micah tomorrow. He knew it was a good plan, but he also knew it was useless. He couldn't rest until he knew what had happened.

CHAPTER 18

Acapulco, Mexico
July 2002

Thomas and Daniel, Edmond's lawyers, looked over all the facts they had assembled. Edmond's fate looked dismal, but they knew they had to do whatever was necessary to see that he was exonerated. Their futures depended on it.

"We'll fax all of this information to Atlanta and have the whole team get on it. We must leave no stone unturned," Thomas said. "I have a few ideas."

"I do, too. We just need to make sure about the laws down here. They will be able to research everything in no time."

"Right. I know it's an uphill battle, but I also know we've got to make this thing happen in the right way."

Edmond was in custody, and perturbed he hadn't been released. He spent the night in a dirty cell, just inches away from two smelly derelicts. He lay on the dingy cot and allowed his mind to drift. He couldn't wait to get back to the good ole US of A. The first thing he'd do would be to contact Pepper. He knew she was waiting for his call.

Damn, Pepper. It is you I need. I need you now.

He focused his mind, reliving that stormy night—the last time he'd seen her. She groveled at his feet, proclaiming her undying love. He remembered her face, grotesque and swollen, looking up at him.

He was crazed with desire, his hand pumping frantically. His legs stretched, he moaned aloud, and a powerful stream shot from him. His cum covered his lower region, soaking his underwear and pants. He needed an immediate shower. He called for the guard, but no one responded. He couldn't tolerate the thought of his body fluids seeping back into his body.

He jumped from the narrow cot and stripped away his clothes, standing naked in his cell. Word spread fast. The inmates reacted—rattling the bars, catcalling, stomping. Utter and complete disruption swept the prison.

Two guards rushed in, guns cocked and aimed. They were frightened, hoping their mere presence would calm them. Edmond was frantic, pacing, eye twitching, butt-naked and uncontrollable. He was dangerous and delirious. He resembled some wild, possessed animal, and the vibes he emitted, his feral manner, incited chaos.

The guards panicked, didn't know how to proceed. "Every   _ down. Now!" one of the guards shouted.

When the commotion escalated, he panicked and fired his rifle. He frightened himself as well as the prisoners, but the gunfire worked. He hushed the inmates, brought the noise to a standstill. Edmond halted his tirade and stared, stood perfectly still.

The second guard reacted quickly. He rushed forward. "Everyone in bed. Now!" he yelled.

He looked at his assistant and blared, "Throw the lights." Because of their fear, they had restored order.

Ed crawled onto his cot, covered himself with the coarse blanket and slept naked all night, refusing to touch his clothing.

Twenty-four hours later, a distraught twenty-two year old Italian male from the Bronx confessed to the murder of Consuelo Menendez. Samuel Conte knew every aspect of the murder. How she was killed, how the scene looked, the time of the murder—not one thing was amiss. The police released Edmond, and he, along with Angelo and his lawyers, left the country, bound for Atlanta.

Pepper's private phone rang at 10:35 p.m. "Hello," she said.

"Hello, Pepper. This is Edmond. It has been a long time. How are you?"

She was stunned. Her heart raced. She knew she should hang up, but she held on. He was back again—the formal cadence of his speech, his heartfelt sincerity—and she was hooked. All kinds of thoughts flooded her.

"Pepper? Are you there? I have been concerned about you for months. I have been out of the country. I just got back. You are the first person I have called. Hello?"

"I'm here. I'm doing as well as can be expected."

"I want to apologize for all the trouble I caused you. I know I have said it before, but I have sought help. In fact, that is the reason I was out of the country. I have made a lot of headway in these last few months. Please forgive me," he said, lying, but knowing how to control her.

"I'm happy for you, Edmond. I wish you much luck."

"You did not say you had forgiven me. Have you or could you even find it in your heart to do so?"

She paused before she answered. "I forgive you."

"Thank you. I am so pleased. You don't know how much that means to me. I have suffered as much as you over this thing. I would like to make amends some how. Could I take you to dinner or do…?"

"I'm scheduled for surgery, Edmond. I can't possibly do anything before that."

"Surgery? I am so sorry. When is it? What kind of surgery?"

"Facial surgery, cosmetic," she said.

"If it is connected with what I did, I insist on paying the expenses. Is it?"

"Yes, it is. The surgery's quite extensive."

"Please let me take care of everything. I insist. When is it? Where will it be?" he asked, concern and regret seeping through.

She was hesitant about relaying details, so she said, "I will call you when it's over. I'll make sure the expenses are sent to you."

"Thank you for that. It is the least I can do. I know it is late, and I will not keep you. Just give me a call when you return home. Do you need any recommendations? You should have the best doctors. If you need anything, just let me know."

"We have everything arranged. I'll call you when I'm released. Thanks."

"You're welcome. Goodbye…Oh, Pepper?"

"Yes?"

"I have missed you terribly."

"Goodbye, Edmond."

She'd been doing so well. Now this. She wanted to see him, but she knew it was absurd. Her surgery was scheduled in three days. Her recuperation would take weeks. She'd have time to think.

When Edmond hung up, he smiled. She was putty in his hands. He was confident and in control, and because he'd never failed, he knew this time would be no different. He would give her a little time.

He walked into his bathroom, retrieved one of his thick towels and lay down on his bed. He kicked off his shoes and let his mind wander—

Acapulco. Consuelo Menendez sprang to mind—a tall, elegant woman with dark, flashing eyes and jet-black hair. He remembered the crimson kimono, the red bra and the full crimson lips.

His intensity mounted with each detail he uncovered. When he focused on the filmy red panties, his body jerked. He relived the power; he smelled the fresh breeze of soap; and he could feel the muscles of her narrow, virgin passage tighten around him as he sodomized her. Her agony threw him on the edge, but he held on. His mental playback of the beaten corpse sent him reeling over the brink. He came powerfully into his towel, milking his memories and his penis until he was depleted.

My God. How have I ever survived without her? Pepper, how I need you. We're meant for each other. It won't take much longer.

He went into his bathroom, closed the door and shed his clothes. He washed his hands. He rearranged all his belongings—his toiletries, his medicines, and every one of his expensive artifacts. After he convinced himself that everything was in order and immaculate, he stepped into the shower and spent seventy minutes scrubbing himself.

His compulsive behavior had escalated. He poured himself a scotch, added the required three ice cubes and spent fifteen minutes folding his bed covers, matching and aligning each fold. His right eye, twitching, had a mind of its own.

He picked up his phone, called his guardhouse and issued one instruction. "Angelo will be in the city tonight. Make the arrangements."

CHAPTER 19

✿

Atlanta, Georgia
July 2002

Johnny met with his two bodyguards, who also served as his bounc-
ers, in his office in Club Eden. He needed to divulge his plans about
Edmond Windbrook to Rubin. He rarely involved himself in the
details of their covert activities, but he gave instructions on how he
wanted them conducted.

"I've got an important job for you. Rubin, it's up to you to decide
how to handle it. You can hire it out, if you'd like. Just make sure it's
tight. We haven't been involved in this kind of thing in a long time,
but I need someone in North Atlanta taken out. He's high-powered
and rich, so it's serious. Twenty-five grand each when it's done. I'll let
you know when."

He reached into his desk drawer and handed Rubin the detective's
report on Edmond's activities along with several recent photographs.
"Get familiar with these details, scope out his place and wait for my
instructions. Any problems or questions, let's hear 'em now," he said,
always direct and to the point when he talked business.

Rubin skimmed the report. "Is this the Windbrook who buys cor-
porate buildings and property around the world...the one whose
company just merged with Amflac?" he asked.

"The same family. The father's dead. This is the son." Johnny was not surprised. Rubin knew of Windbrook because he was well read, college educated, and intelligent.

"All right, we'll take a look at this," holding up the report, "and I'll let you know the plan."

"How soon you think this might go down?" Ernest asked.

"Soon, but I don't know when. I'll let you know. What about the twenty-five G's?"

"It's cool…no problem. I'll get back to you," Rubin said.

Johnny looked at Ernest. "You okay?"

"Yeah, I'm cool."

"Good. Let me know what you come up with. All right?"

"We square," Rubin said.

"Later," Johnny said, reaching for his phone and dismissing them in the process. Gia had been calling off and on, keeping his expectations vivid. Rubin knew Johnny well. He was ready to accommodate him in whatever way he could when it involved Cantoni. Rubin and Gia's dislike for each other was well known by employees in both camps. "Both of you stick around. I need to talk with you about Cantoni."

"Right," Rubin said, pulling the door shut as they left to wait outside. "May I speak with Juanita Sanchez, please?" Johnny said.

"She's on another line at the moment. Would you like to wait or would you like her to give you a call?"

"Just have her call Johnny."

"Yes sir, I'll give her the message. Does she have your number?

"Yes, she does."

"Thanks. Goodbye."

"Goodbye," he said, leaning back to think. He had seen Juanita almost daily, but she hadn't given him the word to proceed. She appeared okay, but she hadn't asked him one thing about the arrangements. He just wanted to hear her voice. He wouldn't mention the plans he had arranged.

Johnny got up and opened his door. "Come on in. We need to talk."

"Right," Rubin said. He and Ernest entered Johnny's office and closed the door.

"I want you to set up a meeting with Cantoni and me. I want you both present, and I want it away from the club and definitely not in Gia's office. A lunch or dinner somewhere in our territory. You arrange it Rubin. And do it soon."

He told them his plan; he wanted to keep it simple. Rubin nodded. He knew the perfect place.

Twenty minutes after he left the message, Juanita called. Johnny dismissed Rubin and Ernest, saying, "We'll talk more about this tonight. I want to get this settled. Later." When they closed the door, he picked up the phone. "Hi, baby. How are you doing this morning? You busy already, huh?"

"Somewhat. We're putting the finishing touches on the outfits for the show. We're having a meeting this afternoon with Lila. I think we may be going to Paris and Milan next month just to get a feel for the spring fashions. Got to keep the creative juices flowing, you know."

"Paris and Milan? How long will you be gone?"

"About a week. Wanna come?"

"Nah. You don't want me tagging along."

"We'll have plenty of free time. Give it some thought, please. Micah might have somebody coming over for a few days.

"Somebody? What does that mean?"

"Uh, it's a little complicated. I'll tell you tonight."

"Oh, am I seeing you tonight?" he teased.

"Uh-huh, you sure are."

"Good. I can't wait."

"Me neither. Bye."

He sat holding the phone. A vacation in Europe might be just the ticket. He would love to spend some quality time with her. If he decided to join her in Europe, he'd resolve his issue with Gia before he left. He made a mental note to talk with her about Europe tonight.

❀   ❀   ❀

Armstead sat in Micah's beige leather chair trying to decipher the convoluted, preposterous tale she'd just told him. If anyone could follow it and keep it straight, he'd have to be a genius. It was the most improbable lie he'd ever heard.

"What you're trying to say is…?" he asked, extending his hand.

"Armstead, I will not go through that whole thing again. Now I've told you what happened. And why the third degree? Do I scrutinize your comings and goings? I think not! I'm tired tonight, and I'd love to get some sleep. Let's meet for lunch. Perhaps we can talk more civilly in a neutral environment."

"What's going on, Micah? This is just too ludicrous. I know you well. Are you trying to tell me something? If so, let's have it. I'd much prefer the truth, good or bad."

"Armstead. Nothing is going on. Believe me. I'm just exhaust. You know how we've been working trying to get ready for the sho '

"All right, Micah. I'm going home, but we'll talk about this at lunch tomorrow. I hope you'll be able to tell me in plain English where you disappeared to and what went on."

"I will not rehash all this, Armstead. We'll just have to move on." She stood up, indicating she wanted him to leave.

"We can't just *not* talk about it, Micah, but I'll leave so you can get some rest. I'll see you tomorrow." He wanted to pull her to him. He needed to hold her, but he didn't. He decided to not push the issue. He didn't even kiss her goodbye. "I'll call you in the morning. Goodnight." He opened the door and walked away.

"Okay. Bye," she said, knowing she couldn't continue this way. She knew she'd hurt him terribly. He didn't deserve it. She'd just have to tell him the truth.

She needed to talk to someone. When Juanita didn't answer at home, Micah called her on her cell phone. Juanita picked up after several rings.

"Hey, where are you?"

"I'm at Johnny's. Why? You all right?"

"No, I'm not. Armstead just left and I…" She started to cry. She hadn't done that in years.

"Micah, do I need to come over? What's wrong? What happened?"

"He asked me where I was last night, and I came up with the most fucked-up lie you ever heard."

"Nah, what did you say?"

"I told him some crazy-ass tale about having to go to D.C. because of something in the report Mick brought back on Edmond. It was just too stupid, and he picked up on it instantly. He knew I was lying, but I couldn't tell him the truth. Oh, Nita. What am I going to do? I don't want to hurt him, but I need to move on. It's Mick I want. It's just not fair to Armstead. He's such a good guy. He deserves more," she said, sniffling and blowing her nose.

Juanita got out of bed and sat in the chair by the night table. "You need to tell him the truth. It'll be hard, but it'll be over, and you can move on. Otherwise, you're going to be lying from now on." She looked at Johnny, who was turned towards her on his side, looking at her. The whole thing amused him. "You sure you don't want me to come over?" He shook his head, answering for Micah. He wanted her to stay right in bed with him. That's where she belonged.

"No, but thanks. I'm sorry to interrupt you two. Hope I didn't disturb anything."

"Uh-uh. We're just sitting here having wine and talking," she lied. Johnny rolled his eyes and fell back on the bed.

"Well, go back to Johnny. I'll talk to you in the morning. Thanks for listening. I feel a little better now. Bye."

"All right, bye." She hung up, but sat thinking, almost in a daze.

"So Micah's going to leave Armstead?" Johnny asked.

"Yeah, I think so. To tell you the truth, I don't think he's ever been the one for her."

"Why do you say that? I thought they were great together."

"Well, he proposed to her twice, but she always had some excuse. She didn't even accept the engagement ring. And now she's *so* excited about Mick. I told you that earlier. She's always been attracted to him, even when she first met him at Deauville. It was obvious he was crazy about her, but they never got together until now."

"So, they've gotten together?"

"Yes, and I shouldn't be telling you all this."

"Why not? You think I'm going to tell Armstead?"

"You know better than that. I don't know. She's my best friend. We're supposed to keep *some* secrets."

"Come on. Get back in bed. Don't you want to watch 'Sex and the City' or something on Lifetime?"

"Yes, 'Sex and the City' at nine," she said, crawling back in bed. "Micah cried tonight, Johnny. She hasn't done that in years. She can be hard as nails sometimes. This is going to be so rough on her. I wish I could help."

"Not this time, baby. This is her ball of wax," he said, spooning around her and pulling her to him. He hesitated a moment, then said, "Do you still want me to go ahead with the plans for Edmond?"

"How did we get back to that? Yes, but I still don't know when. That's why I haven't mentioned it again."

"Okay. Just wanted to be sure."

They settled in for the night, watching Juanita's show.

I can't believe I'm doing all this, but I'm loving it, he thought, content for the first time in years.

❈   ❈   ❈

Rubin set up the meeting with Johnny and Gia. They met in a small cafe on Atlanta's southwest side. Johnny and Gia both had two men in attendance, but they were not privy to the exchange between the men. Johnny arrived first and sat in the back corner overlooking the street. He saw Gia and his men arrive, survey the scene and enter the Cafe Chocolat at precisely 12:15 p.m.

Gia, confident and debonair, greeted Johnny. He and Johnny connected from day one, and deep down Gia admitted, Johnny demanded his respect. Gia was in good spirits, his expectations high.

"Mr. Cantoni, glad you could make it," Johnny said, shaking Gia's hand. "Join me. Would you like something to eat?"

"Nothing," Gia said, his eyes darting, checking the cafe for clues.

"Then sit."

"So, Mr. Diamond, what can I do for you?"

"Back off," Johnny said, deadly serious. "I wanted to talk, face-to-face, so there would be no misunderstanding."

Gia nodded.

"Club Eden is non-negotiable. I wanted to make that clear. Don't want any heat."

Gia stared, thinking of Johnny's comments, amazed at the gall of the man. He had *never* had anyone of Johnny Diamond's stature refuse him. *Unbelievable. And now this…black monkey looks me in the eye.* Gia's eyes narrowed, he grappled for facts and answers, his analysis sharp. He admired Johnny's custom-made suit, liked his direct approach, his respect escalating fast. *He got balls, this omo.*

Gia smiled. "You got coglione (balls), Mr. Diamond. I like it…. We talkin' a lotta G's." He couldn't resist the final bait.

"I'm doing all right. Don't need the help, don't need a partner. You got a lot of interests, Mr. Cantoni. I got Club Eden," Johnny said evenly, never wavering, his eyes steady and sure.

Gia said nothing, his assessment made. Finally, he stood and so did Johnny, the moment intense. Neither broke eye contact, and neither spoke. Gia extended his hand. "I like you, Mr. Diamond. I like your guts. Club Eden is yours." He turned abruptly, without another word. He walked from the cafe with his bruisers in tow. The deal was struck.

CHAPTER 20

❀

Atlanta, Georgia
August 2002

Micah and Armstead met for lunch at Arnold's, the downstairs restaurant in the Fitzgerald Hotel. She had slept restlessly and so had he.

"Would you like something to drink before we order?" Armstead asked.

"I'll have white wine."

He addressed the waiter, "White wine for the lady, bourbon and water for me."

His concerned expression alerted her to what she knew lay head. "Micah, I know you want to avoid this, but is there some reason you're unwilling to tell me what's wrong? Where did you disappear to the other night? Is that too much to ask? We talk every night if we don't see each other. You were gone all night. Didn't you think I'd be worried about you?" He didn't know for sure that she'd been gone all night. He was hoping she'd deny it.

"Armstead, at this point, it's not important where I was, what's important is I don't want to remain in an exclusive relationship anymore. I'm sorry if I upset you or caused you unnecessary worry, but someone else has entered my life, and I want to see where that relationship takes me." She'd said it all in one fell swoop. Relief flooded her.

He had always known, deep down, at some point, they'd have this conversation, but that fact did not make it any easier. He loved her with all his heart. "Is it Mick?"

She looked at him with such helplessness. "Yes, it's Mick. I hope I don't regret this decision, but I have to give this relationship a chance. I'm so sorry, Armstead. It was nothing planned. It just happened."

He wanted to hold her, to make her change her mind, but his pride kept him intact. "I'm sorry, too, but I'll respect your decision. I love you, Micah. I always will, but it's your life, too."

"I hope this doesn't make us enemies. I'd love to consider you one of my dearest friends," she said.

"No, we could never to be enemies, but I couldn't be in your life and not have things the way they are now. If you ever need anything, just know that I'm there."

Tears brimmed her eyes. How she hated to do this. She said, "Thank you. I understand."

She was unable to eat, so was he. They finished their drink and left. As they walked through the hotel lobby, she concentrated on the extraordinary beauty around her—the vibrant paintings; the Birds of Paradise rearing up proudly, poking their colorful heads high above the surrounding foliage; the gilded French furnishings. Her head was spinning. She wanted to run, to get away from her posh surroundings. She wanted to scream, to release it all. But she held it in, felt the lump in her throat, but most of all, she felt Armstead's pain.

They stopped just outside the brass revolving door, and he held her hands, hating to leave her. "I hope you find what you're looking for, Micah. I regret it wasn't me." He was trying to resign himself to his new reality, but he didn't want to face it, didn't want to give her up.

"Please don't, Armstead. Not here…Let's not say goodbye. I just want to thank you for everything you brought into my life. It was so wonderful."

She kissed his cheek, and turned away, heading down Peachtree, walking blindly. He stood for a long time, watching her leave him, tears in his eyes.

Oh, God, how awful! I couldn't bear his hurt, the look in his eyes. Please forgive me. I had no other choice. She walked aimlessly, heading nowhere, just away from his pleading eyes, sobbing uncontrollably.

❧   ❧   ❧

Angelo found a parking spot just down the street from Giovanni's, his favorite restaurant. He had already decided he wanted veal scalopini for dinner. He was deep in thought when two masked men, dressed in black, stepped in front of him. He heard the click as the switchblade opened; saw the glint of the knife as it sank into his stomach.

"Punk," the attacker said.

His accomplice rushed in behind Angelo, jerked his head back and slashed his neck. Blood gushed from the severed artery, and he slumped to the ground. The first assailant decorated Angelo's chest with the proverbial "Colombian necktie" in which his tongue was pushed down through his gullet and pulled through the slash in his neck—a popular mobster tactic. They disappeared into the night, leaving him dead, just a few feet from the door of Giovanni's.

The Atlanta Journal-Constitution headline read, Local Man Found Mutilated. The article stated, "Angelo Gonzalez, an employee of Windbrook Consortium, Inc., was found nearly decapitated just outside the popular Italian restaurant, Giovanni's, Friday night. He was stabbed, slashed and savagely mutilated. No suspects have been found…."

Edmond read the article with relish. He smiled when he finished. The extensive torture pleased him immensely.

When Edmond's lawyers told him Angelo had spearheaded his attack and blackmail attempt in Acapulco, he was enraged. He wanted to slit his neck then, but he brought him back to the states to exact his revenge. It took extreme control to not lash out at the sight of him, but Edmond knew his betrayal would be assuaged.

Samuel Conte, one of Edmond's assailants in Acapulco, told them the whole sordid tale and agreed to confess to the murder for two and a half million dollars. He would split the money with his two partners. He would get a million and a half for his part in the cover-up and his imprisonment, and his partners would split the other one million dollars.

Edmond would tolerate no double-dealing. He knew Angelo had flirted off and on with the mob, but he was small potatoes. He mingled with the lower echelon of the mob world, and Giovanni's was their favorite meeting place. Since he was not a part of their official organization, they didn't bother to avenge his murder. Death was just an ordinary occurrence in their lives, nothing to lose sleep over.

Edmond folded the newspaper, placed it on his side table and finished his morning java. A deed well done always pleased him. N that Angelo was out of the way, his next real job was to focus on Pe̦ per. He needed to formulate a plan to get her back. Getting control was the key. It was essential for his final mission. She was needy and dependent. He would find just the right irresistible touch, something she could not refuse. His time was running out, and he needed to think.

His head began to ache, and he began to rearrange his possessions—the candles on the dining table were out of line, the book he left yesterday lay crooked, the picture slanted a fraction downward.

"Charles! Anna! Where are you? Why is this house in such disorder?" he yelled.

Haymon, his current butler, appeared, concerned by his tone.

"What is it, sir? Charles and Anna are no longer in your employ. They're gone…they've been gone for years. What have we left in disarray? Please—"

"Gone for years? What do you me—?"

His right eye danced rapidly, and his head spun. He was disoriented. "My head is pounding…"

"Sir, you're ill. Let me call a doctor."

He turned to leave, but stopped when Edmond swayed. "Feel faint…" Edmond said, sinking, losing consciousness. Haymon caught him as he fell.

"Susanna, come quickly. Please call Dr. Forester. Mr. Windbrook is ill."

CHAPTER 21

"Hey, sleepy head. Are you awake? It's seven o'clock. I promised to wake you," Mick said.

"I was sleeping so good. What time did I leave you?" Micah asked.

"Around two. I wish you would have stayed."

"I would have, but I have a nine o'clock meeting this morning, remember? If I'd walked back in the office in that same suit, Mom would have fainted, and Juanita would thought I'd lost my mind."

"Then we'll have to rectify that situation immediately. Bring a few things when you come next time. I'll make some room in the closet."

"I'll do that, but I'm warning you, you'll regret you made that suggestion, I assure you. You won't have an un-crammed spot in your closets."

"I can't wait. Promise?"

"Yes, I do."

"I'm going to make my reservations for Europe today. I haven't been in a few years, and I'm looking forward to being there with you. We didn't get around to doing too many things last night, but I'm not complaining. Is Johnny D. going with Juanita?" Mick asked.

"Yes. It sounds like so much fun, Mick. I can't wait. Why don't you see if you and Johnny can fly together if you two can't come with us? That would be terrific."

"Yeah, I'll check with him to see what he has planned. I'll call you after everything's booked. I'm hoping I can leave with you. I'll know this morning. You'd better shake it if you're going to be on time for your meeting. I love you."

"Mick? Are we still going to the range tonight? I'm a little nervous about the guns. I know they're your first love, but don't expect miracles from me, okay?"

"I won't, but I'm happy you agreed to come. Everyone should know how to shoot. I think once you get the hang of it, you'll love it."

"I don't know about that, but we'll see. See you tonight…Mick?"

"Uh-huh?"

"I love you, too. Bye."

She stretched her legs and yawned. She'd give herself five more minutes. She just wanted to reflect on her night with Mick. They'd been together only twice, but he made her heart sing. She hadn't felt so alive in years. She thought about the two years she'd spent with Armstead. She was certain she made the right decision. Her heart ached whenever she thought of him. They had never felt remotely the passion she and Mick shared.

What a fantastic lover. I can't believe everything he did to me…and I did to him. Juanita and Pepper would love to hear this story.

If she weren't careful, she'd be addicted to him. She wondered if Pepper's obsession with Edmond stemmed from the passion they shared. Even so, in Pepper's case, the brutality should outweigh any passion she felt. Micah vowed then she'd never love anyone who mistreated her in any way, no matter what.

Mick loved everything about Micah. He was on cloud nine. He'd wasted so much time. Just the thought of it was incredible…*she loves me. I've loved her since I first laid eyes on her.*

Mick could barely wait for their future to unfold. He felt as if he'd spent his whole life preparing for her. He loved Micah with all his heart, and from what she'd gone through already, breaking up with Armstead had been devastating, he felt certain she loved him, too.

CHAPTER 22

❀

The dressing rooms buzzed with excitement as the models prepared for their first time on the catwalk. Micah and Juanita were overseeing the fittings and making sure everything worked smoothly. The commentator opened the show to a rousing round of applause as the jazz combo in the background picked up the pace.

"If we survive this, it'll be a miracle," Juanita said to Micah.

"You got that right. Mom is so jittery. You'd think this was her first fashion show."

"Her name and reputation are on the line every time we do this, Micah, so I can understand why she might be."

"We did the designing. Our reputations are at stake, too. Suppose they don't like this year's line."

"Give me a break, Micah. We have the baddest stuff around. They'll love everything, believe me."

"I hope you're right."

Two hours later, when the last models exited the catwalk, and the commentator had Lila come out for a bow, the audience went wild. They loved the upbeat, fast-paced mood of the show and adored the clothes.

Lila had Micah and Juanita join her on the catwalk, and she paid special recognition to Pepper who beamed from the sidelines. She looked as beautiful and serene as ever, her black patch setting her apart. Her face was not healed, but her makeup covered any telltale signs of the surgery. She glowed. She was proud of her two friends. They'd done a phenomenal job with the designs.

Mick and Johnny were their biggest fans; they were the first ones on their feet, applauding as the crowd stood to acknowledge them. The show was a major success. It took Juanita and Micah well over an hour to break free. When they slipped from the backstage celebrations, they found Mick and Johnny doing very well without them, with a magnum of champagne within reach. They had made plans for dealing with Edmond, and found they enjoyed each other's company.

When Mick saw Micah, he stood and rushed to her. "The show was fabulous. You two outdid yourselves this time," he said.

"Thank you, thank you. We're so pleased the show was such a success. Our clothes were something, weren't they?" Micah said.

Johnny, who had already monopolized Juanita, answered, "They were fabulous, Nini. Really gorgeous." He pulled her to him, absorbing her emotions, not giving a damn about the sexual suggestion of his intimate hug.

Lila and Franklin brought up the rear. They emerged arm-in-? from backstage, walking straight to the designers' personal party.

"Everyone's coming back to the house for the after party, right?" Franklin asked.

"We wouldn't miss it," Micah said, hugging her father around his waist.

"I'm so proud of you two. You did a marvelous job," Franklin said to Micah and Juanita. "Pepper, you'll be back next year. I can't wait."

"Yes, I sure will," Pepper said, excited about the whole thing.

"The limo's right outside. Let's go. I know Ruby is fussing around, looking for us any minute," Franklin said.

They stepped onto the sidewalk and waited for the limousine to ease its way into the circular drive. Flashbulbs went off all around them. Two loud popping sounds startled them. Johnny flinched, and Rubin fell.

"I've been shot. Everyone get down," Rubin shouted.

"I've been hit, too," Johnny said. "Where's Ernest?"

"He's at the limo. He's getting it to us now," Rubin said.

The limousine screeched to a halt, and Ernest ran to them, gun in hand. He helped Johnny up and ushered them into the back, his eyes scanning the crowd and the tops of the buildings. He saw no one. Pandemonium reigned. He jumped into the limo behind them, and the driver took off.

"Get us to Grady," Ernest said, checking out the condition of the two victims.

"I'm hit in the left shoulder," Johnny said. "Where did they hit you, Rubin?"

"Upper left chest. I'm bleeding pretty bad."

"Step on it driver," Franklin commanded. "They need help now."

The driver jumped lanes, and sped through the traffic, weaving in and out, doing all he could to help.

"Johnny, why? What's this all about?" Juanita said. She was in total control, but she was worried about Johnny. Under stress, she was all business. She and Johnny had that in common.

"I don't know, baby, but we damn sure are gonna find out."

Micah clung to Mick, more frightened than she had even been in her life.

"I'm going to investigate this one myself," Mick said. "We'll catch whoever did this. Don't worry about it, Johnny. Consider it done."

His concern was for Micah and the others, too. The bullets could have hit any of them.

Juanita had her arm around Johnny, supporting him as best she could. He leaned into her, his handkerchief saturated with blood.

Johnny and Rubin were rushed inside and into the emergency room. The others sat in the waiting room, excited and wondering why anyone would do such a thing. They all knew Johnny had enemies, but even Johnny couldn't pinpoint why anyone would want to kill him.

Two hours later, Johnny walked out, his arm in a sling. They had released him, but with orders to take his medication and do nothing strenuous. Rubin's wound was more serious. They assigned him a hospital room, and Johnny had already been in to see him as well as talk to the police.

The limo driver took everyone home before dropping off Lila and Franklin. The after party never materialized. It was supposed to have been just a private celebration for the seven of them.

"Do you see why it's important that you learn to defend yourself? You're a natural with the gun, Micah. You did great at the range the other day," Mick said.

"Yeah, if you call missing the whole target good, then I was beyond great," she said.

"Come on, Micah. It only took you a few rounds to hit something, and another box to get near the intended target," he said, bursting out laughing. "You're doing fine. We're just going to keep at it. It'll come. At least, you weren't afraid of the gun. That's a major plus."

"Go on, laugh, if you want to. That's okay. Now, what you don't know is that I'm an expert with the bow and arrow. I got into that before I went to Deauville. Of course, it's been a while, but I bet it wouldn't take me long to bone up," she said.

"I love the bow and arrow, too. We'll practice some this weekend. I have a target in the garage. You're an interesting and sexy woman, Micah. I don't know if you know that," he said, cuddling close, nibbling her lips.

"Now that's a deal. I'll show you something with the bow and arrow...laughing at me," she said.

"Anything you want." He couldn't be around her a minute without wanting to make love to her. He nuzzled her, lifted her hair and nipped her neck.

"Good. Now it's Juanita who can shoot a gun. That girl's a sharp-shooter, if I ever saw one. When she was in public school her boy-friend, Boogie, taught her to shoot. I saw her dismantle one of my daddy's guns one time, and she had it back together in a flash. She showed Pepper and me how well she could shoot in our back yard," beginning to respond to his nipping.

"You're going to be a real pro before we're through, too. Just have a little patience."

They were standing in her kitchen, trying to decide on something to eat. He hugged her from behind, as she stood with the refrigerator door open.

"What would you like? I've got eggs, bacon…"

"How about just a nibble of you" he said, closing the refrigerator door and coaxing her into her bedroom. He stopped in the hallway and took her in his arms. She felt his hardness against her and kissed him, her arms encircling his neck. He moved into her, his hands roaming her hips. He pulled her closer, kneading her buttocks, caus-ing her to call his name and her breath to quicken.

"Mick, you feel so good…"

He led her into the bedroom and unbuttoned her blouse, reveal-ing a nude-colored lace bra. He unzipped her skirt and let it drop. She stepped out of it, her eyes fixed on him.

"You're so lovely, Micah. I've dreamed of you for so long."

She removed her panties, and he unfastened her bra. He took off his shirt and trousers. She took the lead in removing his skivvies, fondling his penis, wanting him more as he stiffened.

"You drive me crazy," he said, at last, steering her to the bed. She sat, but he remained standing. She fondled him, caressed him and then took him in deeply. He stood watching, pushing gently. He lay with her, their expectations building. He put her leg over his hip, opening her to him.

"I love you so much, Micah."

"I love you, too. I've never felt this way about anyone…."

He teased her, moving back and forth, but she wanted him fully. He withdrew and sucked her nipples, laving them with his tongue. His breath hot, his tongue insistent. He was a sensitive lover, knowing just what she wanted. She pressed his face to her as her pleasure mounted.

"Oh, Mick…" she said, pumping her hips until she moaned in satisfaction. He moved on top of her, slipped inside, and steeled his mind to hang on…waiting. He stroked to the hilt, building her intensity. She began to rise again, matching his strokes, pulling him to her with her entwined legs. He talked to her the whole time, sexy…intoxicating whispers. "It's so good, Micah. I'm waiting on you. Tell me when you want it," he said, and she lost her mental footing.

"Ahhh, Mick," she said as her muscles ripped, her body jerking, lifting from the bed. He was impaled deep within her, and he released a hot rush of cum, bathing her inside. They came together mightily, infused, holding tightly. Then they lay spent, satisfied, still connected, unwilling to give it up.

"My God, Micah. I can't begin to describe it. It was…so good."

"It was wonderful," she said, kissing him, meaning every word, wanting him just where he was. She felt his small paunch against her, considered it her personal property and smiled.

He spent the whole weekend with her, loving her and laughing, sharing the details of their lives. They established an intimacy they both cherished. She felt none of the hesitancy she had with Armstead. Mick met all her needs, and she fulfilled him, as he knew she would.

On Sunday morning, Micah said, "I need to call Juanita. We should see how Johnny is doing. We were selfish yesterday—taking the phone off the hook. I know she's mad as hell with us, Mick."

"She'll get over it, but do call. I hope Johnny's doing all right. On second thought, as long as he's with her, I guarantee you he's doing fine."

"Nita? How's Johnny? Is he there with you?"

"As if you care. Yes, he's right here with me. He's been in bed since Friday. I had to fight him tooth and nail to make him do so, though. I tried to call you all day yesterday, but your phone was disconnected…so I assume Mick's with you?"

"You assume correctly."

"You go, girl. Was it all that good? You having to take the phone off the hook and all." She smiled and winked at Johnny.

"Uh-huh. It sure was."

"Well, hallelujah! Thank the Lord, you've come around. Didn't think I'd ever hear this from you. Never heard it with Armstead."

"Nita. I will not go there, okay?"

"All right, Miss Thang. I'll talk with you later."

"Tell Johnny we called."

"He already knows. Bye."

"Johnny's with her. He's been in bed since Friday night. He's doing fine."

"What did you mean when you said, 'I will not go there?'"

"Oh, Juanita's always coming up with some stuff. It didn't mean a thing," she said, again not wanting to go there.

They were well suited for each other, brought out each other's best qualities. Mick didn't leave until six o'clock Monday morning. He was in the same situation in which she found herself at his house.

"Do you have to go now? Can't you just go to work from here?"

"What would Sela think if I came to work in the tuxedo I wore to the show?"

She smiled and said, "Then I guess we'll have to rectify this situation. Bring in the clothes. The only problem is, there's not a damn place to put them."

CHAPTER 23

Depression is a bitch! Pepper had been reviewing her life, thinking about all the mishaps she had encountered, and her eyes welled with tears. Her mother and father had no idea of the changes she had been through. Juanita and Micah had insisted she see a therapist after she kept going back to Edmond whenever he would mistreat her. If they knew all the things she had faced, they would be astounded.

For the first time in a very long while, Pepper allowed herself to think about the summer she turned ten. LaVerne left her often in the care of her neighbor, Connie, while she ran her errands. LaVerne would take the baby, Nicky, with her. Connie's husband, Alan, was always at home, and he drank beer and watched TV all day. Connie inherited her parents' home and all their possessions when they were killed in a car accident. Neither she nor Alan had to work to make ends meet.

Because of her dark memories, Pepper neither watches TV nor enjoys beer today. Unknown to LaVerne, Connie often ran her errands while Pepper was in her care, leaving Pepper alone with Alan. It started very innocently. Alan adored Pepper, and she spend her days with them watching TV. LaVerne and Fred limited Pepper's TV viewing, so it was a treat for Pepper to watch the variety of shows he enjoyed.

Alan and Connie were friendly and jovial, and Pepper looked forward to the time she spent with them. They allowed her to do everything that was forbidden in her own home. Pepper could eat candy and have her fill of sugar drinks. Life with the Andersons was the one thing she cherished.

Pepper's hell began the summer of 1985. The first time Alan approached her was one hot day in July, and he was drinking his Budweiser beer. She remembered it as if it happened yesterday. "Come on over here with me. You're going to love this episode." She thought nothing of it and scooted next to him on the couch. He put his arm around her and moved her closer. She wore her usual tee shirt and shorts. As they watched a re-run of "M*A*S*H", Alan began to stroke her thigh. Before the show was over, he had pulled one leg of her shorts aside and was fondling her private area. She knew it was wrong, but he said he was doing it because he loved her.

That summer, the fondling escalated into full-scale sexual contact. It happened often over the next few years. He told her she was to tell no one, and she never has. He continued to molest her until she left for Deauville Academy five years later.

As she reminisced, tears streamed from her eyes. The long-term effects were still in evidence. She refused therapy because she kr her secret would be discovered. Even now, she could not bear to su fer the embarrassment of being associated with the horror. She has longed to tell Juanita and Micah, but she could not bring herself to do it.

Her reminiscing made her claustrophobic. She needed something to do, something to take her mind off all her troubles. She dried her eyes and decided it was time to go back to work. Activity was what she needed. She would love to go to Europe with Micah and Juanita, but she was hesitant because Johnny and Mick were going, and she didn't want to be an intrusion. She decided to broach the subject with Micah.

"Line one. It's Pepper. She sounds great," Dana said.

"Pepper, how are you doing, girl? Ready to come back to work?"

"I think so. Do I still have a job? It's been so long."

"Get outta here. Do you still have a job? What kind of question is that? Of course, you have a job. We're all waiting for you to come back."

"Good. Uh…Micah, when are you going to Europe?"

"In three weeks. You want to come? I think that'll be a great way for you to reenter the world of work—going on a quasi-business trip where we work a little and play a lot. What do you think?"

"Well, I've thought about it, but I don't want to be in the way with the guys and all."

"What? Oh, come on. We'd love to have you with us. I can't wait to tell Juanita. She'll be delighted."

"I haven't made up my mind yet, but I'm thinking about it. Mrs. McCall's going, too, right?"

"Chile, are you kidding? That plane wouldn't move if she weren't on it. Sure she is. And Daddy's not going, so she'll be alone, too."

"Hmm. That just might work. Let me think about it some more."

"Don't wait too long. We'll need to get the reservations made. We would hate for you to go on another plane or stay in a different hotel. Why don't I go ahead and have Dana make the reservations? If you change your mind, we can always cancel. Your passport's still current, isn't it?"

"Yep, it sure is. Yes, let's do it. Have Dana make the reservations."

"Oh, Pepper. This is such great news. We're going to love scouring the alleyways and finding all kinds of good stuff."

"Yeah, it does sound great. I'm going to do it. It's time."

"Right. We'll take care of everything, and I'll call you back, okay?"

"I'm not going anywhere. Just let me know. Thanks, Micah, and I love you."

"I love you, too, and I'm so glad you decided to go. I'll call you right back. Bye."

Pepper was elated. She was finally ready to get back into the swing of life. She didn't have her left eye, but her surgeon had done a terrific job with her face. She was as good as new. She had a small limp, but it was almost imperceptible.

And I do like the patch. Micah was right about it—it does add mystique. This is going to be so much fun. I'll get a truckload of new things. I can hardly wait.

CHAPTER 24

"Good morning, Mr. Sutherland. How are you?" Micah said.

"Doing *very* well, this morning, Ms. McCall, thanks to you." He smiled, thinking about being with her last night.

"Hmm. My step is a little light this morning, too. Could it be because of you?"

"It damn sure better be." They both laughed, enjoying the intimacy of the moment. "What have you planned for today?" he asked.

"You're going to love this. Nita and I are going to the range, around three, if we can make it. Since I've improved, I can hang out there with her now. What do you think of that?"

"I think that's great. I told you it wouldn't take you long. I'm still trying to get over your skill with the bow and arrow. You're much better right now than I'll ever be, and you haven't picked them up in over ten years. That's incredible."

"I loved the bow and arrow the moment I picked them up. Daddy taught me how to shoot, and I made the team in eighth grade. You should see Daddy with the bow. He's phenomenal."

"I can't imagine what you'll be like after we've practiced more. You're awesome, already. In more ways than one," he said, the sexual innuendo making an impression.

"Happy to oblige in any way I can," she said, her voice dropping an octave.

"Well, you oblige real good, I want you to know." He shifted in his chair. Their flirting already heating things up.

"Hmm. You've got me going already. I can't believe you. Just sitting here talking, and I'm thinking about ravishing you," she said.

"Now that's a hellava thought. Can't we do lunch at the house?" he asked, erect and wanting her.

"Oh, sweetie, I can't. I've got meetings, and then I'm leaving early. But it would be nice, huh?"

"Damn right. I'm sitting here craving you. You're a naughty tease," he said, not wanting her to stop.

"So are you. You started it. But we'll fix it tonight, okay?"

"Okay. Let me get myself together before Sela gets here or she'll have a stroke," he said, laughing at the thought.

"And we can't have that."

"Hubert and I have started looking into Johnny's attack. We don't have anything yet, but we're still digging. We should have something before we leave for Paris. I need to start taking a few things to the cleaners. We've just got a few days before we leave. I haven't had a real vacation in years. I'm looking forward to it. By the way, you had me so enraptured last night, I forgot to tell you I talked with Johnny. He's doing great and is looking forward to going. He'll be going over with us. He was able to work that out."

"Wonderful. Nita's made a real turnaround since she and Johnny tightened things up. Which is a good thing. She's so happy with him." Abruptly changing the subject, she said, "You may not know what clothes you're taking, Mick, but I know in detail everything I'm going to wear. We've got to look like the successful designers that we are. When we're not working, I just want to hang out—jeans and casual stuff. All right?"

"We'll do whatever you want. I'm just looking forward to getting away with you. It'll be our time to kick back."

"Yes, it will be. I'd better go. Got to get some work done. It's almost nine. I'll call you before I leave for the range."

All right. Talk to you then."

Juanita knocked on Micah's door, peeked in and said, "It's almost
three. You gonna make it?"

"I'm almost done. Five minutes tops. See you in the galley. Can't
wait to get out of these clothes. You brought something to change
into, didn't you?"

"Yeah. Let me close down shop, and I'll see you in there."

Thirty minutes later, Juanita pulled up at the range, and Micah
whipped in behind her. Walking across the small lot, Micah said,
"Let's sit out front a minute. The sun feels so good."

"Yeah, it sure does." They sat on the bench in front of the range,
stretched their legs and relaxed.

"We haven't been able to talk much lately. How's everything
going?" Juanita asked.

"Perfect. Mick said he talked with Johnny, and he's going over
with us, huh?"

"Yes, he sure is. I'm happy about that. I have to keep an eye on
him all the time. He works all the time, and he hasn't completely
recovered yet. This trip will be good for him. Rubin came by last
night. Johnny said his wound was a lot more serious than we
thought. He's still moving a little slow, but he's in such great shape,
he'll be back up to speed in no time."

"Johnny's in great shape, too. He's got *some* physique, Nita."

"You telling me? Not an ounce of fat. Nowhere. Chile, please, that
dark brown body is just too much. He eats right, and he exercises.
Pumps a little iron, but not much. Micah, he is the most incredible
lover. God! It gives me chills just thinking about it."

"He is? I can see you're all into him. He's that good, huh?"

"Oh, chile. Don't let me get started. The boy can run it on *down*.
What about Mick? I've never been with a white guy before. What's
the deal?"

"I've never thought about Mick as being white. Never. But I know he is, and it doesn't make one bit of difference. He's great."

"Micah, I'm talkin' 'bout in bed. What's that like?"

"It's terrific. He's sensitive, and he talks you through the whole thing, real soft and sexy-like. Girrrl, he'll make you wanna slap yo' Mama! He can be…wild, too—just kinda out there. He does everything. And Nita, he's got the cutest little paunch. To be honest, I've never been more satisfied sexually…but to just get right down wit' it, the boy's off the chain. Just talking to him on the phone, and I'm ready to snatch off all my clothes and go jump his bones."

"Damn! He's all that?"

"And more."

Juanita paused a beat and said, "You wanna trade?"

They burst out laughing, acting like the raunchy sisters they were.

"Girl, you're too crazy. Nita, I want you to give me some pointers in here. I want to get as good as you. When you shot Daddy's gun in the backyard that time, I couldn't get over it. You were something. You know Mick laughed at me the other day when he brought me here. I want to just show him, make him eat that laugh. So, we're going to practice at least twice a week until I'm up to snuff, all right?"

"Yeah, that's cool. I love to shoot anyway, so it's no problem. You ready? Let's get with it."

When they got their guns and goggles, Juanita took the first round.

"Here goes. I haven't done this in a long time. Let's see how much practice I need."

When she finished, she took off her goggles and said, "Not too bad, huh?"

"Not too bad? Girl, just look. I see only one hole up there, and you took six shots. That's awesome. You have *got* to teach me how to do that, Nita."

"You got the basics. All you need is practice. It took me a long time. Boogie just wanted me to be good, and I loved it as much as he did. So, come on girl, show me what you got."

They practiced until five, and Micah felt great. She had improved with the tips Juanita gave her. Juanita was right. It just took practice. Her goal was to show Mick just one hole, when she'd fired six rounds. When she made up her mind, there was no stopping her. And, about that, she'd already decided.

❦   ❦   ❦

"Johnny? Mick. We just got some information I thought you ought to hear."

"Yeah? About the shooting?"

"Uh-huh. You'd better sit down because you're going to be shocked."

"What is it? Who did it?"

"Edmond Windbrook had it done. Can you believe that?"

"Pepper's ex-boyfriend?"

"The one and only. What we don't know is why. You got any ideas?"

"Not one. I don't even know the dude. I can't imagine why he'd try to waste me. It has to be connected somehow to Pepper."

"That's what we thought, but we're still dealing with it. Johnny, just keep this under your hat for now. We don't want to spoil the trip. Pepper might just back out if she knew that, and we'd have two dissatisfied females to contend with."

"Yeah, you're right. I'll see if we can unravel something from this end, too."

"Okay, let me know if you come up with anything. Hey, Johnny, while we were probing this whole thing, we found some discrepancies in the investigation of his parents' death back in '82. We're looking into that, too."

"What? You think he might have been involved with that?

"Maybe. We're thinking he did it, but we don't know that for sure."

"Well, I be damn. If that's true, we're dealing with someone much worse than we imagined. Keep me posted on all that. Later."

Mick and Johnny sat in their respective offices trying to figure out why Edmond Windbrook had ordered the hit. It didn't make sense. Johnny had decided to have Rubin and Ernest dig a little deeper. They were already scoping out his home, but they would need more money to coerce someone in the know to spill the beans. He'd take care of that first thing in the morning.

Johnny didn't need Pepper's go-ahead to follow through with the plans he had laid for Edmond anymore. As soon as he returned from Europe, he would get personally involved.

Of all the things that could happen, that motherfucker wanted me whacked. Well, the tables have turned. This shit's going to really hit the fan.

CHAPTER 25

Paris, France
September 2002

Excitement reigned supreme. Micah was hyped, and Mick got such a kick out of her reactions. She had quizzed him about everything. He assumed she'd do the same thing about Milan. Johnny looked at him and shook his head when the three friends said something indecipherable and laughed.

Lila had several former modeling friends in Paris. She had put them on notice that she'd be in town, and her social calendar was already chock-full.

Pepper was the oddity. She was a striking woman of extreme height and beauty. Her opposing characteristics attracted immense attention. At first glance, she exuded the refined elegance of the rich and well bred. Yet, when observed by an experienced eye, she emitted a smoldering, sensual intensity that hinted at a darker side of her personality—one of an extremely sexual woman who harnessed her deepest desires.

Pepper was unaware of her extraordinary beauty and her sensual appeal. Mick was aware of it and felt certain Johnny was, too. He knew most European men would sense it and pursue her unrelentlessly. She would have to either ignore them or succumb to her innate nature and take them as they came.

Their party was in full swing by the time the plane touched down at Charles de Gaulle Airport, just outside the village of Roissy. Thanks to the champagne the girls insisted they have, they were revved up and in high spirits, ready for their week of fun.

The driver of the hotel limousine awaited them as they stepped outside into the fresh air and sunshine. It was a glorious French day, balmy and bright. The driver whisked them through the countryside and into the renowned city 17 miles away. He spoke English quite well, and he pointed out interest spots along the way. When they entered Paris, he showed them the famous two arches—the *Arc de Triomphe* and the *Arc de Triomphe du Carrousel*—and the Eiffel Tower. When they neared their hotel, they saw the Louvre and the Tuileries Gardens.

The Place Vendome was lined with Mercedes, BMW's, Fiats and Renaults. Adjacent to the hotel they glimpsed Cartier, Armani, Mikimoto, Van Cleef & Arpels and their beloved Chanel's, all discreetly displayed. They could barely wait to visit them all.

The driver stopped, and they got their first glimpse of the fabulous Hotel Ritz. The familiar white canopy with the Ritz imprint greeted them first. Micah and Juanita chose it because of its reported charm and glamour and also because of the celebrities who sang its praises. The Ritz was expensive, but they wouldn't dream of going to Paris without staying there. Besides, it was close to the fashion houses they had come to see.

When they stepped out of the limo, Micah whispered, "Pepper, Nita. We can't gawk at anything. Remember, we're successful designers on a routine trip."

"Pinch me, I don't believe we're here. Look at this place, the square. It's everything I ever dreamed it would be," Juanita said.

"I'll see you girls inside," Lila said, familiar with the whole scene.

Pepper stared in awe, speechless. She looked around and noted the angled, slate-covered roofs. The imposing obelisk, the *Vendome*

Column, rose high above them. It was erected in the 1800's to celebrate one of Napolean's victories, if she remembered correctly.

"Micah, we're ready," Mick said when he and Johnny finished their conversation with the driver.

"Okay, we're coming."

They stepped through the door and were transported into another world.

"Is this the lobby?" Pepper asked.

Mick smiled and said, "Yes, it is. Isn't it gorgeous? They don't allow sightseers and photographers, which makes it different from any place you've been."

"I can't wait to see our rooms," Pepper said.

"Me, either. We're all near each other," Micah said, grasping Lila's arm. "Mom, this is so fabulous. I think this is one of the best ideas you've ever had."

"Yes, I can see why," she said, wondering whether she'd get any work out of them on this trip. "Just remember, we're here to look at the spring collections first, Micah, all right?"

"I know, Mom, first things first, but we're checking out the Ritz tonight."

They were taken to their rooms, and they couldn't get over the impeccable service or the accommodations. After ten minutes, Juanita called Micah.

"Girl, can you believe all this? A full bottle of Shalimar with matching shampoo and lotion. And champagne already iced-down in a silver bucket, two fabulous chandeliers, and a bidet. What a setup. This is something, Micah."

"It sure is. Mick is getting a kick out of my reaction to all this, but it's mind boggling. And Nita, I've never even *seen* a towel warmer before. I'm about to shower and use one of these big, thick peach Porthault towels. I'm knocked out, too, that's all I can say. I've seen some pretty snazzy hotels, but the Ritz is beyond magnificent. Or, should I say it's just plain *ritzy*? Do you have a fireplace?"

"Chile, please. Yes, we do. I think it's solid marble. I'm going to call Pepper to get her reaction. I bet she's walking around in a stupor touching everything in sight. We're still meeting at six for dinner?" Juanita said.

"Yeah. What are you wearing?"

"I don't know…perhaps my green dress with the diagonal neckline. What about you?"

"I'm trying to decide. Maybe the black dress. It's quiet and sophisticated. I don't know yet, but it'll be something like that," Micah said.

"I'll call you before we leave. What's the name of that restaurant?"

"The L'Espandon. Call me when you're ready," Micah said.

Juanita opened the door to the balcony and walked out. Johnny joined her, hugging her from behind and taking in the magnificence of the formal garden.

"Johnny, this is like a dream. Isn't it stunning? I'm so glad you decided to come. I can't imagine being here without you."

"I'm glad I worked it out," he said, knowing full well work would never have posed a problem. "This place is exceptional, but so are you, Nini." He kissed her neck and held her, enjoying the view and the feel of her body.

"We've got four hours alone. We're doing nothing until six. Got any ideas?" she asked.

He smiled and fondled her breasts. "How about some champagne? It's just waiting on us."

"That's a refreshing thought. It was a long trip. I'm going to get in that big, beautiful tub. Wanna join me?"

"Uh-huh. I wouldn't miss it. You tired?"

"A little, but not too tired for you."

She turned around to face him and put her arms around his neck. "You make me so happy, Johnny." She looked at him for a moment, then kissed him.

"Hmm, that pleases me. I want to make you happy. You've changed my life, you know that?"

"I hope it's for the best."

"It *is* for the best." He kissed her then, molding her to him. "I love you, Nini. I get so…lost in you when I'm with you."

"I like that…lost in me," she said, still holding him close. "Are we having that champagne or are we're going to stand out here all day?"

He sighed, and pulled back. "Right now I don't give a damn about the champagne, but yes, we're having our champagne." He took her hand, and they went inside.

"You pour the wine, and I'll run the bath," she said.

"Deal."

They took their bath and almost finished the champagne while in the tub. They retired to the bedroom, determined to rest before dinner, and drifted off to sleep. Juanita's alarm clock buzzed at five o'clock.

"Do we have to go to that restaurant? I don't want to move. I'm enjoying it right here," she said.

"Me, too. We have plenty of time for the restaurant. We'll order something in. Call Micah and tell her we're not going," he said, pulling her closer.

"Yeah, I will." She snuggled with him a while, then she called Micah and Pepper. She was relieved. All she wanted was to relax with Johnny.

After she'd talked with them, she stretched her legs and said, "Hmm. A free night in Paris with the love of my life. Now that's what I'm talkin' 'bout." She smiled at him and snuggled closer.

"Me, too," he said. "Since this is the city for lovers, why don't you take charge and just love me while I lie back and enjoy it?"

"You're insatiable, Johnny Diamond," she said, rising up and straddling his body, looking him in the eye.

He closed his eyes, already anticipating.

"Don't ever say I don't give you what you want," she said, kissing his eyelids, then the corners of his lips.

"I've never been guilty of that," he said, his hands folded beneath his head.

"I don't want you to move a muscle, do you understand?"

"Yes, ma'am, I won't." He had already started moving some muscles he couldn't control, and he said, "This is going to be good, I can already tell."

"Don't talk. I'm in control, here. Do you understand?"

"Yes, ma'am, I told you I did."

"Then quiet," she said, caressing his long body, using her hands and her mouth.

She flicked his nipples, sucked, and then nipped. She felt him flinch, but she continued.

When she circled his navel, she could feel his stiffness lurching below her.

"Baby—"

"No talking, I said."

She worked around his already erect, pulsating staff, prolonging the thrill. She lingered between his legs, and kissed his bulging sac, sucked on each rigid ball.

"Oh, shit, Nini—"

"You asked for this, now be quiet or I'll stop." She proceeded.

"Yes, ma'…Oh…"She raised her head and looked at him.

"All right, but you're just asking for it," he said, his hands now in her hair.

"Do you want this to continue?"

"Yes, but I—"

"Then, do as I say or else." She smiled to herself, and went back to her caressing. She was as hot and bothered as he, but it was such a delicious game, she wanted to venture further. She sucked each toe, causing him to quiver. She started back up his body, but she could tell he wouldn't last.

She grazed his engorged penis, and he stopped her. "Uh-uh," he said. "Come on up here." He raised her onto him and entered her. He'd tired of her game, and he wanted her then.

"Oh, Nini," he said as he felt her warmth surround him. "Nini…" He pushed upward, clamping her hips to him, reveling, lost, trying to consume her.

"Aahh, Johnny," she said, tightening her muscles, massaging him. She wanted more of him, pushed down on him, wanted him deep inside her. His hands on her hips, he helped her move, brought her onto him, gyrating, on the brink of losing control.

"I'm so wet…"

"Uh-uh, everything's so good…don't stop," he pled. Then he exploded, ricocheting, calling her name, taking her with him.

"Johnny," she murmured, her head thrown back, cresting with him, gripping his hips with her knees, melding into him. He felt her muscles contract, moving around him, pulling him to her. Then down they came, ebbing, landing, their bodies drenched. She lay quietly and still, her head upon his chest, still holding him within her, listening to the subsiding thump of his heart.

They lay together in that position, enjoying the closeness, gathering their strength, and then he said, "Nini, my God. That was incredible."

"Yes, it was wonderful." She eased from him, smiled and said, "So, tell me, big boy. How was your first night in the city for lovers?"

He hesitated a beat. "Fuckin' fantastic," he said, nestling with her, satisfied.

❦   ❦   ❦

Mick and Micah skipped dinner, too, but found themselves exploring the hotel, checking out the famous back stairway that Mick said was rumored to be a secret passageway used by the rich and famous for their private assignations.

They visited the health club and the swimming pool area where Versace's final Paris fashion show was held just a week before his death. Micah struck up a conversation with Nicole, a member of the hotel staff, who told them some interesting tidbits about their famous dwelling.

"The Ritz was the first hotel in Europe to do many things," she said.

"Like what?" Micah asked, delighted to talk to someone who could tell her everything she ever wanted to know about this fabulous, old hotel.

"It was the first hotel in Europe to have electricity and...how you say?...indirect lighting."

"Your English is quite good," Micah said, wishing she could speak French half as well.

"Thank you. I try to speak it with the guests. This hotel was the first to have a telephone in every room...also, the king-size beds." Her scheduled guest arrived, and she had to leave them. "Please come back. Schedule an appointment," she said as she left to attend her customer.

"She's right. We've got to use this health club before we go. It's got everything we could ever want," Mick said.

"Tomorrow when we get back. How about a massage? Let's set an appointment while we're here," she said.

"Now that's a winner."

Mick wanted to stop for a drink in Hemingway's. He told her he wanted to come back on Wednesday night, which was cigar night in the famous bar. He wanted to talk with the legendary barkeeper, Colin Field. Hemingway's was a man's place, but everyone was welcomed. It had wood-paneled walls and smelled of cigars and French perfume.

Since they had little to eat all day, they ordered a cold seafood plate and champagne. When the champagne arrived, it was served with a rose. All the water glasses contained floating raspberries, and

Mick told her the olives they were nibbling had been soaked in cognac.

Micah loved the stories Mick told her about Paris and their surroundings. He fascinated her. She found him even more stimulating than ever. He was wealthy and low key. He'd traveled everywhere, he was imaginative and sensual, and he kept her in perpetual awe.

"It's after midnight," she said. "We'd better go. I've got to get up in the morning. Are you going to sleep in the morning or eat with us?"

Getting up from the table, he said, "I'll eat breakfast with you, and maybe Johnny and I will prowl the city." They headed to their room. "You know Princess Diana and Dodi Fayed were staying here when they were killed, don't you? Dodi's father, Mohammed Al-Fayed, owns the Ritz."

"Oh, Mick. I'd forgotten that. I remember the video of them leaving a hotel just before the wreck, but I'd forgotten it was the Ritz. How sad."

"Yeah, it was." They arrived at their room, and Mick opened the door. "I've been thinking about that all evening."

"I'm glad you mentioned it. I would have never connected it."

She wanted to hold him, so she stepped into his arms. "Mick, this has been such a wonderful day. I'm so happy you decided to come."

"Me, too." They kissed and nuzzled, always in tune to each other. "I don't think you know how much I love you."

"I think I do. I love you, too," she said, "but why don't you tell me later?"

When they went into the bedroom, everything was back in place. The bed had been turned down in an unusual, diagonal fashion, and the Ritz-produced chocolates were scattered on their pillows.

"We couldn't have made a better choice. This hotel is more than I could have imagined," she said.

"And so are you," he said, unzipping her dress and looking forward to dessert—just a little 'some'um, some'um' is all he wanted.

❦   ❦   ❦

Since no one wanted to go out to dinner, Lila called Sasha, a friend and former model who came back to live in Paris. She and Pepper met her at Natacha's, a small bistro on a residential street in the 14th *arrondissement*, near Sasha's apartment. The patrons were an assortment of the arty and offbeat as well as women clad in vintage Yves Saint Laurent and Jean Paul Gaultier clothing. The people, the clothes and the atmosphere captivated Pepper. It was a city she could call home without any regrets.

Pepper saw a different side of Lila in Paris. She'd known she had been a model when she married Micah's dad, Franklin, but she didn't know she had another life that included friends of the bohemian variety. Lila knew Paris well, and she was comfortable in any setting.

She also had an innate sensibility about clothes. Even though she had never been to Natacha's, she advised Pepper on the right thing to wear. Pepper had chosen a chic beige ensemble with a matching lightweight wrap. Lila suggested she wear her black velvet jeans with her vintage brocade jacket. When Lila finished helping her accessorize her outfit, Pepper exuded an understated Parisian glamour that fit her personality and the occasion to perfection.

Lila chose a stunning black pants ensemble with a snug hot pink top. The only jewelry she wore was fabulous, huge hot pink shoulder-duster earrings. Lila and Pepper were similar in appearance. They were both a smidgen under six feet tall, slender and gorgeous, with innate sensual appeal. When they walked into Natacha's later that evening, they caused all heads to turn. They made a stunning pair.

As they were being driven to meet Sasha, Lila thought about Johnny's earlier attraction to her. She smiled at the memory. The incomparable Juanita Sanchez had swiftly brought him to heel. She noticed how attuned to her Johnny appeared. His total focus was on her. He'd never attracted Lila, but that wasn't to say she didn't think he was a handsome man with a powerful masculine presence. She had to give him that, and a whole lot more. Anyone would. She was happy for Juanita and Johnny. Franklin was plenty, and he was all she wanted.

Sasha was waiting for them when they arrived. She'd brought her friend, Jean Luc Pedescleaux, with her. They stayed late into the night, enjoying the wine and the ambience. Jean Luc and Pepper were attracted to each other. Lila and Sasha detected their instant connection, and Sasha encouraged it.

As they were leaving, Jean Luc turned to Pepper and said, "It has been a most enjoyable evening, Pepper. When you are not working, I would love to show you *my* Paris. Would you like that?"

"I would *love* that," she said, surprising herself.

"Wonderful. And when I call the Hotel Ritz, for whom do I ask? Pepper…?"

"Hankerson," she said, beginning to feel that familiar excitement edge its way into her being.

"Thank you. I will call you tomorrow." He kissed her cheek, and they joined Sasha and Lila.

Jean Luc was dark, with a black moustache that shadowed his full, pouty lips. He was six feet tall, and he was an artist who lived in Sasha's apartment building. Lila was surprised that Pepper gave him a second thought because Micah told her Edmond was the only man she would dare consider. Lila surmised that because Jean Luc was charming and clever, and he'd lived his whole life in Paris, he represented a foreign appeal that intrigued Pepper. She could never have imagined the attraction stemmed from a much darker, secret passion that lurked within Pepper.

No one must ever know. I miss Edmond so much, and it's been much too long.

❧   ❧   ❧

The next morning, everyone ate breakfast together, and Johnny and Mick took off to scour the Left Bank. They decided they would save their special tours to share with the girls. Lila, Micah, Pepper and Juanita headed to *Chanel's*. Shasa, a former model for many years, arranged a private showing for them. They loved everything. The three designers wanted to bring out their sketchpads and record what they'd seen, but it was out of the question. Lila kept them in hand. They just had to remember what they'd seen. Micah was already sketching designs in her head.

They went to *Armani's* and *Chloe's* and scrutinized the clothes and the accessories. Everything they encountered was overly expensive, but they couldn't resist. All of them spent far too much money, including Lila. They returned to the Ritz exhausted, but with bags in hand. Mick and Johnny were relaxing in their rooms.

"Micah, this is the anniversary of the Twin Towers disaster. The news coverage is extraordinary. Look at all this. I guess I'm a little surprised it's this extensive here."

"Well, you can imagine what it's like at home."

"It's been a year already. Where has the time gone?"

"It's flown by so fast. I know the families are reliving that horror story. It was such a useless act," she said.

"Yes, it was."

"What did you two do today?" Micah asked.

"We explored the Left Bank, had lunch at some cafe and just checked out all the women," he said, smiling at her.

"Oh, you did, did you? What did you find?"

"Nothing like you, I assure you. Come here," he said, pulling her down on the bed with him.

"Tell me anything," she said, kissing him.

"You don't play fair. You're a vixen," he said, referring to the sizzling kiss she'd just given him. "Did you pick up many ideas for the spring season?"

"Oh, Mick. These French designers are incredible. Yes, I did, and I'm going to capture some of them on my pad tonight. It won't take long, okay?"

"Okay. I know this is a partial business trip. I'm fine. Do you want to sketch now?" He saw President Bush, and turned the TV volume up. They listened to his brief statement, talked about his comments and resumed their conversation.

"When are you going to do your sketching?"

"A little later. I want to finish it tonight so I can have tomorrow free, and we can do whatever we want. We'll see the sights tomorrow."

"Uh-hmm, I'm all yours. Just do with me what you will."

"Now that's an interesting thought. Put a pin in that," she said, kissing him and taking off her clothes. "I just want to get comfortable. My feet are killing me."

"Come on and get in bed. Let me rub them for you."

"Oh, Mick, you're so sweet. That's one reason I love you."

The next day, Pepper and Jean Luc spent the entire day together. He took her everywhere. They didn't spend a long time in each place, but Pepper had a good sense of the places he took her. They visited the Eiffel Tower, the *Arc de Triomphe*, the Louvre and *Notre Dame*.

She invited Jean Luc back to the Ritz, and he accepted. They recognized each other to be what they were, and he wasted no time in getting right to the point.

"I know you're attracted to me, Pepper, as I am to you." He took her in his arms.

"Yes, I am attracted to you. I was right away. I believe it's called chemistry."

"Yes, chemistry. That is the correct word. We have chemistry. And I like the black eye piece," he said.

"It's called a patch."

"Then I love the black patch, Pepper. I find it bewitching. I want to imagine what happened. The truth would not be as exciting."

Then it's your loss, Jean Luc. If you only knew.

He kissed her hard, forcing her to respond. He teased her tongue, explored deeper. She allowed him full entrance, and she moved closer to him.

He undressed her, piece by piece, awakening his senses. He found her exquisite. By the time he had her undressed, his passion was in full bloom. He pulled his belt from his pants and removed them. He placed her face down on the bed, and he removed his shirt and shorts.

He picked up his belt and flogged her, raining blows upon her, but making sure they struck only her butt. She cried out in pain, and most of all in pleasure. She loved the pain, savored and anticipated it, her mascara smearing her face.

"Harder," she demanded.

When he saw her tears and the blood he'd drawn, he entered her from behind without any further foreplay—the beating was it.

When he heard her beg him for more, insist that he harm her, he could contain himself no longer.

"Bitch, you are nothing but a cunt," he said, pounding into her.

"Yes, yes…" she said, crying and coming as he ground himself into her anal passage.

He expelled his sperm, then stopped and withdrew from her. He went into the bathroom, and she heard the splash of water. He came out fully dressed.

"Thank you, Pepper. I will call you. We will see each other tomorrow night. Goodbye."

"Bye," she said, still on the bed. She pulled herself up, and went into the bathroom. She stepped into the shower and winced from the pain as the water bathed her rawness.

God, help me, please. I just can't resist him.

Juanita and Johnny roved the entire city, relished its tightly connected secret sections. They toured the Egyptian Antiquities area of the Louvre extensively. Juanita wanted to see as many of the 5,000 Egyptian displays as she could. She told Johnny if there were such a thing as reincarnation, she would have been an Egyptian in her former life. She had always been drawn to Egyptian jewelry and artifacts. To their surprise, Johnny loved it all.

They spent five glorious days in Paris, and it was a whirlwind experience. They accomplished their goals of previewing the spring collections and also enjoying themselves. They pursued their interests separately during the day, but on two occasions, they visited several well-known nightspots together.

The two couples spent considerable private time together. Pepper saw Jean Luc daily without their knowledge, using the famous back stairway for the purpose it was rumored to have been built—pursuing their private assignations.

To Lila's surprise, Sasha threw a lavish party for her at one of her friend's villas. She invited all of their old friends who were still in the city. They partied long into the night. Sasha took it upon herself to invite Armand, Lila's first real love and lover. He arrived after midnight, looking every bit the dashing, successful actor that he was. Armand DuBois. Standing before her, magnificent as ever. When Lila saw him, her heart thumped, and her eyes skimmed him, his black pants hugging his thighs, his bulge prominently displayed.

My God, Armand. Why did Sasha do this?

"Lila, my love. How beautiful you still are," his accent thick and seductive. He took her hand and kissed it, his eyes riveting, boring straight through her.

"Armand," she said, still startled.

"I could not resist it. When Sasha told me, I could not stay away. I've longed for you so long."

Their attraction was undeniable. The chemistry as strong as ever....

Lila's taxi pulled up to the hotel at 7:00 a.m. Their flight to Milan left at three. She had no sleep and knew she wouldn't be able to. She packed her belongings, took her shower and relaxed on her luxurious lounge. She closed her eyes and sighed. All she wanted to do was think.

"This was the best five days of my life," Micah said on the way to the airport.

"Amen to that," Juanita said.

"What about you, Mom. Did you have fun with your friends?"

"More than you'll ever know. Sasha's a *real* miracle worker."

"Amen to that," Pepper said, smiling at Juanita and thinking of Jean Luc.

"Milan will be different. I just want you to absorb the style of the city and the women. That should help you in designing this r line. We'll just relax and do whatever we want. Nothing's on the agenda," Lila said.

"We can handle that," Juanita said.

Mick and Johnny said nothing, but they had made plans of their own regarding Edmond. Their time was drawing near.

CHAPTER 26

Milan, Italy
September 2002

When the Atlanta crew set foot on Italian soil, the weather was foggy and overcast, everything muted and dismal. It was nothing akin to their sun-kissed, balmy arrival in France. They looked forward to a relaxing two-day holiday, and the gloomy weather did not deter them. The women were excited about getting another glimpse of European fashion at its best. They were there to observe the fashions and the cultural aspects of the second largest fashion city in Europe.

The Westin Palace Hotel, a five star establishment, was as different from the Ritz as the Milanese were from the Parisians. The Ritz was incomparable as far as customer service. The Westin Palace was excellent in that regard, but it was not in the same league as the Ritz. Milan was a conservative, laid back city.

The women dressed in basic, somber colors of olives, grays, taupes and beiges. A bright color never reared its head in this well-known fashion capital. The Milanese left anything colorful and showy to the Romans.

Pepper had snapped back miraculously. Europe intrigued her as no other place she'd been. She arranged an outing for a stroll along the mosaic-paved, shop-lined *Galleria Vittorio Emanuele II* leading up to the magnificent Duomo, the central city cathedral. Mick and

Johnny declined the tour of the shopping area and hung out by themselves, drinking and enjoying the scenery. The women bought scads of leather shoes and purses from the shops in the cathedral square. Mick and Johnny could glimpse them occasionally as they trekked in and out of the shops.

Juanita figured out the best place to observe the locals was in the *Quadrilaterral*, the elegant and expensive high-fashion area around Via Montenapoleone. They analyzed the well dressed and the rich, and they compared them to the ordinary workers who moved about the area. By American standards, everyone was sophisticated and chic, but their discerning eyes registered the higher quality of clothes the rich wore. The fabric and cut of the clothing the wealthy wore were far superior to the average worker's clothing. They vowed their clothes would be of high quality, yet also be affordable to the masses. That thought would remain uppermost in their minds when they designed their next collection.

They visited the famous La Scala Opera House, but were unable to attend because it was closed for the season. September through November featured classical concerts and ballets. They had planned to go to a concert, but they never did because they always found something more enticing to do.

On their second night in Milan, they went to dinner at Trattoria Milanese, a small family-run restaurant, recommended by one of the locals they met. The food was typical local fare, but it was exceptional. The patrons were energetic and friendly and were very curious about their American lifestyle. They adored the Milanese, the food and the camaraderie. Pepper struck up a private conversation with a young man named Mondo who bought them wine all evening.

They boarded the plane the next day at the Malpensa Airport and said goodbye to a wonderful week of European fun and inspiration. The three girls were eager to get on with their designing tasks for the upcoming season.

Juanita and Micah were ecstatic about their experiences. Pepper was in high spirits and seemingly back on track. Lila was quiet and reflective. Mick and Johnny, relaxed and jovial, had their separate plans in place. Edmond Windbrook was their top priority. Their activities would be hectic and dangerous, but they had prepared for the inevitable.

CHAPTER 27

Atlanta, Georgia
September 2002

Micah had mixed feelings when their plane landed at the Atlanta International Airport. She hated to let go of their world of make believe and face reality again, but the thought of home brought comfort.

"Mick, it was such a wonderful trip. You made it so much fun."

He put his arm around her and smiled. He looked out the airplane window as the it taxied into the terminal. "It *was* great, wasn't it? I could have gone anywhere with you, and it would have been fantastic," he said, looking into her misty eyes.

"I love you," she said.

They swept through the terminal, moving fast, and Micah was caught off guard. The Atlanta airport was a hubbub of activity. As Mick moved her along, her eyes focused on a familiar figure. When he turned, their eyes locked. It was Armstead. They were on a different path, but she stared.

She'd read somewhere that whenever you locked eyes with someone, that person had a message for you. She'd read that in the *Celestine Prophesy,* she thought. She made a mental note to check it. Did Armstead have some message for her? If so, she'd never get it.

She also noted he was arm-in-arm with a beautiful cafe au lait-colored woman who leaned in close, talking intimately. She knew instinctively they were headed for some private, seductive getaway; something she'd never had time for with him.

He acknowledged her with his eyes, followed her until they'd passed. Micah's last glimpse caught him responding to his companion as Mick squeezed her hand. It was a fleeting moment, occurring as they walked, but it was etched forever in her mind. Seeing him touched so possessively by someone so beautiful made her jealousy, but she'd made the decision.

His eyes told her he still loved her, but he'd been forced to move on. Her heart tugged with that thought. It was ridiculous. She had told him she wanted Mick. Now that he'd moved on, she was jealous. How fucked up was she? She grasped Mick's arm and pulled him closer.

"You okay?" he asked, shifting his bag to his other hand and hugging her as they walked.

"I am now," she said, closing that chapter of her life forever.

CHAPTER 28

❀

Mick opened his office door at 6:35 a.m. All of them planned to take the next day off to adjust to the jetlag, but his mind wouldn't rest. He had spent the night with Micah, but he woke up early, left her a note and went home. He showered and made his way to the office. The Edmond Windbrook case controlled him. He'd struggled with it in Europe, but he was back now, and he needed to make some headway. He had an unexplainable feeling of dread.

He'd talked with Hubert twice while he was in Europe. He had not mentioned it to anyone. He didn't want to disrupt the trip. When he saw the thick report in the middle of his desk, he knew some of its content. He scanned his messages and made some coffee.

He clicked on his TV and went to make a pot of coffee. He switched the TV to CNN, sat back with his feet propped on his desk and opened the report. He read for over an hour, horrified by most of it. Edmond Waverly Windbrook, III had to be destroyed. He had no other choice. He was a sadistic, calculating predator whose victims were the weak and less fortunate.

He would have to do something himself because he feared for them all. He just needed time to think, to formulate his actions. He had always been able to work within the realm of the law, but this was personal. This problem was a private, moral issue, and the long arm of the law held no claims.

"Juanita. This is Mick. I hope I didn't wake you, but is Johnny there?"

"Yes, he is, and no you didn't wake me. I'm rummaging in this kitchen trying to scrape something together for breakfast. You still at Micah's?"

"No. In fact, I left her asleep this morning. She hasn't called me, so I know she's still sleeping."

"Oh. Hold on a minute, I'll get Johnny." He could hear her muffled call.

Johnny picked up. "Mick, what's up?"

"I'm sorry to disturb you, but I have something here in my office you need to see. Take your time. Juanita told me she's fixing breakfast. I'm going to be here all day. Come at any time."

"It's serious, huh?"

"Yes. See you when you get here."

"Right. Later."

"What's going on? He went to the office anyway. It must be something serious," Juanita said.

"Yeah. He didn't want to talk about it on the phone. I gather it's something about the shooting. I'm going down to his office to see what he has after we eat something. What's for breakfast? You n   ¹ any help?"

"No, but I have some of everything. I've learned to keep this house stocked. You know how your appetite is after I've brought you to your knees," she said, smiling at him. "You want anything special?"

He grinned back, tweaked her silk-covered nipple, and said, "Yeah, right. I'm craving some down-home stuff. How about some grits, eggs and sausage. This will be my last splurge before I hit the gym this week."

"Okay. I'll get it going. You take your shower. Wonder what's so important that Mick couldn't tell you about it over the phone?"

"Don't know, but I'll find out soon," he said, walking back toward the bathroom, deep in thought.

An hour and a half later, he walked into Mick's office and greeted Sela. "Hello. I'm Johnny Diamond. Mick called me earlier and asked me to come by. Is he in?"

"Yes, and he's expecting you. Go right in," Sela said, giving him *more* than the once over. *Good God a' mighty! What a hunk.*

Johnny knocked.

"Come on in."

"Hey, man. What you got?"

"This," Mick said, indicating the report. "I think Windbrook is planning on whacking the four of us—you, Juanita, Micah and me. He's trying to wipe out Pepper's whole support system, as he sees it. At least that's what one of our informants said. I guess he doesn't think her family is much support."

"What? Damn crazy bastard. Then we need to get the girls protected, and they need to know what's going on. Otherwise, they won't do a damn thing we say."

"Right. I've already gotten someone on Micah and me. You need Ernest or someone on Juanita, and keep Rubin by your side."

"Uh-huh. It's good as done. I haven't talked with Rubin or Ernest since I've been back, but I'm going to the club as soon as I leave here. I'm looking for them to have something on all this, too."

"Man, Johnny, that's just a fraction of what's contained in this report. This dude is all fucked up and has been for a long time. The evidence shows he was the chief suspect in his parents' death, but the case was dropped. I bet some bigwig was paid to make it happen," Mick said, marveling at the corruptness that's present within the ranks of our upstanding men in blue. "I'd like to find his childhood *au pair* and the longtime family butler. They're both back in England. It shouldn't be too hard to track them down. They should be able to give us some firsthand information."

"Killed his parents? Now that *is* some fucked up shit. I tell you, Mick, and I know you're a man who upholds the law, but I made up my mind before we left for Europe, that he's my personal property. Take that any way you want, but he's mine, especially since I know his plans," Johnny said.

"I *am* a man who believes in upholding the law, but this is different. He's used his money to do whatever he damn well pleased. You might be surprised, but I vowed the very same thing this morning when I finished reading this report. He's a sick motherfucker. Some of the things he did in childhood pointed straight to where he is today. His parents either didn't give a shit about him or they turned their heads the other way. I'm in, whatever the plan. I want to be in on the action as well as the planning."

Johnny stood. "You're in. I'll let you know what's going down after I talk with Rubin. Later." He left Mick's office, bracing himself for the plans he made in Europe.

CHAPTER 29

Atlanta, GA
September 2002

"Pepper. This is Edmond. How are you? I saw pictures of you when you were at the McCall fashion show. They were breathtaking. I am so pleased the surgery was successful. If it is at all possible, you are more beautiful than were before. I was stunned when I saw you in *People.*"

"Thank you." Her heart raced, heightening her desire for him.

"I am just so thankful you were not injured. How is Juanita's boyfriend doing? He was shot, wasn't he?"

"Yes, he was. He's recovered. The police are investigating the shooting, but they haven't come up with anything. We were so frightened. I've never been through anything quite like it."

"I am sorry you had to witness all that. As I said, the most important thing is you were not hurt," he said, caring and concern evident in his voice.

"Johnny's such a wonderful person. It's just a shame he and his bodyguard were shot."

"From what I have read about Juanita's boyfriend, Pepper, he's some kind of petty gangster. When you associate with people like that, you can expect any kind of trouble. I am afraid for you. I wish you would accept my offer for the protection of my home. You know I have the gate, the dogs and the guards. You will be safe here."

"I don't think any of us is in danger. We think it has something to do with the business Johnny's in. I think you've misinterpreted the whole thing. No one is after the rest of us," she said, trying to convince him.

He felt he had the control back, and he said, "I insist, Juanita. You have no idea what kind of people you're dealing with. You *will* come here until this whole thing is resolved."

He does love me. He's just concerned and protective.

"I don't know, Edmond. I'm starting work next week. I've got so much to do to get ready. I've got to unpack and get things in order."

"Unpack? Where have you been?" He didn't have her under surveillance, but he knew she'd been missing for a week.

"I'm just getting back from Europe. From Paris and Milan. I went with the McCall staff."

"Please. Micah and Juanita? Who else accompanied you?"

"Lila, Mick and Johnny. We had a wonderful time. We saw all the new lines, and we got a chance to tour the cities. We just had fun. It was terrific," she said, not revealing the two encounters she allowed.

As she talked with Edmond, her mind flashed to Milan. She was intoxicated with the wine, the view and Mondo, the handsome stranger. It was her one and only one night stand, but it was glorious. It was almost as wonderful as her encounters with Edmond, but her experiences with Jean Luc were what she cherished.

"I'm even more concerned now than ever," Edmond said. "Your continued association with the underbelly is unthinkable. I insist you come here at once. I will send the driver for you tonight."

"Edmond, I can't come tonight. I've got too much to do to get ready for work next week. Now I appreciate your concern, but now is *not* the time."

He could not believe she was defying him, but he took another path. "All right, Pepper. I respect your opinion. I will allow you to get your things in order. But next week, you *will* come here. I insist," he said, deciding to relent. *I thought she had learned her lesson. Got to do something about her outright rebelliousness.*

"All right. Next week. I must go, Edmond. We'll talk before then. Bye."

"Goodbye. Pepper, while you are unpacking, you might as well pack some things to bring here. In any event, we will talk next week. Goodbye."

A silent bell went off in her head. She sat thinking about their conversation. She was so caught up in Edmond's renewed possessiveness that she couldn't see the light. With Edmond, it had always been one her faults.

❦   ❦   ❦

Johnny called Juanita from Club Eden. He'd been busy all day. He had assigned Ernest as her full-time bodyguard. He needed to talk with her about everything he had discovered since he'd left her.

"Hey, Nini. What are you doing?"

"The same ole drudgery—washing and trying to get everything back in order. Are you still with Mick?"

"No. I left hours ago. I'm at the club, but I'll be back there soon. I need to talk with you about some things."

"Hmm. That sounds interesting. Can you give me a hint?"

"Not now, but I'll be there in a couple of hours. Since you've been slaving in the house all day, would you like to go out to dinner?"

"I'd *love* to go out to dinner. You choose the place, okay?"

"All right. Put on something fetching, something that will get my juices flowing."

"Johnny, your juices are always flowing. I don't have to do anything special."

"That's because it's you. You just got it like that, huh?"

"You got that right. And don't you forget it," she quipped, smiling.

"No ma'am, I won't," he said, for the first time realizing Juanita has *always* had his number. She knew he enjoyed that take-charge brassiness she clobbered him with sometime.

"See you, baby. I'll be there soon."

"Bye, sugar."

❀   ❀   ❀

Mick rang Micah's doorbell, and she looked through her peephole. She couldn't see his face, but recognized his thick bush of gray hair. She opened the door immediately.

"Hello, Mr. Early Bird. Where have you been? I've tried to call you off and on all afternoon."

"I've been involved with Hubert. I've got to talk with you about some things. You want to go out for dinner?"

"Not tonight. I took out some steaks. Thought I'd just bake a couple of potatoes and make a salad. Is that okay with you?"

"Not only okay, it's a relief. I'm bushed," he said, bringing her close to him. "You smell so good."

"I took a long soak in the tub this afternoon. It's good to be back home." She touched his face, looked at him lovingly and kissed him. She adored his touch, loved his solid body. She was happy with him and the course their relationship had taken.

He pulled her closer, skimming her buttocks, lifting her to him. He moved, and she sighed, freeing herself for him. He detected her acquiescence, and he hardened. "Ah, Micah, what you do to me."

"Hmm. It's what you do to me. I can't explain it. Every time you touch me, I can't help myself. What kind of bewitchery have you practiced?"

"Don't know, but I'm taking advantage of it while it lasts," he said, lifting her thin dress, surprised and delighted she had on no panties.

"Well, what do we have here," he asked, looking at her nakedness.

"Just a little some'um, some'um I thought you might like."

"Oh yeah? You thought I might like it, huh?"

"Uh-huh, I sure did."

"Here, let me show you how much I do." He lifted her onto the kitchen counter, bend down to her, and teased her."

"You're a naughty boy. I think I just might spank you tonight," she said, smiling.

He stood between her legs, hugging her around the waist. Can I take a shower, too? It'll revive me."

"Sweetie, you can do whatever you want, but reviving, you don't need."

Mick got up from bed and padded into the kitchen. "White or red?"

"White, I think."

"Okay." He poured two glasses of white wine and returned to the bedroom.

Micah was propped up on several pillows, leaning back, trying to second-guess him. She reached out for the wine and said, "Thank you, sweetie. Now what do you need to talk with me about?"

He crawled in beside her, careful not to spill his wine. "It's about the shooting incidence. We found out who shot Johnny and Rubin."

"You did? And you haven't even mentioned it. Who did it?"

"It was Edmond."

"Edmond? My God. Why? What did Johnny do to him? I can't believe it. He doesn't know Johnny, does he?"

"No, he doesn't. Edmond didn't do it personally, but it was either someone on his staff or he hired a hit man. In any event, Edmond issued the order. We have an informant who told us *we* might be in danger—you, Juanita, Johnny and me. He wants Pepper to suffer, and he thinks getting rid of her closest friends would hurt her more than anything. He's sick, Micah. He's been sick a long time, since childhood. He's the classic sadistic killer."

"Mick, tell me this is some sick joke. He wants us killed? What will we do? Have you reported him to the police?"

"No, I haven't, but I've hired a bodyguard for both of us. They've been on the job all day. I'll introduce you to your guy tomorrow. His name is Donald Myers, and he's one of the best, has lots of experience."

"Mick, this can't be. I'm frightened. A bodyguard? What will this do to our lives? What about Juanita and Johnny? Does Nita know? Pepper? Does he want to kill her, too?"

"Right now, Pepper's all right. She just needs to keep away from him. She was fine in Europe. I hope she's gotten over him. Johnny has Ernest guarding Juanita, and Rubin's guarding him. He's telling Juanita all about this tonight, too. You must be observant of your surroundings, but it's nothing to be paranoid about. Donald will be with you or near you at all times. Johnny and I are trying to come up with some kind of plan for us. It's not finalized, so I can't talk about it yet."

"Who's guarding Pepper?"

"No one, at the moment. She's not in danger."

"Mick, work it out now. She needs protection, too."

"Micah, we've taken care of everything. He won't harm her."

"Does Juanita know?"

"I told you, Johnny's telling her tonight." Tears rimmed her eyes, and her body trembled. He pulled her into his embrace, rocking and soothing her.

"It's okay. Everything's going to be all right. We've got everything covered. He just needs to make one mistake, and we'll have him. I had to tell you so we can protect you the way we should. Just do as Donald says. Please don't worry about it. It's under control."

❈   ❈   ❈

The doorbell rang. "Shoot!" Juanita said as she put down the hair dryer and started to the door. She hadn't finished drying her shoulder-length, full head of hair, and she wanted to be ready when Johnny arrived. She had on her new leopard bra, panties and half-slip. Johnny left her a voice message that he would pick her up later than he'd planned. He was going to his house to shower and change clothes first.

She opened the door and said, "My goodness, sugar. Look at you. I love the suit. I'd better make it clear you're with me tonight."

He walked in smiling, "Ah, shucks. This is just a little 'some'um, some'um' I thought you might like," he said. The both laughed.

"You're too much. You look *so* handsome, sugar," she said, kissing him and feeling the texture of his well-tailored, navy wool suit.

"Thanks, baby. Where did Micah get that expression anyway?"

"I don't know. She's always had her favorite sayings. It wouldn't be Micah, if she were just plain ordinary. I'm almost ready. Just need to finish my hair and slip into my dress. Where are we going?"

"It's a surprise. We've got plenty of time. The reservations are at seven-thirty."

"Okay. Want a drink?"

"Maybe. You want something?"

"I've got some wine. Fix yourself something, and I'll hurry up."

"Okay."

She shouted from the bathroom, "I'm curious about today's events. What did you want to talk to me about?"

"We'll do it at dinner. I want to be able to sit down and just talk about it."

"Oh-oh. This sounds serious. What was it that Mick couldn't discuss over the phone?"

"That's part of the story. I'll tell you everything at dinner," he said, mixing himself a bourbon and water.

Johnny took Juanita to the revolving restaurant on top of the Fitzgerald Hotel. It was new, and she'd never been there.

"Johnny, this is so romantic," she said, looking out at the city lights.

"Yes, it is. I thought you'd like it."

After they were seated, they both ordered grilled salmon and salad. They had no dessert, but Johnny ordered them two cognacs. He waited until the waiter brought their drinks, and he said, "Mick found out who ordered the hit…the foiled hit, I should say."

"Hit? Is that what the shooting was? A hit?"

"Yes, an attempted hit. On me."

"Johnny, why? Who wants to harm you?"

"Edmond Windbrook."

"*Edmond?* You don't even know him. Why would he want you hit?"

"Mick thinks he wants all of us out of the picture, then he'll have total control over Pepper."

"All of us? Me, you, Micah…?"

"And Mick."

"I can't believe it. I can understand why he would want me whacked. He's always known I didn't like him. But the rest of you? It's incredible. He's got to be crazy, Johnny. I know I don't even need to tell you to go ahead with the plans you'd made, do I?"

"No, I'll take care of it. I'm going to have Ernest guard you until we get through all this. It could be a while. That's what I wanted to tell you, Nini. He's going to be with you day and night. You might not always see him, but he'll be there."

"Oh, Johnny, is that necessary?"

"It's imperative. You've got to cooperate with me on this, Juanita. I don't want any slip-ups, no antics from you. Okay?"

"I guess. If it's got to be done." She thought about what he had told her for a moment then said, "Johnny, I need a piece. You've got a small arsenal at home. I'd feel so much better if I had my own gun."

"I've got anything you'd want, but are you sure? Will you be able to handle it?"

"Let's stop by your house after we leave here. Let me choose what I want, okay?"

"Sure. But let's talk about this some—"

"What about Micah? Will she be guarded?"

"Yes. And Mick, too. He's arranged it all."

"Johnny, is Pepper in danger?"

"Mick doesn't think so, but I've asked Rubin to guard her. She won't know it, but he'll be there."

"But Rubin always guards you. Who's going to cover you?"

"I'll be okay. I'm going to be packin' my own stuff." He didn't tell her he had a second motive. He felt the need for his own protection because of grist from the rumor mill. He'd had a rash of employees quitting lately without any reasonable explanation. Rubin told him word on the street was that Gia Cantoni was the culprit. Johnny and Gia had remained friends, and their bargain had been upheld. He didn't believe Gia had reneged on their deal, but he had to be sure. He refused to be baited by rumor, but he had Rubin fishing for the details.

"Oh, Johnny. Shit! This is scary, but that bastard—excuse my French. He's *got* to go. I don't think we ought to tell Pepper just yet. I'm not sure she can handle it now. Johnny, please be careful."

"I'll be fine. Pepper's still at home with her folks, but if she does decide to go back to her place, we'll have to tell her."

"Uh-huh, you ready? I want to see what you have at home."

"Yeah. Let me pay the bill."

When they got to Johnny's house, she went straight to his gun cabinet. She saw what she wanted. She picked it up and said, "This is it."

"Juanita, this is a Glock. You've got to learn—"

Before he could finish his sentence, she'd broken it down, checked it out and had it closed within seconds. "Yeah, this is a Glock model 20, ten millimeter."

"What? Where'd you learn all that? It's quite obvious you've done the breakdown many times, but where?" he asked, stupefied.

"In my former life. It's a long story. I'm a sharpshooter, Johnny. That's just the way it is," she said, fishing in his bottom drawer for bullets.

"Damn. Where did you learn all this? What other tricks you got up your sleeve?"

"Baby, I doubt if you'll ever scrape the bottom of this barrel." For the first time ever, she didn't pretend to be a kick-ass woman, she just performed like the gun moll she was, and Johnny thought she was magnificent.

CHAPTER 30

Atlanta, Georgia
October 2002

Juanita, Micah and Pepper dedicated themselves to the task at hand since returning from Europe. They were back at work, but their lives had taken a different turn. They had agreed nothing would keep them from designing their best collection ever. Pepper was still in the dark about Edmond's alleged plans.

They were working day and night on their new line because they were determined to be ready for the annual McCall Fashion and Design Center Holiday Extravaganza the second week in December. They were enthusiastic and confident about the designs they'd already produced. When they were in Europe, they realized everyone in the design center would have to spend the next few months working exclusively on their collection. Lila wanted to postpone the fashion show until the spring, but they would have no part of it. They would be ready on December 14th.

The three VP's decided to refer to the holiday show as their seasonal collection. They decided to design for all four seasons, not just for the spring. Their creativity soared with their newfound freedom.

Even before the holiday season, their clothes were flying off the shelves. The publicity from their previous show and the shooting incident were still fresh in everyone's minds. They were elegantly and impeccably dressed whenever they were interviewed or talked to the media. The sales for *MJP* went through the roof. They had finally made it. Everyone had high expectations for their new collection.

❧   ❧   ❧

Micah decided to buy herself some new archery equipment. Her parents had bought hers when she was in eight grade. She located a specialty shop in the phone book and found it on her lunch hour.

"Hello. I'd like to see some of your bows and arrows," she said.

"We have many as you can see. Are you looking for one in particular?"

"No, but I own a Krim bow now, and I want something of better quality."

The owner showed her every bow in his shop. She was thoroughly confused, but she decided on an expensive Horse bow that was well made and beautifully balanced. She placed the set in her trunk because she wanted quick access to it when she practiced at Mick's on the weekend. She and Juanita would resume their twice a week practice at the gun range today, and she looked forward to gaining insight from her. As she pulled from the curb, she saw Donald in his large gray van pull out behind her.

Micah and Juanita met at the range after work. "Now that I'm getting the hang of the gun, I think I like it," Micah said. "Let's get something to drink next door and sit awhile."

"Now that's a winner. We haven't really talked since we got back from Europe."

They ordered their drinks, and Juanita scanned the cafe for a seat. "I told you it would be fun once you got into it. The better you get, the better you'll like it, I guarantee you. Let's get that table by the window."

"Okay. I've been wanting to ask you for a while, how are you feeling about the bodyguard? It's been a few weeks now," Micah asked.

"It's not my favorite thing, but he hasn't cramped my style. It's comforting to know he's there, even though I don't see him all the time. I just wonder when it's all going to end. I don't think Edmond's going to do a damn thing."

"Me, neither. Donald does all he can to *not* disrupt my life. I wonder where they are now?" Micah said, looking around, but not seeing them. "He's nice, and Mick says he's an expert at what he does. I'm just thankful he's with me. This thing scared the shit out of me when Mick told me about it, I can tell you that. Mick has been incredible, Nita. He's the most caring man I've even known, and we have so much fun together. I think I'm in love."

"Really? Micah, I am telling you no lie, I never thought I'd ever hear you say that."

"Why? Am I all that different from everyone else?"

"Yes, you really are. When the rest of us were falling in and out of love every week, you were the stable one. No one ever fazed you. You always hung tough."

"That's what you all thought. It really wasn't that way at all. I wanted to have someone in my life, but for some reason, the right person never showed up. You think I might have been waiting on Mick?"

Now Micah, how the hell would I know that? Don't get me to lying all up in here."

Micah laughed. "Are you in love with Johnny?"

"How would I know? I've never been in love before. I do know that I care for him a lot...a whole lot. But love? I don't have a clue."

"Just from what I've observed and from what Mick's told me about him, he's in love with you. Has he ever said it?"

"Uh-uh. We don't talk in those terms, but I know he cares."

"Nita, Mick says you're carrying a gun yourself. Are you? And, if you are, why the hell didn't you tell me?"

"Yes, I am, and I thought you'd freak if I told you. I just feel better having my own protection."

"And Johnny's carrying his own gun, too, since Rubin's guarding Pepper?"

"Yep, he's packin'. Micah, you should see him when he takes off his jacket. Man. He has a holster that goes around his back, and the gun is tucked to his left side. Just the sight of it is mind-blowing."

"See, there you go. I told you, you were crazy. You're fucked up bad, girl, that's all there is to it."

"Well, anyhow. When he takes the gun off, he has this little black case that it fits into. It looks like a little briefcase. Girl, it's just too cool."

"Uh-huh. Right. Why you like all that thuggish shit? I *can* say a few things for Johnny, though. He's smart, and he's decisive. And above all else, he loves you. That's why I like him, not because he acts like a gun-carrying thug."

"Ah, *excuse* me, Miss Thang. I'll have you know Johnny is *not* a thug, but you really think he loves me, huh?"

"I have not one doubt about it. And he is *definitely* eye candy," Micah added, smiling at Juanita.

"Sho' nuf! Now that's what *I'm* talkin' 'bout," Juanita said, doing that neck thing, confident Johnny was a real hunk. "Now tell me about Mick. It's been too long since we talked. Has Mick said the "L" word to you?"

"Yes, many times. He's generous, kind, romantic, definitely ﹃ ﹄ and…just everything as far as I'm concerned."

"Well, I'm really pleased. It's about time you joined the human race."

"Well, thank God it's with someone I'm passionate about. I've never mentioned this, Nita, but when we deplaned from Europe, I saw Armstead arm-in-arm with some woman going somewhere on vacation, I think."

"You did? And none of us saw him?"

"Nope, just me. He saw me, too. His eyes just followed me for as long as he could without having to be obvious about it. He hasn't gotten over the break-up. I could just tell by the way he looked at me. And Mick had my hand and was leading me through the airport. And guess what, Nita? I was jealous. Can you believe that dumb shit? When I saw them, I think it was what I needed. I was able to let it all go without all that guilt. I'm happy he's found someone who can give him all the things I didn't or couldn't, whichever."

"What did the woman look like?"

"Some funky lard-ass."

"Nah! Not Armstead. He wouldn't be attracted to anybody like that."

"No, Nita. She was stunning—creamy brown, dynamite figure and all into him—that's about all I saw. I was just so damn jealous, I couldn't even see straight. It was crazy. After thinking about it, it was like I wanted to be the only one who could go off and find somebody else. It was so fucking bizarre. I was kidding just then about how the woman looked. She could put me to shame, if truth be told. She was a goddamn brick house if I ever saw one," Micah said.

"Micah, get over it. Life is a roller coaster. Sometimes we're up, sometimes we're down. When we were at Deauville, no one could have told any of us we'd experience some of the things we have. I'm just glad you're happy with Mick, and I'm delighted you were tough enough to wait for the right one."

"Yeah, me, too. But Pepper is still out there floundering. I wish she could find somebody to love who would treat her right. That's what she needs."

"You're right. She's been locked up in that office since she came back to work. She doesn't even relate to us the same. She says she's catching up on all the reading and previewing the new designs. Let's get her out to lunch tomorrow, okay?" Juanita said.

"I'm with that. We've got to remember not to mention the bodyguards. I think she'd go berserk if she knew.

"Uh-huh, she would. Since tomorrow is Friday, maybe we could all hang out like we use to. We've never been to Club Eden. Johnny would love it if we showed up. Wait 'til you see the club, Micah. It's top notch, and the trio is terrific. And the best thing is, it'll be on the house.

"Now that's a deal."

"Okay, let's roll. It's time to practice."

"Yes, Mick is cooking dinner for me tonight at his house, and I can't be late."

"How sweet. Can he really cook?"

"I'll find out tonight. Let's go. Wonder where our protectors are"

"Hiding out somewhere, but you can bet they've got us in their view," Juanita said, scanning the cafe, but not seeing a damn thing.

❦   ❦   ❦

Edmond was getting desperate. He thought by now he'd have Pepper under his spell. She'd been defying him since he'd been back. His headaches were beginning to get more severe and more frequent. He knew it was because of her. *Why is she doing this? I'll have to make sure this will never happen again.* He knew it was time to move forward with his plans.

❦   ❦   ❦

Micah appeared at Mick's door in a huff. "Mick, I'm so sorry I'm late, but Nita and I got carried away at practice and lost track of time. Have I ruined your dinner?" Her arms were filled with a lightweight duffel bag and some clothes in a hanging bag.

"Not at all," he said, taking the load from her arms. "You look quite fetching. Come on in." He kissed her cheek, amused by the sight of the always-impeccable Micah in her jeans and baggy shirt. He found her adorable with a lock of hair standing at attention.

"I need to just run through the shower. It won't take me a minute."

"Go right ahead. Take your time, dinner's fine. You want some wine?"

"I'd love some wine. You're a sweetheart. I'll be right out," she said, hurrying through his large family room.

Mick took her things to the bedroom, came back and poured the wine. He checked the oven and decided everything was ready. He freshened his drink and returned to the sofa. He had been enjoying one of his old CD's, "Unforgettable" by Natalie Cole, and it was still playing. He propped his feet on his coffee table and made himself comfortable.

How could I have lived without her? She's made such a difference in my life. I'm happier that I've ever been. I think it's about time for her to meet Mother.

Mick laid his head back to think. His broken relationship with Gloria sprang to mind. She had been upset when he called the whole thing off, but he didn't want to lead her on…not for a minute. She had been cool initially, but before the evening was over, she had become venomous, displaying her innate, highly publicized, artistic temperament. They had been friends all their lives, and it was an unspoken fact that they'd marry one day. The last thing she told him was he would never be happy without her, and he would find himself begging to come back. They've never spoken a word since, which saddened him.

He had always been fond of her, but he knew now, he had never loved her. His mother, Lucy, was heartbroken when he told her they had separated. Gloria and Mick were reared in the exclusive Belvedere section of Northwest Atlanta, just two doors from each other. Both fathers had started with nothing, and through hard work and determination, both became solid members of the *nouveau riche*. Mick's parents migrated south from Boston in the sixties, and they never returned. Mick, Sr. held a variety of low-paying jobs until he accumulated enough money to pursue his lifelong dream.

He opened the Sutherland Investigative Service in 1968, and acquired Hubert's father, Randolph, as a partner in 1972. Mick,

Sr. died of a massive heart attack five years ago, and Randolph retired that same year. The sons, Mick and Hubert, stepped into a prosperous, and sometimes dangerous business. They had increased the profits two-fold in the last five years. Sutherland-Bailey Investigative Services was successful and well respected nationwide.

Mick and Hubert had a specialized team of thirty-six detectives nationwide who handled their routine cases. They opened offices in Miami, New York and Los Angeles since taking over five years ago. Headquarters remained in Atlanta. Mick was thinking of expanding into Boston, but he and Hubert couldn't agree on that decision, so he'd dropped the idea for now. Mick and Hubert worked cases that were lucrative or the ones that interested them. Otherwise, they manned the shop.

Gloria and Mick first parted when Mick went off to Harvard, and she went to UCLA. He opted for a traditional education because he wanted to work with his father to expand his business. Gloria and Mick's relationship floundered, but it stayed intact. She wanted to pursue life as an artist, and convinced her parents that Los Angeles would be the perfect place to test the waters and decide in what area she wanted to specialize. They were dead set against L.A., but allowed it because her mother's sister, Sylvia, resided in Long Beach. They gave her two years to make up her mind. Four years later, she received her degree from the UCLA Department of Art, specializing in painting and drawing.

She also had tremendous potential as a sculptress. She returned to Atlanta and found a beautiful home that her parents converted into her personal studio. It's a shady hideaway, set among huge oaks, where she paints, draws and sculpts. She has acquired a tremendous following, all clamoring for her latest work. Her paintings are in constant demand in the upscale museums in New York.

Mick told Micah he was involved in a relationship, but he never told her he had been on a strong course to marry the beautiful, successful and, oftentimes, tempestuous artist, Gloria Manning. He told Micah soon after they started seeing each other that he, too, had broken off with the woman in which he'd been involved. Micah has never asked him a word about her or the details of the relationship. She said she didn't want any more information to clutter her already overwrought brain.

"Wake up, Sleepy Head. Are you exhausted? Should I do the honors with dinner?"

"No, to both questions. I was just relaxing and listening to the incomparable Miss Cole. There's your wine. The dinner's fine," he said, drawing her close and kissing her deeply. "You spending the night, I see."

"Uh-huh. I got the work clothes thing covered this time," she said, sipping her wine and leaning back with him. "Didn't want to worry about leaving at 2:00 a.m. again."

"How was practice?"

"Great. I can't wait to show you how much I've improved. You're going to be so proud of me."

"I'll let you tell me when you're ready to show me, okay?"

"Okay. I bought a new bow today, Mick. You're going to love it."

"You did? I'll get it out of the car after dinner. We'll set up the target this weekend and shoot a little."

"Right, that's what I want to do. But you might get better than me."

"Not by a long shot," he said, enjoying the relaxed intimacy. "Are you hungry?"

"I'm fine right here for now."

"Me, too. Just want to do what we're doing."

"What did you cook?"

"Chicken sauterne with rice and asparagus on the side. It's one of my specialities. I think you'll like it."

"It smells scrumptious. Oh Mick, Nita and I are going to Club Eden tomorrow night. We're hoping we can get Pepper out with us. We'll be all right with the bodyguards, huh?"

"Yes, but they'll be right there on you, though."

"Not obviously on us, I hope."

"No, but close. Just keep your eyes open," he said, not liking the idea at all.

"I'll be so glad when we can live a normal life again."

"Me, too. This should all be over soon, I hope."

"We're also going out to lunch with her tomorrow. She's just got to get back into the swing of things."

"Well, good luck. I hope you can get a handle on what's going on. I get the feeling we don't know half of what's happening with her."

"We feel the same way, but she won't tell us a thing," Micah said.

"Has she always been so secretive?"

"Somewhat. Especially about Edmond. That's why we don't know a whole lot about him."

"Humph, now that's interesting. I've located Anna, Edmond's childhood au pair, in Berkshire. We're still trying to find Charles, the former butler. Once we locate him, I might take a quick trip over there to see if they can shed some light on the mysterious Mr. Windbrook. They were with him a long time, so they would know a lot about him and his family. I want to know what they think about his parents' death."

"Edmond's frightening, is all I can say. He's always been elusive. You think he might have done something to his own parents?"

"Yep, I do."

"Man, we had no idea we were associating with a freak. For the life of me, I can't understand Pepper's attraction to him. He's not bad looking, but he has no personality whatsoever, and he's just flat-out weird."

"He's definitely that."

"I hope he's changed his mind about trying to hurt us. I find myself looking over my shoulder all the time. I know Donald is somewhere near, but if someone wanted to get to us, I'm sure they could."

He couldn't deny what she'd just said because it was true. "That's why you shouldn't put yourselves out there too much. I don't want you to stay cooped up, but just don't tempt fate either. We'll have all the guards in the club tomorrow night. They won't disturb you in anyway, but they are going to be right there with you."

"Yeah. I hope they'll be able to blend in. We don't want to arouse Pepper's suspicions in anyway."

"She won't suspect a thing. Just be careful. Johnny will be there, too."

"We will. Come on, let's eat. That food is tempting me."

"Micah, before we eat, I want to talk with you about something else."

She could feel the shift in him. Something else was bothering him. "What is it, Mick? You sound so serious."

"It's just that I've been thinking…I'd like for you to meet Mother, and I don't know how you feel about that."

What? I can't believe it. "Mick, you've caught me off guard. Meet your mother?"

"Yes. I'd like you two to get to know each other. Do you think it's too soon? How do you feel about it?"

"I'd love to meet your mother, but…" she said, looking at her hands.

"But what?" he said, looking up into her downcast eyes.

"That's an important step, I think. Let's give it a little more time." She wasn't sure she was ready to meet her. She'd told him the truth.

"I'm ready for you to meet her, Micah, but we'll wait. I love you, and I want her to know you. We don't have to rush it. We can talk about this later. Now let's eat."

She put her arms around him and held him for a moment. "I love you, Mick. With all my heart, and I don't want you to doubt that. I'm just...skittish and afraid. Just give me a little time."

"Oh, Micah, you don't have to be afraid. I understand. You tell me when, all right?"

"Yes, I'll tell you when. Thanks for understanding." She released him then and said, "Let's go get that food. It smells so good."

"You got it," he said, feeling the depth of his love for her.

CHAPTER 31

Edmond made his second call to Pepper that week. He could stand it no longer. "Pepper? This is Edmond. I hope you've come to our senses about letting me provide protection for you here."

"I'm doing fine right here, Edmond."

"Before you say another word, I've just found out that one of Johnny Diamond's enemies, of whom he has many, is targeting his closest friends. The informant said that's the best way to hurt him. You must disassociate yourself from them immediately. You need my protection until this thing is over."

"What are you talking about? I don't believe it, Edmond. I think you're exaggerating. I think you've always controlled me through manipulation and force. I've had some time to think things through, and I don't think what you're saying is true. Don't call me again." She hung up, allowing him not one final plea.

She'd finally come to the realization he was a skilled manipulator and a control freak. She knew she'd have to fight for her freedom, but at the same time, she craved his possessiveness, and most of all, his violence. She needed to overcome her dependence on him, and she was moving toward that goal, but she wasn't quite there yet.

❀   ❀   ❀

The next day at work, Juanita knocked on Pepper's door.

"Come in."

"Hey, girl. Have you caught up on all your reading? Thought you might join us for lunch today. How about it?"

"Not today, Nita. I'm almost done, but I have just a few more things to get through."

"Oh, come on, Pepper. You've got all the time in the world to read this stuff. We're going to Slim's. You haven't been there in a long time. You need some stick-to-your-ribs kind of food. I won't take a *no* today. So, let's go and get Micah," Juanita said, not allowing her a choice.

Pepper sighed, and reached for her purse. She was reluctant to the core, but Juanita was insistent. "Nita, you don't know—"

"Come on, Pepper. Micah's waiting."

They arrived at Slim's in the middle of the noonday rush. "This is like old times," Micah said. "Remember how we use to wait almost an hour to be seated in here, and we didn't even care? Slim's making a bundle, but the food is still fantastic."

"Yeah, and it'll put ten pounds on you in one sitting," Pepper said.

"True, but it wouldn't hurt you. You've lost weight, but you look terrific. Let's see if I can convince Slim that we made reservations, and some incompetent person failed to record it."

"Micah, Slim doesn't take reservations, remember?" Juanita said.

"Oh, yeah. Well…let's see what I can do anyway. We're faithful, longtime customers."

They were being stopped to sign their names on napkins, to talk to everyone and a request to take a picture with a tourist. Slim came out and ushered them to a table.

"Sorry 'bout all the commotion, ladies, but you *are* celebrities now," Slim said. "I'll send someone right over."

"How did you do that? What did you say to him? We've got all those people in that line mad as hell," Juanita said, grumbling.

"I don't think so. Let it drop, Nita. Leave it to the pro. I know how to deal."

"Yeah, you always have," Pepper said in awe.

They ordered their lunch and sat back to talk. "We haven't seen you out of that office not once since you've been back. Why are you shutting yourself off like that?" Micah asked.

"I'm not shutting myself off, and there is a lot to catch up on."

"Yeah? Like what?" Juanita asked.

"Like the designs you two have finished and all the stuff Lila passes down to us. It's a lot. I was out a long time, you know."

"Okay, Pepper. But it's over, all right? We gave you a week. That's long enough to catch up on anything," Juanita said, getting straight down with it.

"I was thinking…let's go out tonight. We haven't been to Club Eden, Nita. You've been bragging about it; so, let's check it out. We'll have a good time. You said the trio was great, huh?" Micah said.

"Da bomb, chile. That's a fabulous idea. I'll let Johnny know we'll drop by. He'll have everything set up and taken care of. What about it, Pepper? You need to get out of that house. LaVerne said you don't even step outside the front door unless you're going to work. Let's do it."

"I don't think so. I know you're worried about me, but I'm not up to all that just now."

"And if we left it up to you, you'd never be. So, we're on for tonight. Around nine. I'll pick everybody up," Juanita said, taking charge of the situation.

"Wonderful. I'll be ready. Juanita, I promise I'll be ready when you get there."

"I guess there's always a first time, but you'd better be. I'll pick you up first, Pepper. Then, we'll get Micah. It's settled."

Pepper was disgruntled. She wanted to tell them what Edmond had said about them being in danger, but she didn't want them to know she'd been talking to him. So, she sat in silence, dissatisfied and sulking. She'd also made up her mind about what she needed to do to free herself from Edmond permanently.

❧   ❧   ❧

Edmond was losing it big time. He paced about his home, ranting and raving. His eye twitched constantly now, no longer an occasional problem. For the first time in the twelve years since he's known Pepper, she was beyond his reach, completely out of his control.

I will not have it! She will not defy me. I'll have to deal with her, too. Personally.

❧   ❧   ❧

Just before the girls showed up at Club Eden, Mick received further details regarding Edmond's proposed actions. His reliable informant told him Edmond's latest plan was to shoot Juanita *and* Micah this week. His plans were changing erratically and fast. Mick and Johnny would be targeted later. Everything was chaotic. Rumors were running rampant, and it was hard to tell truth from fiction. Johnny and Mick decided their best plan was to keep all five of them, Pepper included, under even tighter scrutiny. Edmond could and might do anything.

Juanita rang LaVerne and Fred Hankerson's doorbell at 9:03 p.m. Dr. Hankerson answered the door.

"Juanita, come in. Pepper told us you were picking her up tonight. We're so happy she's finally getting out again. I've been very worried about her, but I'm hoping this is the sign we need. Hope she's on the mend now."

"We hope so, too, Dr. Hankerson. Hi, LaVerne. What are you doing? Not working? I can't believe you. It's the weekend, and Dr. Hankerson's at home, too."

"I'm not really working, just looking over some of our new designs. Fred and I are watching a news special. Have a seat. I'll see what's keeping Pepper."

She sat on the sofa waiting for Pepper. She glanced around. LaVerne was extremely talented. Her home was beautiful, deep greens and burgundies everywhere. Dr. Hankerson indicated concern for Pepper. She wanted to question him about it, but she refrained. She couldn't understand why Pepper craved Edmond. Her parents were normal, everyday working people. No different from her parents or Micah's. It had to be something inherent in Pepper's personality.

"Hi," Pepper said, bubbling. "I'm ready."

Juanita turned to Pepper, and was rocked by her beauty. "Girl, you know you got it going on. You're absolutely gorgeous." Pepper had on a simple red dress that fit her voluptuous figure like a glove. She was understated, but undeniably stunning, black patch and all. Her attitude was completely different tonight.

She's having mood swings, Juanita thought.

"Pepper, you do look lovely," Dr. Hankerson said, looking at Laverne for confirmation. Pepper smiled, happy her father approved.

"This is one of Pepper's designs that she sketched while she was recuperating," LaVerne said. "I finished it just last night."

"It's perfect, and just so…like you, Pepper. You'll sell a ton of them," Juanita said, meaning it from her heart.

"She is the very best with these simple designs. She knows exactly what she wants," LaVerne said.

"Now that's for sure. Well, let's hit it, girl. We've given Micah plenty of time to get it together."

"I'm ready."

LaVerne and her husband walked them to the door, arms around each other's waist, looking at them depart. "Have a good time," Dr. Hankerson said as they backed out of the driveway.

"You've got great parents, Pepper. You're so fortunate. Where's Nicky tonight?"

"On a date, as usual. She's in love at the moment. And yes, I do have wonderful parents. They've been so supportive through all this. I'm about ready to go back to my own place, but they want me to stay a little longer."

"Why don't you just relax and stay with them a while. You can always go back home," Juanita said, worrying about her being on her own just now.

"I might stay another week or two, but no longer. I'm missing my own space."

"Just take it day-by-day. They seem to like it that you're there. Take advantage of it as long as it lasts."

They picked up Micah, who for once was on time. Pepper was upbeat and looking forward to the evening. It was really like old times.

When they arrived at the club, Juanita took the lead. "Hi, Marv. Johnny's expecting us."

"Yes, please come on through. Denise will take care of you from here."

They were treated like royalty. When they walked in, they caused the usual commotion. Everyone recognized them as the top local designers that they were, and they all had on their respective designs. They waved and talked their way to their table, moving as quickly as they could. Juanita and Micah spotted the guards who hovered near, eyes on all the customers.

"Here you are ladies. What can I get for you? Everything's on the house."

"Is Johnny here?" Juanita asked.

"Yes, he has someone in his office, but he wanted me to let him know when you arrived. As soon as I take your order, I'll let him know."

"Great. Okay. I'm going to have a margarita. Pepper? What do you want?"

"Just white wine. You know I'm not much of a drinker."

"And I'll have an apple martini," Micah said.

"Got it. Mr. Diamond should be out shortly."

Juanita looked around. "What do you think of the club?"

"It's beautiful," Pepper said. "Johnny has great taste, if he had anything to do with the decor.

"He sure did, and yes, he does have great taste. He's got me, doesn't he?" she said, laughing and enjoying the whole scene.

"It really is a wonderful club, Nita. But knowing Johnny, he'd only involve himself in the best," Micah said.

"Look, here comes Johnny," Pepper said excitedly.

Juanita looked around and smiled. She turned to her friends and said, "Is that a fine hunk of man or what?"

"Uh-huh," both of her *compadres* answered.

"Hey, baby. How are you doing? He bent to kiss Juanita's cheek, taking her all in with his eyes. "Welcome, ladies. Just wanted to greet you, that's all. Order anything you want. And have a great time. I'm stuck in the office tonight, so eat, drink, dance and be merry."

Johnny was immaculate. He had on a precision-tailored, double breasted navy, wool suit, with a custom-made Egyptian cotton, white shirt with cuffs and a navy and burgundy silk tie. He was expensively dressed and conservative, but his flair showed in the details—the cut and the fit. His appearance was quiet, upscale and refined.

"Johnny, this club is awesome. We'll be back, I assure you," Micah said.

"It's terrific, Johnny. Thanks for rolling out the red carpet," Pepper said.

"Thank you both. Nothing's too good for my friends." He looked at Juanita, raised his eyebrows and smiled, indicating he liked what he saw. He kissed her again and admired her openly. "You look beautiful, baby. Let me know when you're leaving."

"I will."

"Girrl, he's too much. What did you do to mesmerize him like that?" Micah asked. "He talked to us, but he couldn't keep his eyes off you."

"I just got it like that. What can I say?"

"And he has such beautiful chocolate skin. He's some good looking man, Nita."

"Don't I know it. And he's all that in *everyway*, chile," she said, smiling broadly.

"We've just got to get Pepper involved and in love with someone," Micah said.

"I don't think so. I'm not ready for any involvements. I'm going solo from now on."

"Maybe for now, but not from now *on*," Micah corrected.

"Whatever," Pepper responded.

"Here you are ladies," the waitress said. "Enjoy. I'll be back soon. Anything to eat?"

"Not yet. We'll let you know," Juanita said.

They ordered two more rounds, and decided they just *had* to dance. They all got up, danced wildly with each other deep wit the crowd and finally admitted they were all a bit tipsy.

"What should we eat?" Micah said. "We'd better get something in our stomachs or we'll all pass out up in this swanky club."

"Here's a menu. The steak sandwich in here is delicious," Juanita said.

"Yeah, a steak sandwich for me," Micah said.

"And I'll have one, too," Juanita joined in.

They looked at Pepper and saw tears streaking her face. "Pepper, what is it? What's wrong?" Juanita asked.

She shook her head, not wanting to talk.

"Sweetie, what is it?" Micah said, touching her hand. "Did something happen?"

She shook her head again.

"Then what is it?"

"It's so awful. I feel so awful…" Pepper stammered.

"Why? Did we do some—"

"No, it's not you two. It's me," she slurred.

"Let's get her out of here. She's had it," Juanita said.

Juanita beckoned to Denise who rushed right over. "Tell Johnny we're leaving. Pepper's not feeling well."

"Right. I'll let him know right now."

She spotted Ernest, who'd moved in slightly. She shook her head, indicating they'd handle the situation. Micah had already silently communicated with Donald, but Rubin was hovering closely, concerned about Pepper.

Juanita spoke up, "Sir, can you help us get her to the car? She's not feeling well."

Rubin moved right in. "Yes, ma'am. I'll take her. Your car's outside?"

"Yes, not far from the front door." *As if you don't already know.*

Rubin helped her up, gripped her solidly under her left arm and shouldered her weight, helping her walk outside. She brushed his crotch accidentally and felt a sexual twinge. "Don't I know you? You look familiar," Pepper said, squinting, trying to remember just where she'd seen him.

Johnny came out immediately. "What is it? What happened?" concerned, eyes skimming the crowd. He touched his left side, reassuring himself his gun was in place.

"Pepper just had too much wine on an empty stomach. Everything's okay. We're taking her to Micah's. Don't want her parents seeing her in this shape."

Johnny moved his head slightly, wanting all the guards covering them. "Let me drive you home. Leave your car. I'll take care of it later."

"You don't have to do that. I can drive," Juanita protested.

"I'm driving you, Juanita. Let's go," he said, at that moment, nothing but business. "I need to do something in my office. I'll be right out. Wait for me, Juanita." His look and his voice indicated he didn't want any funny business out of her. He meant what he said. She didn't move a muscle.

He walked into his office and said to Mick, "I'm taking them home. Pepper's had too much wine. We're going to Micah's apartment."

"All right. Just get them inside, and I'll take it from there." Mick had just heard a rumor about Edmond's latest plan, and he was there to tell Johnny about it.

"Later."

Johnny drove them home, reassured by the fact he had a four-man back up, including Mick. *It's overkill, I know, but I don't give a fuck. Don't want any surprises.* He wanted them safe. He helped Pepper inside, got her settled on the sofa and turned to Juanita. "Lock up tight. Don't open the door for anyone."

She looked at him, puzzled by the fanfare, questioning with her eyes.

"I'll explain later," his tone softening. "I can't right now. Just do as I say, Nita, please."

She trusted him implicitly. "Okay, but call me later."

He pulled her to him and whispered, "I don't want anything to go wrong here. I couldn't stand it, if anything happened to you. I love you, Nini." He released her quickly and stepped through the door. "Lock it now."

She threw the locks, including the chain.

My God, he actually said it. He loves me. At that moment, she was happier than she'd been in her whole life.

CHAPTER 32

Mick and Hubert finally got some much-needed information from Anna Bradshaw, Edmond's former *au pair*. They talked with her extensively, eliminating the need for a trip to England. Anna told them she had not heard from Charles in over a year, but the last time she did, he was living just outside of London. She would find his address and phone number when she returned home from shopping.

Anna told Mick that Edmond had been an extremely controlling child, completely caught up in his private world of make-believe. He ruled the staff with an iron hand, even as a child. His parents were rarely in residence in the Atlanta home, so his instructions were followed strictly and without question.

Anna related how his infrequent summer vacations in England resulted in disaster at every turn. His relatives complained bitterly of his extreme fastidiousness as well as his controlling maneuvers. All of his cousins were either afraid of him or repulsed by him. His father discounted the reports he received, staunchly encouraging Edmond to stand fast in his beliefs and never submit to people beneath him; consequently, he pursued his controlling instinct with vengeance.

His mother was never privy to his misdeeds, and her love for her husband overshadowed any misgivings she might have had about him. Edmond took his mother's lack of interest as a lack of love. He longed for her attention, and he wanted his father's respect. That deadly combination of desires was the impetus for his actions from early childhood to the present time.

When Mick reached Charles, the former butler, he was afraid to divulge any information about Edmond. He knew him for what he truly was—a vicious, sadistic killer. Charles eventually told Mick he felt certain Edmond killed his parents. When he found out Mr. and Mrs. Windbrook's car careened out of control, he suspected Edmond immediately.

Charles and Anna worked for the Windbrooks for years and knew of his violent nature. They had seen the animals he'd mutilated, witnessed his compulsive cleaning habits and his strict code of order. All of these traits, he believed pointed to his consuming killer instinct. Charles said Edmond had a particular fondness to kill with the knife even though he used various methods on the animals that he captured.

Charles and Anna said they'd long wanted to leave the Windbrook household, especially after his parents were killed, but they feared for their lives. Charles told Mick the sordid tale, and swore him to secrecy about the source of the information.

CHAPTER 33

"I'm going to make a pot of strong coffee. That should help her snap out of it," Micah said.

"I don't want any coffee. I'm fine...just got a headache. You got any aspirin?"

"Yes. Juanita, would you get the aspirin from by bathroom cabinet, please?"

"Sure. Just hang on a minute, Pepper. I'll get them."

They got Pepper settled down, and she wanted to talk. Her wine was still working. Micah and Juanita poured their coffee and sat in the family room with her.

"I need to tell you something. I just don't know how to go about it," Pepper said.

"What do you mean? We've always been able to talk. What's so different this time?" Juanita said.

"Well, this time it's a whole lot more serious. I've wanted to tell you two everything that has been going on with Edmond and me for all these years, but I could never bring myself to do it."

"Well, we've had an idea of some of the things, but, go ahead, we're here to listen now," Micah said.

"I guess I should start with my childhood and work forward. I decided I would tell you everything when I was at home recuperating. Well, here goes," she said, sighing.

"When I was a child, my neighbor's husband, Alan, molested me from age ten until I entered Deauville Academy."

"What? My God, Pepper! How awful," Micah said.

"Pepper, you could have told us. We've shared all kinds of things with you," Juanita said.

"Yes, I know, but this was just so awful. You'll never know how terrible it was. I've never told a soul. He told me he loved me, and it was our secret. No one ever suspected. Momma would be devastated if she knew, even now. Well, anyway, Momma would leave me with her neighbor, Connie, when she ran her errands. Daddy was always at his office or the hospital. Connie would run her errands when I was there, and she'd leave me at home watching TV with her husband, Alan. Momma never knew that. He would watch TV all day and drink his Budweiser Beer. When I got to the academy and met Edmond, I was hooked. The first night I met him, I fell in love instantly. Remember?"

"How could we forget? And we couldn't figure out why. I've never liked him…I'm sorry about that, Pepper. That's just the way it is. He's a strange, arrogant motherfucker, that's all I know. What is it about him?" Juanita asked, for the first time being one hundred percent truthful.

"The first night I met him, he slapped me for asking him a simple question, and that did it. In fact…this is *so* embarrassing."

"Go on, Pepper, it's okay," Micah said.

"Yeah, we want to understand," Juanita said.

"The only way I can enjoy sex is to be violated in some way. I need to be hit or beaten to be able to feel loved. When I'm defenseless in some way, I can have one exquisite orgasm after another. I've never experienced normal sex. Never. I'm completely dysfunctional sexually." She began to cry, and Micah hugged her.

"My attraction to Edmond is based on his need to hurt and control and my desire to suffer. In our relationship, when I grovel or plead or make him think he has me within his grasp, he'll ejaculate on me or in...my anus, but never inside me normally." Then she broke down, moaning.

"Micah hugged her, tears in her eyes. "It's okay, Pepper. It's all over now." She looked at Juanita and shook her head pitifully.

Juanita wiped a tear with the back of her hand. "Yes, it's over," is all she could manage.

"Sometimes he would use instruments as a tool—a bottle and once a gun barrel in my vagina. It's so despicable. We're both *so* sick and disgusting."

"It's not your fault. It's the trauma you suffered as a child. That cocksucker should have been strung up by his balls," Juanita hissed.

Neither Juanita nor Micah could believe it. They listened and stared at each other, speechless. They'd never heard of some of the horrors she told.

"We're here to help, Pepper. You need therapy," Micah said, already planning a strategy.

"I've known that for a long time, but I was too misguided and ashamed to admit it or do anything about it. If Edmond feels he has me in hand, he's ecstatic. If his self-esteem or confidence lags or he feels he's lost control in any way, he becomes enraged...almost like a trapped animal. When his eye begins to twitch, I know he's violent and at the point where I know he could kill. That's the way he was the last time he beat me. He was so frightening, and I was unable to help myself. And to think I thought it was love. God, I need help. I want to be free of this affliction. Please help me," Pepper begged, crying so hard she had trouble breathing.

"That sick bastard! I'd like to kick his ass. It's okay, Pepper. You should have told us. We could have done something...gotten you help or put his ass in jail," Juanita said, ready to kill him with her bare hands.

"I just couldn't do it. It's a vicious cycle. Edmond told me the other day that—"

"Hold up! You mean, you've talked to him since he beat you?" Micah asked, horrified by the thought.

"Yes. He's called me several times. He apologized for blinding me...for the beating."

"I bet he has," Juanita said, "He just wants you back so he can kick your ass again. Don't you see that?"

"He wants me to come live with him because he said I was in danger...from Johnny's enemies...some ruthless, petty gangsters, who want to kill all of us. Just to get back at Johnny. He said—"

"I don't give a fuck what he said," Juanita spat out. "It's a goddamn lie. Edmond ordered that hit on Johnny. Something went wrong, and he and Rubin were just injured. *Edmond* had it done. Do you understand that? He wants us out of the way so he can control you. He's psyching you, Pepper. His main goal is to control *you*." She was so mad she could spit. *I'd like to stomp his motherfucking ass!*

"Mick and Johnny have bodyguards covering us, Pepper. Rubin has been guarding you all week without your knowledge. Rubin was the big, bald guy who helped you to the car tonight," Micah added.

"So, that's who he was. I knew I'd seen him before. I can't believe it. Guarding me? You knew about all this and didn't tell me? Why not? Did you think I was too sick to cope with it?"

"Something like that," Juanita admitted. "We just didn't want to upset you."

"My God, this is too much. It's worse than I thought. There's something I want to ask you two. Did you suspect I was involved with Mondo?"

"Mondo? Who the hell is that? What are you talking about?" Juanita asked.

"Mondo...in the restaurant in Milan? The guy who bought us all that wine?"

"I remember, but he left the restaurant well before we did. We stayed so long, the waiters practically threw us out. We were the last ones to leave," Micah said, not getting the connection.

"You're right, but I passed my room number to him in a match book before he left."

"Oh, fuck! You have *got* to be kidding. I don't believe it," Juanita screeched, now wanting to kick *her* ass.

"Yes, I did. Please listen. I need to get all of this out."

Yeah, to worry the shit out of us, Juanita thought, pissed as hell with Pepper.

"He came to my room late, and he whipped me horribly, but just on by butt and thighs where it wouldn't show. And I loved it. I'm attracted to men who are sadistic. Don't you understand? I can spot them a mile away. It's wacked, I know. I'm counting on both of you to help me," she said, sobbing again.

"Pepper, we'll do everything we can," Micah said, embracing her and patting her back. She was angry, too, and knew she'd have to do something about this herself. "Starting tomorrow, we'll get you some help."

"Something's going on tonight. Johnny was too protective. I've got my Glock, and the door is locked," Juanita said.

"I'm calling Mick. He'll come over or do something," Micah said.

"Yeah, let him know what's happening. I think you'll be fine with some psychiatric help, Pepper. I know you didn't want to go that route, but it's the only way. You can't go around it. You've taken the first step. You admitted you have a problem and asked for help. We're here to support you. We're with you no matter what," Juanita said, talking fast and back in charge.

"Thanks, Nita. I wish I had told you all this a long time ago."

"So do I," Micah said, her cell phone to her ear.

Pepper started to tell them about Jean Luc in Paris, but even she knew when to quit. She had told them enough. The weight of the world had been lifted from her shoulders. She had carried most of that burden alone for over twenty years. She was even more determined to carry out her latest plan. *I've got to take care of this myself...even if he kills me.*

Micah reached Mick on the phone. "Mick?" she said. "Where have you been? Thank God, I've found you. I'm at home, and Pepper and Nita are here with me. It's been a terrible night. Huh? You're outside? Why?" She listened for a long time. "My God, that's why Johnny acted the way he did, then. Yeah, I'll tell them. No, I'm fine...Love you, too. Bye."

"Well, what is it? What did he say?" Juanita asked.

"He said Edmond has upped the ante. Mick's informant told him tonight that Edmond ordered his men to shoot us tonight, Juanita. He said he hadn't told me because he thought I'd just lose it. Who the fuck he thinks he's dealing with? But anyway, he ordered the hit this week. He's doing all this to show Pepper he told her the truth about Johnny's enemies seeking revenge. He said Edmond's gone over the edge and is crazy as hell, which we already know. Johnny left here alone tonight, Nita. Mick's afraid he's gone to maybe...do something to Edmond himself."

"Oh, my God. No," Juanita shouted. "I've got to stop him."

"You've got to keep your ass right here. Did you hear what I just said? They're planning to shoot us, Juanita. You can't get out anyway. Mick and the other guards are staked out all around here. They're right outside, right now. Four of them. Johnny didn't say where he was going. Just got in his car and roared off without a word. Vernell's on alert."

"Who is Vernell?" Pepper asked.

"He works for Johnny...in the club. He's at the bar sometimes," Juanita said.

"How could I have been such a fool?" Pepper said.

"Goddamnit, Pepper. The point is, your eyes are open now. So, just keep them that way, okay?" Juanita snapped, preoccupied with thoughts of Johnny.

"Is there anything we can do?" Pepper asked.

"We can't do a goddamn thing, but stay put," Juanita answered.

CHAPTER 34

Johnny took several trips through Edmond's neighborhood trying to determine his method of attack and an advantageous strategy. The whole tree-lined street was deep in cover with foliage. Edmond's large ranch-styled home sprawled across his property, well away from the street. Black wrought iron gates shielded the entrance, and a six-foot stone wall protected the surrounding property. Just to the left of the gate was what Johnny assumed was a well-tended guardhouse. Entrance into the compound undetected was virtually impossible.

Johnny decided to park his black van off the street and well away from the entrance. The dense greenery obscured the van. He selected a spot that allowed him to observe any activity that occurred at the front gate. His tactic tonight was to observe the pattern of activity in and out of the compound.

Rubin and Ernest gave him a full report of everything they had observed over the last few weeks, day and night. Rubin told him they were trying to contact someone special to take care of Edmond. They declined to do it themselves. Things had escalated since they'd talked, so Johnny had to take another tactic. He did what he'd vowed before he left for Europe. He took matters into his own hands.

Johnny could see several muted lights burning across Edmond's acreage, enabling him to see two large dogs roaming the front entrance. His binoculars and his nightscope were on the seat beside him. He checked his watch. It was 1:23 a.m., but he was prepared to stay until well into the daylight hours.

He settled in and had plenty of time to think. Johnny's employee problem had disappeared as quickly as it had appeared. This time, the rumor mill had been mistaken. Rubin and Ernest's probing revealed the employees who left Club Eden a few months back, did so for legitimate reasons. Gia Cantoni's reputation as a man of his word had been substantiated.

❈   ❈   ❈

Pepper made a decision after she cleared her mind of its wine-soaked hideaway. As the sun was rising, she said, "Micah, Juanita, I've decided I'm going back to my house. Since I now have the luxury of a personal bodyguard, there is absolutely no reason why I shouldn't."

"You mean you're leaving your parents' house?" Micah asked.

"That's exactly what I mean. The sooner, the better, as far as I'm concerned. I'll have the protection that you seem to think I need as well as the comfort and familiarity of my own home. It's the perfect solution."

Juanita looked at her and wondered about her sanity. "Pepper, why must you always muddy the damn water? We've discussed all night the possible harm Edmond could cause any one of us and now you want to traipse back to your own house? I don't get it."

"Well, give me one good reason why I shouldn't. That burly body-guard will be there. I've made up my mind. How do we get him the word?"

Micah shook her head in disgust, looked Juanita in the eye and said, "I'll call Mick and tell him. He'll make the arrangements with Rubin or Johnny." She took her cell phone out of her purse and rang Mick's number. He answered immediately. "Mick, Pepper wants to move back into her house today. Rubin will have to accompany her there, I guess. Please let him or Johnny know what she wants to do." She listened, then said, "She'll have to move her belongings from her parents' home."

When Micah hung up from Mick, she said, "He'll call us back shortly. As long as Rubin is with you, he doesn't see it as a problem."

"See, I told you," Pepper said. "At least something good has come of this mess. It's what I've wanted to do for a while."

Mick called a short time later and said everything was arranged. Rubin would pick her up whenever she wanted to leave.

"I'm ready now," she said, while Micah was still talking to Mick.

Rubin pulled the van up to the front door of the apartment and went inside for Pepper. Micah answered the door. "Hello, Rubin. Please come in."

"Hello, everybody."

"Rubin," Micah said, "I don't think you've officially met Pepper, have you?"

"No, I haven't. Nice to meet you," he said, extending his hand.

"Hello, Rubin. It's a pleasure. Thanks for your help last night."

"No problem."

She hugged Juanita and Micah who were clearly not pleased with her decision. "Thank you both so much. I'll call you when I'm settled. It won't take long," she said, wanting to leave as soon as possible."

"Pepper, please be careful," Juanita said.

"I will. Rubin will be with me the whole time. Don't worry."

Pepper and Rubin stopped at her parents' home to retrieve her few belongings, and arrived at her house an hour and a half later. They'd stopped at the grocer's for food and gone directly to her house. Rubin took her belongings inside, and she carried in the food.

"Come on in, Rubin. Put the clothes in the bedroom...through that hallway on the right. I'll make us something to eat."

He put her clothes on the bed and re-entered the family room area. He had checked the layout of her house already. "I've been thinking, before you start, I may be here for a while, and I'll probably need some things from home. I'm sorry to do this, but you've got to come with me."

"Right now?"

"Yes. I don't live too far. It won't take long. I apologize."

"No, don't. Then let's go get it done."

As he drove, she thought about what she'd gotten herself into. She would not be able to make one move without Rubin by her side. She'd have to readjust her whole life, but, as she viewed it, it was a fair trade-off—at least she was back at home.

He pulled into the driveway of his small, but well kept home. "Come with me. This should take no more than a few minutes."

Rubin's home was clean and comfortable, with lots of pictures of what appeared to be family. She picked one up of a much younger Rubin and asked, "Look at you. Who is this attractive lady?"

He glanced at the picture and said, "That's my younger sister, Beverly."

"Are you from Atlanta, Rubin? And look at all your hair."

"No, from Houston."

"A city I've only been through. I've never really been there to see anything."

"I think you'd like it...there's a lot going on. Let me get a few things. Make yourself comfortable."

She walked around his family room, looking at his pictures. *He's a reader. Books are everywhere,* she thought, surprised.

He came back in with a small black bag. "That's it. That didn't take too long, did it?"

"Not at all. Ready?"

"Yes." He looked around, checked his doors and windows and left.

As he backed out of his driveway, she said, "I see you like to read."

"Yes, I do. It's my greatest pleasure, I'd say."

"So do I. You might find something at my home that you might like. Just help yourself, if you do."

"Thanks. I scanned your bookshelves. I see you're interested in a variety of things."

"Uh-huh. Anything from the classics to the most outrageous fiction. Seems you do, too."

"Yes, that's true."

When they returned to her house, she went straight to the kitchen.

"Breakfast or lunch? Which would you like?" she said. "I'm starving."

"Whichever is easiest for you. It doesn't matter."

"All right. I say breakfast. Make yourself comfortable...there's the TV remote. I never watch it, but help yourself. It's here for my guests. What does a bodyguard do in a situation like this? I don't really know."

"My job is to make sure you're safe. That's all there is to it. Just go about your day as if I'm not here. I know that's a stretch in a house, but I'll try not to cause you any distress. Do your best to overlook me."

"Better said than done, but I'll try."

She started breakfast and called Micah's home number. "Hi. Just wanted you to know I'm back at home and dong fine. Rubin is here with me. Have you heard anything from Johnny?" They talked awhile as she fussed about the kitchen. Micah told her she and Juanita had decided they should all take the next week off from work. She'd talked with her mother and explained the whole thing to her, and she agreed immediately. She hung up and said, "They haven't heard a word from Johnny. You think he's all right?"

"I think he's fine. He'll call us all later," he said with confidence.

"We're also taking next week off from work since Edmond is rumored to be planning something this week."

"Good idea," he said.

Pepper went about her normal activities—she washed her clothes, cleaned and dusted a few things and spent hours in her closet doing her favorite thing—assembling and accessorizing outfits. She offered Rubin her guest room, but he preferred the couch in the family room. Their first day passed without one difficulty.

Rubin was quiet, but friendly when she spoke to him. She was comfortable with him and trusted him immediately. He appeared competent. He'd quietly checked her doors and windows, inspected the yard and basement, and when he was obviously content, he chose a book from her shelf, Q *The Autobiography of Quincy Jones*. He didn't initiate any conversation, merely responded to her, when needed.

I've got to find a psychiatrist. I'll ask Daddy for a recommendation…just tell him I need help to work through the beating. He'll like that. I think Rubin's going to work out fine. He's professional and respectful and, most of all, I feel safe and secure. I'm just happy to be back home.

CHAPTER 35

Edmond listened to the report Ben, his honcho, gave him on Pepper's most recent activities. "I cannot believe it," he said, pacing around his large family room. "I should have had you covering her earlier. I misjudged her. She has taken a man into her home? Who is he?"

"It's Mr. Diamond's bodyguard. He's the one that was shot at the fashion show. Here are some pictures we took," Ben said, handing them to him.

Edmond looked on in fury, his right eye twitching at a rapid pace. "I want to know why he's there. She could not be attracted to this brute. He has to be protecting her." He surveyed Rubin's massive arms and zeroed in on his muscled abs that were in plain view through his tight, black tee shirt. His baldhead and his muscular body gave him a strong, menacing appearance. Edmond's head pounded. He was disturbed and unable to contain his jealousy. "Whose home is this?"

"We think it's his. I have someone already inside. We'll know soon," Ben said, getting more nervous with each question.

"Goddamn bitch!" he screeched, when he saw a picture of them smiling, entering her house. He lost it when he saw Rubin's hand on her waist, possessively helping her inside, with his black bag in full view. "I'll take care of them myself," he roared. "I want all the motherfucking information you can find on him, and I want it fast." *She's fucking him, bodyguard or not. It's quite obvious by these pictures.* He stamped from the room and headed for his shower.

"We're already on it. I'll let you know as soon as we have something," Ben said, now terrified of his distraught employer.

Edmond was disoriented and delusional when Doctor Forester was called to his home last month. The doctor recommended he seek immediate psychiatric help. Edmond became violent and had to be restrained. His mental state had declined rapidly since then. At present, he was a stark, raving maniac who was on a full course to destruction. Under ordinary circumstances, Doctor Forester would have had him institutionalized, but Edmond's money was his shield, and he wielded it powerfully.

❧   ❧   ❧

Johnny sat, alert, and with his tape recorder beside him and his binoculars to his eyes. He had witnessed quite a bit of activity through Edmond's gates in the last hour. He had recorded every tag number and car make and style. Something was up, and his adrenalin surged. Two cars and one van had entered the gates, but none had left. All three vehicles were black.

Johnny picked up his cell phone and dialed Rubin who answered on the second ring. "Hello."

"Rubin, Johnny. Are you at Pepper's?"

"Yes. She's doing fine. I'm settled in with her."

"Good. Just keep her close. I'm staked out across the street from Edmond's. Just wanted to see what's going on out here. They've been coming and going here all morning...don't know what that's all about. I'm staying longer than I planned. I need to get cleaned up and check out a few things. I'll call you from home later."

"Okay. Have you talked with Ernest?" Rubin asked.

"Not yet. I'll call him from home. I talked with Juanita, and he's staying right on her. She knows about Edmond's plan to have them shot this week, so she's cooperating. Lat—hey, Rubin?"

"Yeah, I'm still here."

"How's Pepper doing? Does she seem all right…mentally, I mean?"

"She's fine. She's a nice lady, and, as you already know, she's a stunning woman."

"She is that. Don't get sidetracked…just keep it professional, all the way."

"Nah, everything's copasetic," he said, feeling just a little deceptive.

Rubin hadn't been involved in a serious relationship since he'd graduated from Texas A&M, years ago. He'd ended up with Johnny by a stroke of fate. He had just been in the right place at the right time, as he viewed it. Seven years ago, he'd been seated at a table next to Johnny and a young woman in a small, out-of-the-way club in southwest Atlanta when a fight broke out. Rubin stepped in to aid Johnny just as a he was about to be worked over by two men who had staged the fight to get at Johnny. Johnny was appreciative, has never forgotten it and Rubin has been with him ever since. He made twice the money with Johnny as opposed to what he would have made had he worked as a social worker or coach, fields he'd been educated to pursue. Furthermore, Johnny didn't restrict him in any way.

He and Johnny had an unspoken bond that goes far beyond any friendship either has ever had. Today was the first time in seven years Rubin had not been one hundred percent truthful with him.

CHAPTER 36

Atlanta, Georgia
October 2002

Micah picked the phone up and called Mick. "Hi."

"Hey. I'm just about ready to leave. We need to talk. You okay?"

"Yes, I am. Mick, I want to come over there. I want to practice with the bow. We haven't had a moment for anything other than this whole drama thing. How about it?"

"That's fine. Come on whenever you want to. I'll take something out for dinner. Are you spending the night?"

"I sure am. I've been missing you. Can't wait to see you. I need some of your tender loving care."

"I'm willing to please. How long?"

"An hour. See you then. Bye."

A little over an hour later, Micah rang Mick's doorbell, and he answered after one ring. "Hi," he said. She had her hands full as usual—clothes and a small bag. "Here, let me help you."

He peeked out to see if he could see Donald. He was right there on duty. Mick took everything to his bedroom, and she went into the kitchen.

"Steaks tonight, huh?"

"Uh-huh. They're easy and quick. Okay with you?"

"It's fine with me," she said, snuggling into his arms.

"Hmm, I've missed all this. These last few days seem like a lifetime," he said, kissing her neck and nuzzling.

"They sure have," she said, releasing some of her tension.

"You and Donald doing all right?"

"Yeah, he's great. Stays on the job, but he's a champ at being concealed. I have to look for him sometime."

"Good. You're in great hands."

"I know he must be right outside somewhere. When does he sleep?"

"His van is his home when he's working. He's got everything in it. It's almost like a small apartment."

"What? You've seen it?"

"Yes, before I hired him," he said, kissing her for the first time in days.

"We need to talk?" she teased, knowing that was the furthest thing from his mind at that moment.

"Later," he said. "We need to get reacquainted." He led her to the couch and brought her to him. "We must get our priorities straight. First things, first," he said as he unbuckled her sandals. He started from her feet and ended at her lips. He pulled off her white leggings, revealing her silkened body. "You're so enticing, Micah, and I can't get you out of mind. Even when I'm working, you invade my thoughts. You're in my blood," he said in a halting, smoky tone.

"I feel the same way. It's such a…wonderful feeling. I love you, Mick."

"God, I've wanted to hear you say that in just that tone. You don't know how much I've always wanted you." She could feel his sincerity, see it in his eyes.

"Even at Deauville?"

"Particularly at Deauville."

"But you never said a word. Why?"

He stopped to explain. He'd never told her all this. "Because I couldn't imagine you giving me a second thought. You were so popular, so sought after...I just thought you were above it all."

"Oh, Mick, you were so wrong. I thought I was just a friend. You never gave me the slightest indication how you felt even though I think I surmised it."

"You were so in control, so unlike your giggling friends. You didn't need anyone or that's what you conveyed."

"I heard that same thing from Juanita recently. It was such a facade. I wanted you, but I couldn't make that first move. I thought you were head over heels in love with Lorraine Spencer. You sure had us all thinking so, or maybe she had us believing it. She thought you were the cat's meow. Did you bewitch her like you've done me?"

"Not in the least. In fact, if I remember right, I kissed her once, and I knew she was *not* the one."

"No way. She told some fantastic lies, if that's the truth."

"Believe me. It's the truth. But I don't want to talk about Lorraine Spencer, I want to make passionate love to you," he said, proceeding on his mission in the most amorous fashion possible.

Go for it, Mick. I'm all yours....

❦   ❦   ❦

Pepper wanted seafood for dinner, but she had none in her freezer. She and Rubin went to the market, and he stopped by to check his house. He knew something was wrong. He spotted the cracked windowpane as he drove into his driveway.

"Something's wrong. Stay here. I need to take a closer look."

"What's wrong? How do you know?"

"I have a missing windowpane right there, at the front entrance. Do you see it?"

"Yes, now that you've pointed it out. What do you think?"

"I don't know, but I need to check it out. I'll be right back."

He noted the footprints behind the shrubbery. He took in the whole scene. Someone had been in his home. He drew his gun, opened the unlocked door and looked for telltale signs of the break-in. Nothing was askew, nothing was missing. It was an entry for information. Someone was interested in him. He picked up the phone and called the police. "Someone has been in my home. Would you send someone out for a report? My name is Rubin Burke, 2108 Whitmore Ave. I'll wait." He hung up, and went to get Pepper.

"Come on in. I've called the police. They will be here soon. Someone's coming to take a report. I don't have anything missing. Just want the facts on record."

She walked in, looking about. She saw no disarray, nothing out of place, as far as she could tell. "What does it mean? Nothing's missing. What were they after?"

"Information. Someone's interested in me. Edmond has to be involved. Otherwise, this place would be empty."

"My heavens, it's unending. What is this all coming to?"

"I don't know, but we'll find out. Don't be concerned. We'll get to the bottom of it," he said, holding her before him, convincing her with his eyes.

"I hope so. It's just such a mystery. You said Edmond could be behind this?"

"Yes, but we'll never be able to prove it. Have a seat. We'll wait for the police."

She sat on his couch, wondering what it all meant. Edmond was not to be discounted. She knew she still had to face him at some point. That frightened her more than anything, but it also convinced her to move ahead with her plans. No one knew him as well as she did. She had a missing eye, a permanent limp and multiple unseen scars to prove the kinds of things of which he was capable. She knew deep within her, he would never let her go. He would see her dead first. She was convinced of that unless she struck first.

CHAPTER 37

Atlanta, Georgia
October 2002

When Edmond saw Ben enter his family room, he said, "I hope you have the information I need."

"Yes, I do. The man with Ms. Hankerson *is* Rubin Burke, and he is the owner of the house in the pictures. He has worked for Johnny Diamond for the last seven years. He is Mr. Diamond's body-guard...the one that was shot as I told you earlier. He's also a bouncer in Club Eden, Mr. Diamond's nightclub. He's unmarried, college educated and has the strength of a professional weight lifter. He's from Houston, Texas, and he has one brother and two sisters, all living in the Houston area. His parents are dead. He's devoted to Mr. Diamond and has been shot twice trying to save his life."

"He should have been killed the last time," Edmond said.

"He has no special woman in his life, but he dallies with several. He's both tough and smart and has been known to kill. It's not known why he's in Ms. Hankerson's home, but in all probability, he's there to guard her as you surmised. Mr. Diamond heard the rumor we put on the street...about the plan to kill them. The rumor worked. He's worried. Bodyguards are everywhere. If Mr. Burke had to be described in one word, it would be *deadly.*"

"Deadly, my ass! We'll see just how fucking deadly he is. Pepper is screwing him. I know that much. Since no one around here seems to be able to follow instructions, I will take care of them myself. I want this list of items assembled and in my hands by 9:00 a.m. tomorrow. Not one minute later. I would like one of the small vans readied for my use by 6:00 p.m. Wednesday night, and I want it kept ready for my use at all times. And Ben, I don't want any problems this time, not *one* motherfucking slip-up. Understand?" he enunciated precisely, staring into Ben's eyes, looking like the deranged killer that he was.

"Yes, Mr. Windbrook. I understand. Is there anything else you need?"

"Just the items on that list." He stomped from the room, as angry as he'd ever been, trying to control his one identifying trait, his twitching right eye. He went straight to his bathroom, took out a hand towel, and unzipped his pants. He pulled his engorged member from his pants and jerked it back and forth, releasing a hot rush of stored semen into his towel, draining himself.

Pepper, Pepper, if only you knew how much I need you. Why are you doing this to me? We'll be together soon, and the real bonus will be the desperate, dying pleas of your terrified lover. And I will do it myself, and you will watch. Then you and I will end it all—together.

He turned on his shower, stripped himself nude and stepped in, scrubbing himself for the next fifty minutes.

When Edmond left the room, Ben perused the list with increasing anxiety and finally understood.

❈   ❈   ❈

Johnny's contact called him back and told him all the tag numbers he gave him earlier were assigned to vehicles that Edmond Windbrook owned. He had nine vehicles registered to him. He owned two Mercedes, one Jaguar, one Lincoln Continental, four vans of varying sizes and one truck—all black.

Johnny knew Edmond's employees were on some mission he'd ordered. He was uneasy about Edmond's plans. In his mental state, he was prone to erratic actions. He wanted to be prepared. He was ready to give his life to prevent anything Edmond Windbrook tried. Most of all, he was prepared to kill him with his own hands with just the slightest provocation.

🍁   🍁   🍁

"Good morning, Rubin. That sofa couldn't have been too comfortable. How did you sleep?" Pepper asked.

"It wasn't too bad. I tossed a little, but I did manage to sleep…with one eye open," he said, smiling and abandoning his professional stance for the first time.

What a wonderful smile. He should do it more often.

"You should use the guest room. You would be so much more comfortable. I can't imagine you resting well on the couch for any length of time."

"If it gets unbearable, I might change my mind."

"Believe me, you'll be sick of that couch in no time. What would you like for breakfast? I'm a pretty decent cook when I put my mind to it."

"I'm sure you are. Can you make French toast? It's one of my all-time favorites."

"I sure can. It's one of the first things my mother taught us to make. Let's just have the works. I'll get started, if you can make the coffee."

"I can do that," he said, walking into the kitchen. "Just point me in the right direction."

"The coffee's in that cabinet, and there's the coffee pot. They're all yours."

"Right."

Thirty-five minutes later, they sat down to Pepper's sunny breakfast table that was loaded with French toast, ham, sausage, eggs, orange juice, coffee and a variety of syrups. It was a meal for ten people, but Rubin managed to put quite a dent in the whole thing.

"That was delicious," he said, patting his flat stomach.

"How do you do it? You can't eat like that too often and look the way you do. It's impossible."

"No, I don't do it too often, just on special occasions. And this is surely one. I haven't eaten that much in a long time. Thank you."

"It was no bother. Just make yourself comfortable, and I'll clear this all up."

"I've been known to dry a few dishes in my day, if you'd like," he said.

"Don't be ridiculous. I'll get them in the dishwasher, and we'll both be through. Thanks, anyway."

Rubin found himself becoming drawn to her. She was sensitive and funny, as well as beautiful and enticing.

He thought of Johnny's last comment to him…"Just keep it professional, all the way." Well, he'd already overstepped that boundary, but he couldn't help himself. She was just so engaging. He could never have imagined this assignment would entail all these pleasantries.

> Rubin's one serious relationship ended at his college graduation. He found his fiancée entwined in the arms of another man, just after they'd both accepted their diplomas. He was hurt beyond measure, and he called the whole thing off. He had never involved himself in a meaningful relationship since. He dated here and there, indulged his sexual appetite, but becoming entangled was not on his current agenda.

Pepper had all the characteristics that Rubin desired. He knew he might be in trouble when he watched her in her parents' home through his binoculars, when she appeared depressed and forlorn. He had the disturbing notion he'd like to see her smile, that he should be the one who made her smile. He had already fulfilled one of those notions, but he felt himself being pulled under by her, down where he longed to be, but he had to just…keep it professional, all the way.

CHAPTER 38

Atlanta, Georgia
October 2002

Mick made his decision. He'd vowed he would be the one to take Edmond Windbrook out. He had extensive knowledge of his background, knew the sickening details of his life from childhood to the present time. Edmond exhibited every characteristic of the classic sadistic rapist and killer—manipulative, cunning, desire for power and control, eroticized aggression that's vented on the victim by acts of sadism, similarity in appearance of the victims (in Edmond's case, similar in appearance to his mother), arrangement of the victim's hair and/or body, object raping of the victims as a substitute for his own sex organs and often, in the case of death, sexual intercourse with the corpse.

Edmond derived immense pleasure from being able to appear normal in every respect. He never realized he had failed miserably in that regard. Those who knew him well, his paid henchmen and staff, knew him for what he was—a pathetic killer who ruled by fear and intimidation.

Edmond infuriated Mick because he was able to buy himself out of every malicious beating or murder he'd committed. He knew Edmond felt himself to be untouchable and above the law. Mick understood that as long as Edmond lived, he would continue his murderous pattern and pay for his freedom. It was a vicious cycle that Mick had to stop. He'd formulated his plans. His only concern was Johnny might get him first.

❦   ❦   ❦

"Hello, my name is Pepper Hankerson. I'm calling to schedule an appointment with Dr. Ellerby. My father, Dr. Frederick Hankerson, recommended her. She's expecting the call."

"Yes, Ms. Hankerson. She told me to expect your call. Would you like a morning, afternoon or evening appointment?"

"An evening appointment, if there's one available this week."

"Let's see…we have one at 6:30 p.m. on Thursday or an afternoon appointment at 4:30 p.m. on Friday. Which would you prefer?"

"Thursday at 6:30 p.m."

"All right. We'll expect you then. The appointment is for an hour."

"Thank you. I'll see you then."

She walked into the family room to find Rubin. He was seated in the green arm chair, just to the side of the fireplace. "Rubin, I've just made a doctor's appointment for Thursday evening at six-thirty. Just wanted you to know well in advance." She sat down on the sofa, feeling the need to explain. "I haven't mentioned this to you, but I've decided to seek therapy to help me resolve some issues that I've been facing for a while. The attack hasn't made things any easier. I just wanted you to know that."

"Pepper, you don't need to explain anything to me. I'm here to provide you protection. You have no obligation to me. I don't want you to feel as though you need to explain anything. I have no right, no say in what goes on in your life."

"I realize that, Rubin. I just wanted you to know. We've talked a lot, and I've enjoyed our camaraderie. I know there's nothing you can or should do, but I wanted to tell you that. Sorry I disturbed you."

She got up to leave, and he said, "Thanks, I appreciate it. We'll be there on Thursday at six-thirty sharp."

She said nothing more, just returned to her bedroom.

Why the hell did I say that? She was just trying to be thoughtful. I'm going overboard trying to stay detached. I need to lighten up. I've hurt her feelings. Damn!

CHAPTER 39

Atlanta, Georgia
October 2002

Juanita glimpsed Johnny through her peephole. He had called to let her know he was on his way over. She opened the door. "Hi, baby. It's so good to see you. You've just been away from me for a day, but it seems like a year."

"It sure does," he said, stepping inside and squeezing her. "Hmm, you feel good." His hands roamed her body, possessing her.

"So do you," she said, lingering in his embrace, enjoying the feel of him. She pressed into him and closed her eyes. She released him, but kept her body intact. "You've been a busy man. Have you found out anything useful?"

"Uh-huh, and I'm going to be out at Edmond's place every day and night this week. He's going to make a move soon. I just know it, and I want to be there when he does. I've got Vernell out there now." He broke away and walked into the family room.

"You want anything?" she asked.

"No, thanks. Come on in here with me. I just want to talk. What did you do yesterday on your first day of vacation?"

"Nothing much. Just the usual house stuff. Did you spot Ernest out there?"

"Yep. He's on the job."

She placed her head on his shoulder and drew her legs up on the couch. "I wish this was a real vacation where you and I could get away and do whatever."

"Yeah, me, too. But this will be the first and only time we will ever go through *this*," he said with conviction.

"Johnny, are you going to get involved in…our plan?"

"Why? Does that bother you?"

"I just don't want anything to happen to you. When we discussed it, I didn't think you'd be involved. Have you done it before?"

He moved away from her and looked into her eyes, trying to determine where she was going with her questioning. "You having second thoughts?"

"Just worried about you, that's all." She hesitated before she continued. "Have you ever killed anyone?"

He thought about the question and decided to answer. "Yes," he said, "a long time ago."

"Who was it?"

"An enemy. An enemy who wanted to kill me. I don't like remembering, don't like talking about it. It's not something I enjoyed, Nita. It was something I had to do. I really don't think I could do it again. I was depressed about it for months. I would only consider it if the person posed a definite threat to me or someone I loved. And Edmond Windbrook *is* a definite threat."

"You said something to me the other night that you've never said before."

"Uh-huh."

"Did you mean it?" she asked, looking down.

He raised her chin, forcing her to look at him, and said, "I never say anything I don't mean, Nini. Yes, I love you very much, and I hope you feel the same way."

She stared at him, thinking of what he'd just said. "Yes, the feeling's mutual. I love you more than anything." She kissed him, desired him as she never had, inflamed him with her passion.

"Oh, baby, I never thought I could feel this way about anyone. You've captured my soul," he whispered.

She moved to the floor, pulling him down with her, the thick carpeting cushioning their bodies. "I want you here, *now!*" she said, her eyes never leaving him.

He lifted her skirt and eased down her panties. He unzipped his pants and entered her. They were fully clothed, but neither cared. She rose her hips to him, needing him, moving with him, moaning. "Tell me," she said. "Please, tell me, Johnny."

As they moved in perfect sync, escalating to the goal they sought, he said the words she'd been waiting for him to say, "I love you, Nini. I love you."

When she heard his whisper, she lost it, urging him on, talking to him the way he liked, grinding into him, gripping him tightly. She came, but she couldn't stop, couldn't contain herself, and she experienced a series of continuing tremors that overtook her, bringing her to the brink over and over. "Oh, Johnny," she said at each ultimate moment, as her pleasure continued, wave after wave.

She lay quiet and subdued, cradled in his arms and she said, "That was magnificent, the most beautiful experience I've ever had, and I love you so, Johnny Diamond."

CHAPTER 40

Atlanta, Georgia
October 2002

It was 7:00 a.m., and Ben was assembling the contents of his employer's list. It took him 45 minutes to complete the task. He reviewed it to make sure he had included every item. The list, scribbled and almost indistinguishable, included:

- Beretta Model 92, 9 mm
- Bullets
- Gloves
- Saran Wrap
- Binoculars
- Tape Recorder
- Handcuffs (2)

- Flashlight & Batteries
- Rope
- Switchblade Knife
- Small Toolbox
- Nightscope
- Duct Tape
- Digital Cameras (2)

These items confirmed that Ben's views of Edmond Windbrook were accurate—he was a warped killer who had progressed beyond the point of no return. He could not stand by and allow him to murder another innocent person. He just needed to find a way to deter him. Edmond's request for the van tomorrow evening at six o'clock led him to believe he had about 35 hours to stop him.

❦   ❦   ❦

Micah lay wide awake in bed. She'd pulled it all together at last. The plan she had decided to pursue when she had that in-depth discussion with her father was now in place. She'd concocted it beforehand, mulled it over, and she remembered the *exact* moment she'd decided to move ahead with it. It had nothing to do with what her father said, it was just that his mere presence gave her the impetus she needed. She would never tell a soul, not even Juanita or Mick, about it, but she'd felt a desperate drive, deep down, that kept her on track over the last few months.

She had determined that Edmond Windbrook, III had to be stopped. He'd preyed on Pepper for years, mauling and mistreating her, and as she found out, he'd done much worse to others. Pepper did her best to conceal it, but she'd known every time he'd done it. Not every detail, but she'd known of the insults and beatings, known that Pepper was helpless, unable to muster an ounce of resistance, for they were embroiled in a battle of wills—the have's and the have-not's. She had scoured many books about people who enjoyed playing their respective roles—the sadists and the masochists.

She felt she knew Juanita's temperament, and she felt she didn't have the inner strength to come to Pepper's aid. Micah had never considered herself a person with strong convictions nor someone who was revengeful. But seeing the constant humiliation that one her dearest friends suffered and endured for years, steeled h . reserve, enabling her to rise up to confront the situation head-on. No, she was no Joan of Arc, no Robin Hood, but she was a decent, caring individual who *had* to destroy a man who'd spent years satisfying his inner desires, his warped needs, to the detriment of the helpless and dependent, and all to appease his insatiable desire for power and control.

No, I will not have it! I just will not tolerate his fucked-up, misguided deeds not one minute longer. God, help me. Please forgive me, for I am surrounded by hatred, which is consuming me. And you, above all others, know what's in my heart.

CHAPTER 41

Atlanta, Georgia
October 2002

"Rubin, I'd like to talk to you about what I wanted to say to you yesterday, but couldn't."

He took off his glasses and crossed his legs. "All right."

"To tell you the truth, I can't, for the life of me, figure out why I want to share this with you. I've just met you, and you did let me know yesterday where I stood with you."

"Pepper, I want to apologize for the way I responded. It was uncalled for. I was out of line. Please forgive me. Yes, it's true I'm here for your protection, but if you would like to talk about anything, please do. I've enjoyed our camaraderie, too, and I don't want to jeopardize it in any way."

"Thank you. That does make me feel better. I won't belabor this, but I want you to know the reason I'm going to see the psychiatrist is because I have an emotional affliction, if I can term it that."

He was now puzzled, and he leaned forward. "An emotional affliction? What does that mean?"

"It means…Oh, Rubin, this whole thing is so complicated. But in a nutshell, when I was a child, a neighbor's husband molested me for years. No one knew. When I went off to school at Deauville, I met Edmond Windbrook. He's sadistic, I believe, and…you probably already know this, but he beat me seven months ago. He blinded me in this eye," she said, pointing to her patch. "And he broke my arm and leg. I was in a coma for a couple of months. I've had this emotional problem that stemmed from repeated molestation. Oh, God. This is so hard to verbalize." She paused, tears brimming her eyes.

"Pepper, you don't have to do this. Please, I believe I understand."

"No, I want to do this. Just let me finish…I've never had a normal, physical relationship with a man…" She started to cry, to sob.

He got up and went to her. He placed his arms around her, consoling her, allowing her to release the hurt and embarrassment. He said nothing, just held her in his arms.

When she composed herself, she resumed. "Rubin, I'm so sorry. I don't want to burden you with all this. I just want you to know for some reason."

"It's okay. Don't say anymore. I understand."

"This is just all too bizarre, but thank you. Thank you for listening."

"It's all right. You don't have to thank me. You made the right move, with the psychiatrist. You'll feel some relief. I've spent many hours with a psychiatrist. It helped me through some things, too. Thank you for sharing this with me. It'll be okay, I promise," he said, his heart wrenching.

"Just let me take a moment to get myself together."

Have to keep this professional.

She composed herself as best she could and turned toward him. She put both hands on his face and pulled him to her. She kissed him then, flickering her tongue, lingering at his lips, sucking gently and sending instant fire into his loins.

My God, help me.

He reveled in her sweetness, wanted her desperately, and he held on, steeled himself, but she wouldn't let him go. She insisted he take her, deliberately taunted him. He disrobed her, longed for her. He removed his clothes, and she saw him then—was startled by his size.

She moved closer, wanting him instantly and pressed her breasts against him, engulfing him, enticing him with her body, commanding him to take her.

He was erect, straining, and she wanted to taste him, wanted to feel him inside her mouth. She bent down to him, taking his perfectly formed mushroom wholly, worshipping his hugeness. She felt his beat as he pulsated. He groaned and pushed lightly on her head, moved deeper into her mouth. She gave him the suction that he wanted, inflamed his desire.

He wanted to taste her nectar, and he stood up to make the switch. She opened wide before him, inviting him to her. She was warm and wet, and he knew the spot and focused on it fully. He sucked, then licked, sending her into convulsions. He moved up into her, sliding deep, sinking within her wetness. He felt her all around him, drawing him further down. He sank deeper; occupying every crevice of her tunnel, stroking her inner sanctum with each thrust and throb.

She broke loose and cried, "Ahhh, Rubin. You feel so good."

She moved around him, his gigantic shaft now lodged deep inside her. Her body jerked, her hips locked and she waited for him, willing him to come with her.

He was beyond his limit, and he thrust hard and probed. He searched her secret hideaway where no one had ever ventured. He was in virgin territory, her private sanctuary, a secret place where he alone had visited, and he staked claim, forcefully released a niagara of steaming sperm, filling her completely. She fell from his embrace and lay silently beneath him as if all life had ebbed from her body. She emitted murmurs of mournful glory and exhaled her spent desire.

"Oh, Rubin. It was the first time. It was so wonderful, so superb." She clung to him; kissed him, and he knew how much he'd pleased her.

She knew then that his enormous staff could bring her the pleasure and the pain. He would be able to satisfy her as no one else had ever done. She knew he could fulfill all her darkest desires.

My Lord! I can't believe it. That was too exquisite for words. I didn't know what I've been missing.

❧   ❧   ❧

When Ben entered, Edmond was pacing the room. "What can I do for you, Mr. Windbrook?"

"I'm putting everything on hold for now. Keep those items I had you assemble close. That's it."

"I'll take care of it." Ben left without another word.

"I will *not* wait forever," Edmond boomed to no one. He clutched his head, feeling the onset of another raging migraine.

CHAPTER 42

Atlanta, Georgia
December 12, 2002
Two Months Later

Edmond had not spoken to Pepper since she told him not to call her. He was totally devastated. He ordered a full report of all her activities, including up-to-the-minute pictures of Rubin and her. He was obsessed with them, wanted every moment of their lives recorded. Dr. Forester prescribed medication for his migraines, but it didn't help. His nerves were stretched, caused him to react irrationally.

He'd put his plan in place months ago and had been primed for action then, but his timing had been off. The waiting unnerved him. He wanted to lash out, but his lawyers advised him to temper his reactions. They needed to dispel all suspicions surrounding the Acapulco fiasco. They were well aware of his activities, but they chose to protect him because his account made the difference in their quality of living.

Edmond had finally made up his mind to move forward with his plans for Pepper and Rubin despite his lawyers' warning. He had waited long enough. He gave Ben specific instructions and told him to prepare everything as outlined. He had Ben bring him the items he'd had him assemble months before. He wanted to be able to move at a moment's notice.

❧   ❧   ❧

The months of delay without any disturbance, confused and frustrated Johnny, Mick and Rubin. The had their defensive actions in place and waited anxiously for him to strike. As time passed, it became more difficult to contain the girls. They thought it was all a hoax and wanted to venture out more and pursue their normal activities. They'd begun to resent their confinement and rebelled against their protectors. They tried the guards' patience, and it took constant forewarning to keep them focused on their own safety.

❧   ❧   ❧

Juanita walked into the galley to see the latest creation LaVerne had whipped together for her. Pepper was sketching near her mother. "Where's that black dress I changed so many times, LaVerne? The one you were working on yesterday. I can't wait to see it on the model."

"It's on the rack in the other room. It turned out beautifully. It drapes just as you said. It's perfect. You were right about the changes. Take a look at everything in there. It's everyone's new designs.

"They are so beautiful, Juanita," Pepper said. "Our European trip really sparked our creativity. I can't wait for the show Saturday night."

"Me, neither. And I think you're right about the trip to Eurc Can't wait to see how everything turned out," Juanita said, heading toward the back room. They'd decided on a seasonal theme, so the show would be divided into four segments—each segment representing a different season. She was happy they'd decided to change their format because they had put together the most incredible selection of clothing she'd ever seen. She stood before the racks, marveling at the new designs and their newfound originality. Everything was fabulous and finally ready.

She pulled one of Micah's designs from the rack, noting its splendor. She knew Micah fashioned the dress using fabric reminiscent of draperies in the Hotel Ritz—heavy green satin that caressed the body, yet hinted at it artfully. Juanita knew instantly it would appeal to a variety of their clients—concealing *and* beckoning would be the allure. Pepper was right; Europe had really pumped them up, unleashed their creative juices. They had used all kinds of unusual fabrics and colors, and their ideas were fresh and unique. She had no doubt this collection would be a major success.

The Christmas holidays were upon them, and the girls were in the final throes of the fashion show details. They were pumped up and confident. All three of them were heady with expectation, and undergoing final fittings for the gown they would wear to the event. They had worked the staff to a frazzle, but the collection was worth it. From all indications, the expense of the European trip would be just a minor expense. Lila was thrilled by the originality of their work and the prospect of new clients.

Even thought Juanita, Pepper and Micah shunned the protection they'd been provided, Johnny, Rubin and Mick were still fully focused. Pepper had been seeing a psychiatrist for months and seemed happy at last. Rubin still occupied her home, but he shared it now as her lover. Their personal relationship appeared to have grounded them, provided the missing element they needed. Edmond posed their only problem. He clouded their future, held them within his grasp and prevented them from moving on freely.

❦   ❦   ❦

Juanita visited Pepper in her office. They had some free time at last. She chatted with Pepper for a long time, filling in all the blanks they'd not been able to pursue because of their congested work schedules. Pepper was so happy. She said she and Rubin couldn't have been more suited for each other.

Before Juanita left Pepper's office, she said, "Well, I guess we better get use to Rubin being with us everywhere we go. Now that's going to be something to get use to."

"What do you mean?" Pepper said.

"Just think about it. Rubin's going to see everything v do. S pose I wanted to just flirt around a little. You know Rubin's going ω run back to Johnny with it. Then the shit's gonna really hit the fan."

"I don't think he'd do that, Nita. He's not like that," Pepper said, worrying about Juanita's comments.

"Humph, that's what you think. But anyway, girl, so glad you're happy and your life is on track at last."

"Yes, me, too. I couldn't be happier, Nita."

Juanita picked up the phone and called Johnny at home. Nine o'clock was early for him. "Hello, there, Mr. Johnny Diamond. How are you this morning? Did I wake you?"

"Not really. I'm still in bed, but I'm being lazy. We had a late night. I'm doing fine, Ms. Sanchez. Wish you were here. You're in a cheerful mood. May I ask why?"

"Oh, I just finished talking with Pepper. She seems so happy, Johnny. She and Rubin are doing great."

"I told you that, baby. Rubin's feet haven't touched ground since he's been involved with her."

"Oh, so you guys talk about your personal relationships, huh?"

"Now Nita, that's not what I'd consider talking about personal relationships."

"Yeah, right. Tell me anything."

"Come on, baby. I don't want anybody getting any ideas about you. So, why would I even mention you? That stuff's for ladies. I'd love to know what you say about me."

"Chile, please. I'd be a fool to tell any woman 'bout you," she lied straight out.

"Nita, I'd be a damn fool to believe that. I've heard y'all on the phone, don't forget that."

"Here's Dana, sugar. Got to run. I do need to talk to you about something serious…something *really* important tonight. Bye."

Ain't that a bitch? That's just like her. To end the conversation with something like that. Damn!

CHAPTER 43

Atlanta, Georgia
December 12, 2002
That Same Day

"Hello, may I speak with Mr. Rubin Burke, please?"

"He's not here. Who's calling?" Vernell asked.

"This is a friend of his from Houston. I'm in town and need to speak with him before I leave. It's urgent. Could you have him give me a call as soon as possible? I'm leaving tomorrow."

"What's your name?"

"Benjamin Donavan. He can reach me at 792-3546. If he could call me this morning, I'd appreciate it."

"I'll try to reach him."

"Thank you. Goodbye."

Ben replaced the phone, hoping the message would be relayed to Rubin. Time was not a luxury he had. He didn't know when his employer might blow. He could cut the tension on the job with a knife. Things were uncomfortable for everyone. He would have called sooner, but he didn't think the staff at Club Eden worked the early shift.

Rubin's cell phone rang at 11:09 a.m. He was reading in Pepper's conference room. He flipped the cover, and saw the call was coming from the club, but it was not Johnny's personal number.

"Hello."

"Rubin? This is Vernell."

"Hey, man. What's up?

"I just got a call from a Benjamin Donavan, a friend of yours from Houston. He said he was in town until tomorrow, and he needed to speak to you. He said it was urgent, so I told him I'd try to find you."

"I don't know a Benjamin Donavan." He frowned, trying to place him.

"He just called you here, just a few minutes ago. I got his number. He was fidgety, said he really needed to contact you."

"What's the number?"

"792-3546."

"Thanks, man. I'll check it out."

"Right."

Rubin could think of only one Ben he knew, and he wasn't from Houston. He decided to call.

The phone rang one time. "Hello."

"Hello. May I speak to Benjamin, please?"

"Speaking. Is this Rubin?"

"Yeah, it is. I don't know—"

"I know you don't know me, but this is extremely important. It's about Edmond Windbrook."

"Edmond Windbrook?" Rubin said. *It's starting....* "What about him?"

"It's a matter of your life, and perhaps, Ms. Hankerson's, I'm afraid. You're the only one I know who can help."

"With what?" Rubin was skeptical, didn't know if this was a set up.

"I know you're wondering exactly who I am and why I'm giving you this information. I don't have time to go into detail. I work for

Edmond Windbrook, and I've seen him do many things, but I cannot allow him to do what he's planning to do."

"And exactly what *is* he planning to do?"

"He's planning to kill you, and, I believe, Pepper Hankerson—sometime soon and in some horrible way. I cannot stop him, so *you* must be prepared. He's a very sick man, really mentally deranged. He's liable to do anything, and he's getting worse. I need to give you the details. Your life is definitely at stake, so please listen carefully...."

Ben told Rubin everything he knew about Edmond's plans, even the items he had assembled for him months ago, but gave to him this morning.

"So, you're saying Edmond Windbrook is planning on killing me and possibly Ms. Hankerson sometime in the near future...and he's doing it because of our personal relationship. And you don't know when. How could that be if you have all these other details? I don't understand why you're telling me all this. What's in it for you?"

"I have nothing to gain. In fact, if things go wrong, and he ever suspects I had anything to do with it, I won't be around for long. Now that's a fact," Ben said, feeling confident that it was.

"Uh-huh. Thanks for the information, Benjamin. If you're on the up 'n up, I'm really appreciative. If you're not, as you just said, you won't be around for long." He hung up.

Rubin called Johnny at 11:35 a.m. Johnny put down his shaver, turned down his Christmas music and answered the phone.

"Hello."

"Johnny, it's me. I just talked to a Benjamin Donavan who said he works for Edmond Windbrook."

"Now that's a twist."

"Yeah, it is. He said Edmond is planning on wasting Pepper and me sometime soon. It's supposedly because we're involved with each other. He said he gave Edmond some things this morning that he had him assemble—stuff like a Beretta, handcuffs, gloves, Saran

Wrap...a whole lot of other shit. He also said that's Edmond's MO when he wants to handle a job personally. He indicated the guy's wacked out bad, and he's liable to do anything. Oh, he also said Edmond would probably be in a small, black van with tinted windows, and he asked to have it readied for his use at the drop of a dime.

"When I asked him why he was volunteering all this information, he just said he'd had enough, and he couldn't sit around and let him kill anybody else. I could tell the guy hasn't been with him too long, but he said there were some horror stories he could tell about what Edmond does and what he orchestrates. It sounded on the Q-T, but I'm not sure. What do you think?"

"I think we better be ready. We can't take any chances. You do what you need to do to get yourself prepared after that little chat you had, and I'll work on how to handle the rest. I'll call you back after I've put something together. Hey, man, just be cool. We're going to get him, make no mistake about that. Later."

It took Johnny a little over an hour to work out his plans. He called Mick and told him what Rubin had said and what he was planning to do. He called Vernell and filled him in, and told them both the role they would play.

At 1:55 p.m., he called Juanita, who had gone home early. She had completed her whole line of designs, and she wanted to relax at home.

"Hi, baby. You busy?"

"Not too busy for you. I was just tired and wanted to get a little rest. I'm so glad those long nights have finally come to an end. Where are you?"

"On my way there, if that's okay."

"Of course, it's okay. You don't have to ask."

"Just need to pick up my tux from the cleaners. I know you got your dress all ready even though I haven't heard a word about it. But don't tell me. I want to be surprised. Nita?"

"Huh?"

"I can't wait to hear all about this serious, really important thing you've got to tell me. I'll be there shortly. Bye."

CHAPTER 44

Atlanta, Georgia
December 12, 2002
That Same Day

Micah was talking to Mick on the phone discussing Pepper and Rubin. "I never would have thought those two would hook up—Elegance vs. Brawn," she said.

"Don't let Rubin's body mislead you, Micah. He's extremely intelligent and well read. I was surprised, too, when I first talked with him."

"Huh? Are we talking about the same person? I know he's not retarded, but 'extremely intelligent' seems to be pushing it."

"Well, get use to it. He is. You've never even talked with him in-depth, Micah. You're being prejudicial, which is unfair. He has a college degree. Did you know that?"

"No, I did not. And that's great, but a college degree tells me only one thing, Mick," she said, determined to pursue the subject.

He was really getting pissed off with her now. "Oh, yeah? What?"

"It simply tells me the person has tenacity. It has nothing to do with intelligence," she said in a haughty tone.

"Oh? Well, thank you very much for your profound explanation. I know you're an expert when it comes to intelligence. You've cleared up my wayward thinking," he said, sarcasm rolling from his lips.

She wouldn't let up. "But I must admit, the college degree does surprise me. It's comforting to know Pepper has someone who *might* be her intellectual equal. She seems to have it all in Rubin, and I'm happy for her...Mick, I know you're fuming over this, but I don't mean any harm," she said. He didn't answer, so she tried to switch tactics. "I don't think Edmond is going to do anything, Mick. I think we can let Donald go—"

"Uh-uh. Don't even try it. Donald stays! I didn't know you didn't like Rubin, Micah. Just why is that?" he asked, mad as hell with her. He didn't like what she'd implied about him one damn bit.

"Oh, Mick. I like Rubin. It's just that...Oh, hell. I don't know why I said all that. I'm sorry. He seems so perfect for her. I really am happy for them."

"Uh-huh." He wasn't impressed. So, we're still on at six? It'll be good to see what you and Juanita have been doing for months at the range."

"Yes, and I'll be most obliged to show you. Got to run, sweetie, work beckons. See you at six. Hey, Mick. You got your tux ready? Just two more days before the show."

"Yeah, just got it out the cleaners yesterday. I know you got it all together. Don't even need to ask. See you tonight."

Shit! I really stepped in it that time. He's pissed as hell.

CHAPTER 45

Atlanta, Georgia
December 12, 2002
That Same Night

Edmond was restless, disconnected and highly agitated. He ranted and raved, checked and re-checked his backpack that contained all the equipment Benjamin had assembled for him. His staff stayed out of his way. He needed immediate psychiatric care, but no one had the courage to do anything. Haymon, his current butler, thought about calling Thomas Langley, Edmond's lawyer, to let him know Edmond's current state, but he decided to drop it. Langley was a money-grubbing coward. He'd proved that on too many occasions.

"Ahhh. This is just what I need. To take it easy. To relax right here with you," Johnny said. He was stretched out on Juanita's long sofa, his head in her lap. It was quiet, with soft carols playing in the background.

He reached up and pulled her to him, kissing her deeply. "You mean everything to me. I want you to know that."

"I love you, too," she whispered.

"You know, I've been thinking about our conversation this morning about Rubin and Pepper. He's been with me seven years, and this is the first time I've seen him really go gaga over some woman. He's usually so laid back about everything."

"And just why is that? No woman ever attracted him? He ain't nothing to write home to Mama 'bout, but his body *is* tight. I have to give the boy that," she said offhandedly.

"Juanita, you're too much. He's dated many women, just no one to hold his attention. I don't know a whole lot about it, but he was engaged in college and something went wrong between him and his fiancé, I believe. I do *not* know the details, Nita, so don't ask me. I guess we've all been through some of that."

"Uh-uh. I know you didn't say that. I haven't. What about you? What happened to you? Somebody broke your poor little ole heart?" she said, pouting playfully.

"Something like that. A long time ago, and I will *not* go into it. It has nothing to do with us. You're what's important to me now."

She looked at him closely. Whatever it was, it was still a sensitive issue. "Did it have anything to do with that person you killed?" she whispered.

Goddamn it! How the hell did she know that? That's fucking unbelievable.

Intuitively sensing his thoughts, she drew away from him and continued, "You might think it strange, sugar, but I do have some psychic abilities. Even if you deny it, I know it's true. We don't *even* have to discuss it."

You're amazing, Juanita. I appreciate that. It was just too long ago to matter."

"Now Johnny, if I really wanted to know, all I would have to do is throw down the cards and consult the Arcana. But that's another matter. I wouldn't do that to you without your consent."

"What cards you talking 'bout? What's the Arcana? Some of that heebie-jeebie stuff?"

She hesitated. "I'm talking about Tarot cards, and believe me, they are far from being heebie-jeebies or whatever you called it."

Uh-uh, don't even go there. That stuff's way over my head...Does it work?"

"One hundred percent," she said, deadly serious.

"Then, we'll leave it at that." He got up for more eggnog, this time pouring in a generous shot of bourbon. "What is it you want to tell me that's so important?" He picked up his eggnog and took a sip. For some reason, he'd been disturbed since she'd mentioned it.

"Oh, Johnny, I hope you'll understand all this. It's crazy in a way."

Now he *was* alarmed. "What is it, Nita? What are you trying to say? Is there anything wrong between us?"

"Oh, my God, no! Johnny, it has nothing to do with us. I'm sorry if I indicated that. Did I?"

"No, you didn't, but you sound so hesitant. I guess it's me. What is it?"

"It's just that I'm thinking of taking a few months off from work soon, and I wanted to talk to you about it."

"Why? What's wrong?"

"Nothing's wrong. Just let me explain. You know Daddy's from Peru, right?"

"Yes."

"Well, I've always wanted to visit Peru. I'm thinking about taking three months off and going to find out some things about my family."

"To Peru? When did you decide that?"

"It's been a lifelong dream, really. It's not written in stone, but I'm thinking about going sometime early next year, and I'd like you to come with me."

"Juanita, you know I've got a business to run, and to Peru? I don't know about that. I'm...shocked, I guess. You've never mentioned anything about it before. Why now?"

"Like I said, I've always wanted to go, and after all we've been through the last few months, I'm just realizing how precious our time really is. Financially, I can afford to do it now, and that's always been a consideration. It's just time. You don't have to decide right now, but I wanted to tell you what I've been thinking, that's all. Sugar, I'm so sorry if I upset you. I would never do that."

"It's probably just my insecurities surfacing. It wasn't you. Let me give it some thought. Three months? That's a long time. What part of Peru?"

"My ancestors were from Lima, but Johnny, I've always been so fascinated with Machu Picchu. You ever heard of it?"

"Uh-uh. Is it a town?"

"It's a city. The whole city sets atop a mountain, and it was lost for hundreds of years. It was just rediscovered by Hiram Bingham in the early part of the 20th century…in 1911. It's all so mysterious, and it has some psychic connection, too. There's suppose to be some kind of door…a door that's believed to be the entrance to another universe. It's intrigued me since Daddy told Juan and me about it. I was about eight years old then. When Daddy would come home from his expeditions, he'd tell us these long, eerie stories. I've been hooked ever since."

"Hmmm. A door to another universe? That's some farfetched stuff, Nini. Let me give it some thought."

"Okay, but I haven't *really* made up my mind yet. I've got to soon, though. They'll have to know at work." Shifting gears, she said, "Micah and Mick are going to the range tonight. It's the first time he's been out there with her in months. She just wants to show off. She's gotten to be so good. She really has."

But not as good as you, I gather?"

"Chile, please. Ain't no way."

"Juanita, you're really a spoiled brat. You know that?"

"Yes, but, I'm *your* spoiled brat. That's the difference. Now that's what I'm talkin' 'bout," she said, with her bravado flaming.

"You got a point there," he said, not knowing what the hell he would do without her. He'd also not forgotten she might be away for three months. *I don't think that's going to happen, business or no business.*

CHAPTER 46

Atlanta, Georgia
December 12, 2002
That Same Night

"All right, Ms. McCall. Let's see what you got," Mick said.

"Okay. Let me get straightened out, here. Oh, Mick, you're making me so nervous. If Juanita were here, this would be nothing."

"Come on, Micah. Why would I make you nervous? I love you."

"I don't know, but you do."

She took aim, and fired off six rapid shots.

He stood stunned, his hands on his hips. "Well, I be goddamn! I can't believe it. How the hell did you do that?"

"Tenacity plus intelligence. They really do go hand-in-hand, you know." He knew it was her way of apologizing for her insensitive remarks about Rubin earlier. "But most all, it's just a little some'um, some'um I thought you might like," she said, smiling from ear to ear.

"I love it, Micah. It looks like you fired one shot. I'm floored. I mean it. So, you've outdone me again—first with the bow and arrow and now with the gun. You never cease to amaze me, my love. That's how you got me hooked."

"Well, thank you kind sir. I've been working hard to be able to see your face when I did that. That'll teach you to laugh at *me*. When I saw Nita do that without having picked up a gun in years, I was blown away, too. And I've been wanting to do the same thing. I can't wait to tell her all about this."

He kissed her lightly and said, "You're really something, baby. That's why I love you."

"Put a pin right there," she said, reveling in his praise.

He called me "baby." Johnny must be rubbing off on him. Now that's what I'm talkin' 'bout, she thought, imitating Juanita.

CHAPTER 47

Atlanta, Georgia
December 14, 2002

The big day arrived, bright and clear. It was cold and wintry, but everyone woke excited. Micah slept late, comfortably snuggled deep beneath her covers, enjoying the warmth that surrounded her. She wished Mick were with her, but he'd worked late and didn't want to disturb her.

She looked at her gown hanging on her closet door, resplendent in the hazed light. She could see it now.

I'm going to emerge from the bedroom in all my splendor. Mick's eyes are really going to bulge. I'm going to prance around in that black spaghetti-strapped gown hanging there and have that fabulous, huge black matching shawl thrown casually around me. I'm so glad I decided to have it lined in that turquoise satin we found in Milan. That's what makes the outfit pop. My dangling diamond earring and bracelet will be my only jewelry. And most of all, it's unpretentious and comfortable, and Mom said it was a masterpiece. We're all going to shine tonight! I can feel it already.

✿   ✿   ✿

Rubin lay silently, but fully awake, encircling Pepper in his arms. He listened to her breathing, soft and sighing, and pulled her closer. His early morning erection needed attention, but he wanted her to rest. Today was her big day. He managed to pull himself away from her and slipped from the bed.

He opened the closet to inspect his tux. He thought it might be a tight fit with his gun and holster, but that's the way it would have to be. Pepper had his onyx and silver studs and cufflinks lined up in his felt-lined chest. And then he saw it—the gown he assumed she'd wear. It was a luscious, navy velvet straight column. The long matching navy swing coat was lined in fuchsia satin. He glimpsed the Monolo Blahnik stiletto pumps peeking beneath the coat. The ensemble was simple and elegant. *Just like Pepper. She's so damn beautiful. I can't believe my luck. I don't give a damn about her patch. Don't think she does either.*

Pepper had planned a small gathering at the house after all the festivities tonight, and the house looked beautiful with all the Christmas decorations. Despite Edmond Windbrook, Rubin was looking forward to his life with Pepper. He was happier than he'd ever been.

✿   ✿   ✿

Juanita and Johnny were both awake, still in bed, but enjoying their private moment. They'd been talking about the show and what lay ahead for the day.

"Let's eat a big breakfast," she said. "I'm going to need plenty of stamina. I probably won't have time for another meal all day. What do you want?"

"Whatever you fix. I'm not choosy. Do your thing."

"I'm going to tell them Monday about my leave of absence. They're all going to freak. Machu Picchu, Peru! Here I come."

"So, you made up your mind?"

"Yes, I guess I always knew I'd go. Have you given it any more thought?"

"Yes, but I haven't worked it out. I'll let you know soon. When are you planning on leaving?"

"Around the first of February, I think. I'll work through January. It's usually pretty quiet after the holidays, but I'll need to see how our sales are going and satisfy any rambunctious clients. Please try to work it out, Johnny. It's going to be such an adventure. I'd love to share it with you."

"I'm thinking about it. This is a busy month, and I just have to see how things roll out in the club." He wasn't divulging all the facts, but he did have a few more things to work through.

"Let me know as soon as you decide. I haven't been able to concentrate on it too much with the show in front of us, but after tonight, I'm going to get it all together."

"You excited? About tonight, I mean?"

"I am. Did you see the gown in the closet?"

"No, I haven't seen the gown. Describe it, I don't won't to see it until you put it on."

"Well, I'm going to be dressed all in gold, from head to toe. I'm going to be an Egyptian Queen in all her finery," she said, smiling at the thought. "I've got this gold beaded Egyptian headpiece with a fringe of beads resembling bangs. The other beads hang to the shoulders, reminiscent of a Cleopatra haircut. I have this strapless gold gown that's fitted at the waist, and it skims the hips and flows into a graceful swirl. Johnny, it's the baddest thing I've ever designed. I'm going to have on the upper arm bracelet you bought me in Europe."

"The gold snake one—?"

"Yes, the one that cost you a fortune in Paris, not the bangle from Milan. I still think it was too expensive. But anyhow, I'm going to line my eyes in black kohl, just like Liz Taylor did in *Cleopatra*. It's going to be something, Johnny. You'll see."

"I can see you already. Did you get any of your designing ideas from the Lourve?

"Absolutely. I have a whole scene devoted to Egyptian-inspired designs. That was the purpose of the whole trip—to inspire our imagination."

"Well, I guess it worked then."

"For all of us," she said.

"Rubin is going to be with us at the table. That's a switch for him. We talked about it last night. He's doing double duty—bodyguard and significant other."

"Yeah, we had a little conversation about that a few days ago, too."

"You did? What did you say?"

"Oh, just how great it was going to be to have Rubin in on everything we'd do from now on."

"Yeah, right. I know just about how that went," he said, chuckling to himself.

He pulled her on top of him, just wanting to feel her body. "You getting up now?"

"If this is all you have in mind, I am."

"Nini, I have never, in my whole life, met anyone like you."

"And don't your forget it!" she said, throwing the covers off and pulling on her robe. "I'm hungry. Stay there. I'll get breakfast together. I'll even serve you in bed. How about that?"

"Now that's what I'm talkin' 'bout," he said, laughing heartily at his imitation of her.

She threw the covers back on him, enjoying their morning banter.

CHAPTER 48

Atlanta, Georgia
December 14, 2002

Vernell pulled from the parking lot at Club Eden at 8:35 p.m. He headed to Edmond's neighborhood and found a concealed location that provided him clear view of Edmond's gates. It was 9:20 p.m. He took out his nightscope and settled in for the night.

The fashion show at the Fitzgerald Hotel was in pump-up mode, and Rubin scanned the crowd. His role tonight transcended his previous one, but his bodyguard radar was fully alert. He sat upfront in a semi-circle arrangement with Franklin, Johnny and Mick, but his strategically aligned seat allowed him clear vision of Ernest.

The winter season segment was causing rousing ovations as each model stepped briskly down the runway. The jazz trio kept the pace upbeat and kept everyone primed for the dramatic scenes. The audience responded enthusiastically.

At 9:50 p.m., a black Jaguar eased its way into Edmond's gates and disappeared within the shrouded grounds. Vernell checked the license plate number, and it belonged to Edmond. At 10:10 p.m., a small black van with tinted windows exited Edmond's gates. Vernell waited a few seconds and slithered from his hideout into the flow of traffic. Both vehicles headed northwest.

Vernell picked up his cell phone and called Ernest. He picked up immediately. "I'm leaving. Just wanted you to know the van just left, and we're headed northwest. I'll keep you in the loop."

"Right. Call me back when you know what's going on."

At 10:55 p.m., the black Jaguar slipped through the gates of Edmond's compound and headed in the same direction as the van. Exactly thirty-two minutes later, it pulled into an exclusive neighborhood twelve miles west of Pepper's house. Dim post lamps along the street lighted the housing area. The Jag parked on the street, and the driver leaned back to relax and made himself comfortable. He had some time to wait.

At 11:00 p.m., the fashion show concluded, and when Lila took the catwalk, the audience went wild. The show exceeded all expecta-tions. She introduced Juanita and Pepper and expressed her gr...tude for their work.

She introduced Micah last because she wanted to make a special comment. "To my daughter, Micah McCall, whose creativity soared to new heights. She has some particularly wonderful news tonight, and I'd like to share it with you. She became the fiancée to Mick Sutherland, Jr., CEO of the Sutherland and Bailey Investigative Services, tonight. Stand up, Mick, let everyone see who you are," she said proudly as the audience greeted the news with thunderous applause and another standing ovation for Micah's work as well as her engagement to Mick.

Vernell called Ernest again. "He's parked in the back of Pepper's house. I'm going to wait a while...see what he does. What do you think?"

"It depends," Ernest said. "Stay put. If things get out of hand in any way, call the police, but that's the last option. Wait it out...he's got a plan. Don't risk anything by yourself. Call me if anything changes. I'll let Rubin and Donald know."

"Right."

Micah hugged Pepper and Juanita. They were delighted and surprised at the early Christmas present. Tears fell as they fawned over the ring. Micah glimpsed Armstead when she turned to hug Pepper and Juanita. When she looked again, his chair was empty. Johnny, Rubin and Franklin were surprised about the engagement, and they congratulated Mick who beamed.

Rubin's eyes scanned the room automatically. He couldn't abandon his training. He noticed Johnny's innate social graces, but he also knew that every time Johnny touched his left chest he did so to reassure himself his that his weapon was still in place. Rubin's observations were keen and completely focused no matter what the situation.

❧   ❧   ❧

Fred and Laverne Hankerson were very proud of Pepper. Fred had been called in for surgery, and he told the girls regretfully that he and LaVerne would not attend the party. Pepper's sister, Nicky, loved the fashion show, but she and her boyfriend slipped from the dance early and headed for the Run-DMC and Jam Master Jay concert featuring Aerosmith and Kid Rock at the stadium.

LaVerne and Fred arrived home at 1:05 a.m. He changed his clothes, kissed LaVerne goodbye and left for the hospital. The telephone rang shortly after he left. LaVerne thought he was calling back for something, and she answered immediately. "Hello."

"Yes, I'm sorry to call so late, but I have an emergency. May I speak to Dr. Hankerson, please? This is David Washington, one of his patients," he said excitedly.

"I'm sorry, he just left. You can reach him at St. Michael's shortly."

"Thanks, I'll catch him at the hospital, then. I apologize for waking you. Good night."

The door to the black Jag opened, and a darkly clothed figure emerged. He retrieved a backpack from the back seat and closed the door quietly. He crossed the darkened lawn and entered the backyard of the large two-story brick home. He jimmied the glass door just off the kitchen, slid it open and entered. LaVerne, barefoot and still in her evening gown, sat with the TV on, studying some sketches she'd brought home from work.

"Hello," he said, frightening LaVerne, causing her to drop her sketches.

"What are you doing here? How did you get in?" she demanded.

"I'm here to see you," he said and yanked her from her chair. "We need to call Pepper."

"What are you doing?" she shouted as she attempted to free herself from his grip. I will not have you barge in here. He maneuvered her to the phone.

"Call her," he snarled.

She dialed Pepper's number.

When the girls arrived at Pepper's house, they all changed from their gowns to their casual designer wear. Pepper chose black cigarette pants and a v-neck black and gold snug top with high heel mules. Micah's choice was a red jumpsuit that skimmed her athletic body. She completed her outfit with red and black slip-in evening mules. Juanita's choice was an upscale version of the gangsta look she adored. She wore soft, black leather pants and a matching leather motorcycle jacket. She slipped a white cotton and silk tee shirt underneath. She chose beautiful black boots and silver jewelry, which gave her a tough, street-savvy edge.

Pepper and Rubin were serving food and drinks while couples danced to the soft music of Luther Vandross and listened to carols by Nat King Cole. The phone rang, and Pepper picked up. "Hello, Momma?" Pepper said, recognizing the number on the caller I.D.

"Pepper, Edmond is here. He broke in somehow. I—"

He snatched the phone from her and said, "Listen, bitch, you should not have left me and did the things that you did. Now *you* have to pay. This will be your last conversation with your mother.

Just thought I'd let you know that." He handed the phone back to LaVerne.

"Momma," Pepper cautioned nervously, "please be careful...get out of there. Has Daddy left for the hospital?" She heard a muffled yell followed by a gurgling sound, then silence. "Momma, what's happening?" she shrieked. "Rubin, Edmond's at Momma's. Something's wrong...my God...he better not lay a hand on her or else I'll kill that motherfucker myself! Momma, Momma," she shouted.

He placed the phone back on the hook and left the lifeless body of LaVerne heaped on the floor. He moved through the side door and headed to his Jag.

"Edmond? What's going on?" Rubin asked, not understanding her previous comment.

"Oh, Rubin," she moaned, "Edmond's at our house with Momma. I think he's done something to her. My God, we've got to do something. I've got to get over there," Pepper wailed, heading for the door.

"No, you can't do that," Rubin commanded, restraining her. "Sit down and let's think this thing through."

Johnny was already ushering everyone outside. He apologized and told them they had an emergency. His cell phone rang. He picked up, and it was Ernest. "I'll call you back."

"I've got to call Daddy," Pepper said. "He must be at the hospital." She picked the phone up, dialing frantically.

"What's really going on?" Micah asked.

"Damn if I know exactly. Edmond's at the Hankersons'. What should we do, Johnny?" Juanita said.

Johnny and Rubin made eye contact. They recognized there was little they could do, at this point, about her mother.

During the time that Vernell was watching the van, he and Ernest kept in constant contact. Johnny attempted to call Ernest back, but his line was busy. Vernell's eyes followed the driver from the van as he walked stealthily through an adjoining yard, heading towards Pepper's house.

"Hey, Ernest. He's out of the van, moving towards Pepper's, I think. He has a gas can…Shit! I may have to follow him…Wait. I can still see him. He's headed towards Pepper's…no, he's veering off…He's two doors west of her…Goddamn! The sonofabitch has torched Pepper's neighbor's house. Got to call 911. I'll call you back," he said, his adrenalin surging.

Ernest, who was staking out the east side of Pepper's house, called Donald and told him what Vernell said. The fire department should be there any minute.

Johnny called Ernest back, and he answered. "You out front?"

"Yeah, Donald, too. Vernell's on the street behind Pepper's. The driver of that van started a fire two doors from here, and Vernell's calling 911. Them damn trucks will be here any minute. Why is everyone leaving? You just got there."

"I sent them home. Edmond called from Pepper's mom's. He may have done something to her mother. You know where they live?"

"Yeah, Rubin showed me once. Why?"

"Get over there fast. See what happened. And call *me* the next time. Later."

"Right."

Goddamn! Everything's happening at the same time. That mother-fucker planned it this way Johnny thought.

Rubin held Pepper in his arms. He heard Johnny's conversation. "Ernest will call us as soon as he gets there."

He said that's the last time I would talk to her, Pepper thought. "Oh my God," she screeched, crying and totally devastated. "He better not have done *anything* to her. This is like a dream. I can't fucking believe it." Pepper rarely cursed, only when she was highly stressed or agitated did she do so.

"I guess it's on," Juanita said. "Believe me, Pepper, this is no damn dream. This shit's for real."

They heard the sirens blaring. "Vernell told Ernest someone tried to start a fire near here," Johnny said. The sirens are the fire trucks. Donald's out front." He looked at Rubin. "Keep your eyes open, man. I'm going to check on Vernell. He's on the street behind us."

Rubin nodded.

Juanita rushed to him. "Do you have to go? Why can't you stay here with us?" Her eyes were wild and red.

"I'm just going to check on Vernell and cruise the surrounding areas. I'll be all right," he assured her. He left her grasp, and rushed from the house.

Johnny didn't see Vernell's van on the next street. *Where the fuck is he?* His phone rang, and it was Vernell.

"Where the hell are you, Vernell? I thought you were on the street behind Pepper's."

"I was, but I'm trailing the van. He started the fire and left. Didn't even go near Pepper's house. I don't know what's going down."

"Well, join the damn club. This is that fucking Edmond's doing. He deliberately caused this confusion to have us do just what we're doing. Everything's going wrong. He's on his way here. I'll bet my bottom dollar on that."

"What do you want me to do?"

"Ditch the van, get back to Pepper's, and stay off the damn phone. Keep your eyes out for anything. Edmond was at Pepper's parents' home with her mom. Pepper thinks he might have hurt her. Ernest is on his way there now. I'll be back in touch. Later." He clicked off and threw the phone on the seat.

"I won't let that motherfucker get the best of me," he said to himself. He glanced at the clock and could see the fire trucks on Pepper's street. He called Rubin.

"Yeah?" Rubin said.

"Edmond is a shrewd sonofabitch. He might be crazy, but he's damn sure still thinking clearly. He used the van as a decoy to divert attention...the fire, too, I'm sure. He's probably on his way over there. He's as unpredictable as hell. Try to keep them calm. I don't feel good about Mrs. Hankerson. Vernell's on his way to you, so call me whatever you do."

"Right."

"I'm going to scout the other areas…just to see if I find anything. I *might* drive to the Hankersons', but I haven't decided that yet. I'll call you when I hear from Ernest."

"All right, man. Check you later." They hung up, and Rubin turned to Pepper. "Did you talk to your dad? What did he say?"

"He said he was going home and was calling the police to meet him there." *Please let Momma be all right,* she prayed.

The fire engines were now leaving the scene after extinguishing the small blaze. Somehow, the house did not become entirely engulfed in flames.

"Johnny thinks the fire and the van were diversions that Edmond concocted," Rubin said. He looked at Mick. "The driver of that black van started the fire and left. Vernell was tailing him, but he's on his way back here now. This is some fucked up shit! Everything going down at once. Excuse my language ladies, but if you'd just go on into the family room, it'll help a lot." He put his arms around Pepper, and held her. He wanted her to stay with him.

"What black van?" Juanita said, refusing to be left out of the loop. "What the hell are you talking about?" She realized they'd kept them in the dark.

"I'll tell you about it later, Juanita. Right now, I need you in the family room," Rubin said.

Johnny drove through the streets of Pepper's neighborhood once more and saw nothing amiss. He checked the surrounding areas, and everything was normal. He called Rubin again. "Everything okay?"

"Yeah. I'll give Ernest another fifteen minutes. If he hasn't called by then, I'll call him."

"No, man, I told him to call *me*. I didn't see a thing in the whole area. I'm not going to the Hankersons'. I'm going to drive around out here for a while. I'm a little concerned about Ernest being by himself."

"Pepper's dad called the police. They're going to meet him at home, so Ernest won't be there alone."

"Good, that was a good move. Call me if anything happens." He hung up.

"Johnny said he's checked the whole area and everything's fine. He's just going to stay in this neighborhood," Rubin said.

"Good," Juanita said. "When is he coming back?"

"I don't know, Juanita."

Pepper paced back and forth, unable to settle down.

Rubin's phone rang. *Goddamn!* "Hello?" Rubin listened intently for a long while. "Uh-huh...okay. Bye."

"What is it, Rubin? Is Momma all right? Was that Ernest?"

"No, it was Vernell," Rubin lied. "He just wanted us to know he was out front."

"I cannot stand this another minute!" Pepper yelled. I've got to know if Momma's all right."

Rubin wrapped her in his arms and looked at the others. "Please, baby. Try to calm down. You're getting yourself all worked up, and we don't know anything yet."

Johnny had delivered the word about her mother. *I can't tell her yet. She'd go berserk.*

"I can't forget that strange sound I heard. It was...gobbled...I don't know, it just didn't sound right." She snatched up the phone again and dialed home. The line was busy. "Shit! Who the hell is on that line?" she said, frustrated.

"I wish he would show his goddamn face in here," Juanita said, whisking up her bag and taking out her Glock. She placed it beside her on the end table.

"Mick, since Nita has her gun, would you get my bow and arrows from the car? I'd feel better with them inside with me."

"Micah, you don't need them, I assure you."

"Mick, please. I'd like them in here with me."

"All right. I could use a smoke. I'll be right back."

Mick got the bow and arrows from the trunk and handed them to Rubin at the front door. He walked to the side of the house and lit his cigarette. He inhaled deeply, and wondered if Mrs. Hankerson were okay. He walked around the side of the house, checking the windows as he moved.

CHAPTER 49

Atlanta, Georgia
December 15, 2002
Very Early Morning

Edmond entered Pepper's neighborhood choosing the same route as the van. He parked and surveyed the scene. It was pitch black, so he retrieved his nightscope and backpack from the back seat. He eased the door of the Jag shut, tiptoed through a neighbor's shadowy lawn and entered Pepper's backyard.

Using the nightscope, he saw Mick clearly, gun in hand, smoking and looking around in the darkness. He crept closer. When he was within a few feet of him, Edmond stepped on a twig, alerting Mick, who turned in his direction. He rushed Mick and landed a blow to his head with the butt of his Beretta, knocking him unconscious. Mick fell, making a heavy thud, just outside Pepper's bedroom window. Edmond dragged him to the back of the house.

Shortly before Mick's attack, Rubin had the girls move into Pepper's bedroom, out of the line of fire. The lights were out, but the nightlight allowed them to see. "What was that? I heard something," Pepper whispered.

"I did, too," Micah said. She looked at Juanita, "Did you hear it?"

"Uh-uh. What kind of sound?"

Still listening, Micah said, "A muffled sound. Someone's out there."

She picked up her bow and arrow and Juanita grabbed her Glock. They inched the curtain apart and peeped out. They could see nothing.

Rubin heard the sound, too, and was at the kitchen door, listening, waiting.

Vernell, using his nightscope, had clear vision of the east side of the house, but could see nothing on the west side or in the backyard. Donald covered the front and a portion of the west side of the property.

Edmond threw a rock through Pepper's west side bedroom window, frightening them and alerting Rubin. Pepper screamed, and Micah and Juanita turned toward the window with their weapons aimed. Without a second thought, Juanita kicked the window open with her boots. She jumped through and scanned with her gun, crouching low. "Show your face, motherfucker! Where are you?" She peered in the darkness, circling, but didn't see him. "You goddamn coward!" she yelled. She skulked to the front of the house, encountering Vernell who had heard the window smash.

When Donald saw her, he shouted from his van, "What's wrong?"

"Someone broke a window," she shouted back.

"You need to get back inside," Vernell said.

The rock-throwing incident was another distraction by Edmond. He wanted to draw their attention toward the west side of the house away from the east side basement window.

"What's going on?" Rubin called out from the kitchen, moving toward the bedroom, but reluctant to leave his post.

Pepper ran to him, frightened. "Someone's broken the bedroom window, and Juanita's outside."

Losing it completely, he said, "What? Outside?" He stomped to the front of the house. "Goddamn! That girl's crazy as hell. Shit!" He flung open the door and barged outside. "Get the hell back in there. What the fuck do you think you're doing?"

"Trying to kill that motherfucker, that's what!" she snapped. She tramped back inside and found Micah still in the bedroom with her bow and arrow. "Come on outta here. We're going in the family room," Juanita said, spitting fire and ready to fight.

Rubin, still seething, took his position at the edge of the family room, with full view of the kitchen and bedroom door. Pepper clung to his side and refused to leave him.

Vernell crept toward the side of the house, nearing the broken window.

"Be careful," Donald shouted. "If it's him, there's no telling *what* that crazy motherfucker might do."

During the commotion out front, Edmond snuck behind the large oak that separated Pepper's house from her neighbor's. Vernell continued moving, his gun outstretched and cocked. Edmond waited until he was out of Donald's sight and well to the west side of the house. He stepped up behind him quickly and with one smooth stroke, he slit his throat. Vernell was dead before he hit the ground.

Edmond pulled Mick from the backyard to the east side of the house. He removed the screen and pried open the basement window. He pushed the unconscious Mick through it and slid in behind him.

Micah heard a noise in the basement. She grabbed her bow and arrow and opened the basement door, flicking on the lights. She saw Edmond at the foot of the stairs with his knife to Mick's throat.

"You crusty motherfucker," Micah said. "What have you done?"

Using Mick's body as a shield, he started to move toward her. She had her bow drawn and aimed at his head as she ordered him to release Mick. He refused and continued to approach her. She released the arrow with deadly precision. In a millisecond—just before her shot, he ducked behind Mick, and the arrow whammed into Mick's body, killing him instantly. She watched the arrow shudder. Edmond dropped Mick to the floor and bolted to a corner of the basement. Micah dropped the bow and screamed, "Oh, my God!"

Pepper and Juanita ran to her at the top of the stairs.

"Get back into the kitchen," Rubin bellowed.

Micah looked down at Mick. She had accidentally killed the love of her life. She became enraged, pounded her fists against the wall and screamed hysterically, blinded by her tears. "I'm ready to meet her, Mick. I'm ready to meet your mother," she said softly, as she slid to the floor crying.

"Oh, my God, Micah, please, no…" Juanita said, wanting to console her.

Rubin whisked Micah away from the stairs. He saw Mick's body lying on the basement floor. He looked around, but didn't see Edmond. When he heard Micah's horrifying shrieks and saw the arrow protruding from Mick's body, he realized what had occurred. Juanita and Pepper rushed to the basement door as Rubin crept further down the steps, his gun drawn and scanning. Micah was now slumped in a corner of the family room.

"Drop it," Edmond said to Rubin from the basement corner. Rubin turned toward him, hesitated, and eased his gun onto the step.

"In the kitchen. All of you. Now!" Edmond said as he backed Rubin up the stairs. He kicked Rubin's gun from the step. Horrified, the girls obeyed.

"In the kitchen," Edmond ordered. "Pepper, get over here by me." She was frightened. He saw it in her eyes. He was back in command, and his spirits soared.

"What did you do to Momma?" Pepper shouted.

"Forget that, she's history." Just as Edmond uttered those words, his voice changed into a child's singsong voice. He had reverted to his childhood, and was now seeing his mother in the likeness of Pepper. He grabbed Pepper by the neck, awkwardly trying to embrace her, murmuring, "Why did you do it, Mommy? Why did you leave me? I love you so."

He turned to lift his backpack, and Pepper pulled a knife from the knife block and plunged it into his back, striking him repeatedly.

"You should have killed me you sonofabitch! This is for what you did to Momma," she screamed, still plummeting his body with the knife.

Juanita ran to her, trying to take her away. Her gun was still in place behind her, pushed down her leather pants. She was waiting her moment to act, but now it was no use. "He's dead, Pepper. There's nothing more you can do." She put her arms around her, and Pepper dropped the knife.

Rubin rushed to Pepper and cradled her in his arms. "I'm so sorry, baby," he said, trying to console her. She leaned against him heavily, sobbing. She'd struck first as she'd once planned, but she could never have envisioned what he'd done to her mother.

Micah sat on the floor in the corner looking helpless, with tears flowing from her eyes in rivulets. In an incoherent, monotone voice, she cried, "What has this all come to? I killed him…God, help me, I killed Mick."

Johnny rushed through the door, his gun drawn and pointed. Surprised by his entrance, Pepper shifted in Rubin's arms and moved next to where Edmond lay. Edmond moved slightly and fingered the knife. He reared up in one final effort and drew back to stab her. With blinding speed, Johnny dropped instantly to one knee and squeezed the trigger, hitting Edmond squarely between the eyes.

Good riddance, you sick motherfucker!

When Pepper finally realized what had happened, she stared down at Edmond's body, anger consuming her. She kicked him, then spat in his face. "That's for all of us, you sonofabitch. But, most of all, for Momma. It's 'The Big Payback'," she hissed. Rubin pulled her away and brought her to him gently.

Johnny broke the silence. "My God, what a massacre! Vernell is dead outside. And LaVerne…Where is Mick?"

"Mick's in the basement, Johnny," Juanita said. "Micah shot him accidentally with her bow and arrow."

Micah, still shivering in the corner, murmured, "It was so horrible." She began to howl without restraint. Donald heard Johnny's shot, burst into the room and saw Micah huddled in the corner. He went to her, bent down to help her up and led her to the couch. "I don't know what I'm going to do without him." She broke down then completely, her heart breaking, reality taking its toll.

That sonofabitch deserved it, Johnny thought. He looked at Juanita and said, "This was his fate, Nini. I'm not sorry, and I have no remorse. It was his due. I'm putting everyone on notice. Johnny Diamond ain't taking no shit!" He reached out to Nini and enveloped her in his arms.

❧   ❧   ❧

The End

Coming in 2003!

The Arcana Connection

Nini Sanchez and Johnny Diamond are back! Betty Bradford Byers expands the saga of *The Big Payback*'s Nini as she and her cocksure, handsome lover, Johnny Diamond, embark on a must-go trip to her ancestral homeland in Peru. Her sojourn sets the stage for a scorching, new erotic thriller filled with treachery and intrigue.

Nini finds herself spiritually connected to the mysterious mountaintop city of Machu Picchu, a city where her soul is centered, which now beckons for her earthly visitation. She and Johnny become embroiled in a secret world of the occult, sex, betrayal and murder.

The battle for truth unfolds as the Tarot Moon Card professes…

"Beware of deception and hidden enemies. Unexpected changes and disruption are exposed…. This is a card of psychic connection, indicating intuitive sensing and facts revealed through dreams and the subconscious."

0-595-25615-5